Love, Montana

Love, Montana

Deb Martin-Webster

For The Rose and Joe in all of us

Special thanks to Kathleen, Linda, Robert and Donna for their unyielding support throughout this labor of love, BH friends, family members and my devoted husband Pete for his selfless fortitude and brewing endless cups of late night tea and coffee.

Chapter 1

It was hard to believe we were celebrating our third wedding anniversary. It seem only months ago we took our vows. I wanted it to be special. How can one man make such a difference in a woman's life in such a short period of time?

It was my second marriage and his first. We invited our friends and family over for dinner to celebrate. I put the champagne on ice, but I couldn't find our good champagne glasses.

Where did we put them? They were a wedding gift from Paul's brother in London – I hope I can find them. I bet they're in the attic.

As with most of the seldom used doors in our home, the attic door lock had rusted. I wrestled with the latch and after a few tries it slipped open. The smell of old cardboard boxes and mildewed wood greeted me. I switched on the light and waited for the occasional mouse to scurry across the floor.

I'd thought I'd gotten rid of most of this stuff years ago. But there it was – dust covered and still neatly stashed in unmarked trunks and plastic storage containers.

Behind the old roll-top desk we'd purchased from one of our many flea market adventures was a stack of wooden crates. *Our crystal glasses should be in one of them.*

I found a screw driver beside the box and wedged open the lid. Underneath the packing material, I found a pair of old weather-worn cowboy chaps and a large, leather bound book. Brushing off the dust, I gently opened the cover. Pressed between the first two pages were two dried yellow daffodils. I picked them up and held them beneath my nose. The fragrance had long since dissipated, but I clearly remember my first time smelling them and the shit-eating-grin on his face when he handed them to me. They were from the only other man I'd ever loved – they were from Joe.

It would have been his 56th birthday. The fact that our wedding anniversary was the same as his birthday was unintentional. It was the only day in June the church was available. Or maybe it was divine intervention on Joe's part; I don't know.

I continued thumbing through the book reading the letters, emails and newspaper clippings I'd saved. Montana Joe was a celebrated novelist in his genre. He wrote adventure and western novels. The scrapbook took me back to the first time we met.

Chapter 2

It was late April of 1999. I had been at my job as an art critic for a major arts magazine for more than five years. A live-in relationship of seven years ended badly, and the last thing I wanted to do was to hang out at bars to meet guys. My friend Skip used to call bar crawls, "Guys looking for a single night of monogamy." Other friends insisted I go on cruises and peruse singles websites. They even suggested that I try speed dating. None of these activities interested me. I decided I was happy with my overweight cat and my career. I didn't feel the need to run out and find a replacement for my ex-boyfriend.

Two of my best friends, Patrick and Daniel, invited me over for dinner. For years, they'd been my gay hunk shoulders to cry on. Both insisted that I should not jump into the dating pool. I totally agreed. They said I'd been saddled to my job and jerk too long and now that I had no ties, it would be a great time to try something new – to travel to new places, to experience a different lifestyle.

Daniel added, "Why don't you try dating a woman?" I laughed and said, "Oh sure, date someone who is going through the same crap that I'm going through. Double the crying jags, PMS and binge eating rituals devouring pints of Ben and Jerry Chunky Monkey. Thanks, but no thanks!"

After dinner, Patrick walked me to my car.

"I know you would rather sit in your home watching reruns of Star Trek or some dance-your-ass-off show; although watching gorgeous men swiveling their hips is quite entertaining. You've been working non-stop for two years. Why don't you do something you've never done like pick a place on the map and go. Who knows what or who you might find?"

We hugged goodnight, and I told him I'd sleep on it.

Chapter 3

The following week, I requested three weeks of vacation time. I hadn't taken a real vacation in years. The timing was perfect. My column responsibilities always tapered off in the spring. I decided to take Patrick's advice and travel. I packed my bags, took the cat to stay with Daniel and Patrick and said goodbye. It felt good to hit the road with no particular place in mind. Outside the city limits was the most bucolic countryside I'd ever seen. Who knew this beauty existed beyond my metropolitan vista!

Ten hours into my trip, I decided to stop at a rustic country bed and breakfast. The people were sweet, however, like most small town folks had dozens of questions.

"So, what brings you to these parts? Are you traveling with your husband? What do you do for a living?"

I politely skirted around the queries saying I was on a research trip for an article I was writing. I hated to lie, but I couldn't see myself staying here an extra day explaining my failed relationship to a self absorbed jerk.

It was six o'clock, and the sun was still bright in the spring sky. I thought I'd take a walk around town to find some light reading material. The only place open was the library. The cowbell on the door alerted the librarian to my arrival.

"Evening ma'am, welcome to Currysville Library. Can I help you?"

He was your typical librarian with the horned-rim glasses and a bow tie.

"I'm just browsing, thank you."

I noticed a small group of people standing around a seated man signing books.

"He's our author of the month – a western novelist to be precise. Would you like me to introduce you to him?" I thought, *I don't want to meet some local celeb who thinks he's the next Larry McMurtry.*

I also noticed most of the people buying the books were women. As the crowd began to thin out, I realized why. He was an attractive, middle-aged rustic type, wearing jeans and cowboy boots with a shit-eating-smile that younger women would probably find sexy. He had to be at least six-foot two or three.

Not bad looking, but thank God he's not my type – I'm not into pseudo cowboys or any type of wild-west-wanna-be.

I was heading toward the door when I heard a voice from the table, "Excuse me Ma'am, aren't you going to check out my books or at least say hello?" I said, "Hello, nice to meet you and goodbye."

"Whoa, hold on a minute – would you like an autographed copy, a cup of really bad library coffee . . . or to marry me?"

Marry me, this guy is a nut. It didn't take me long to answer, flat out I said, "No, no and absolutely not!"

He grabbed his cowboy hat and came from behind the table. I started to leave when he stepped in front of the exit door.

"Look, it's still early and all I have waiting for me back at the bed and breakfast is a poorly started manuscript and a half-eaten fast food sandwich. You wouldn't be staying at the B and B down at the end of the street, would you?"

"Why? Are you inviting me back to your room?"

"Ma'am, I ain't that kind of fella'. And more importantly, I don't remember your name. What was your name again?"

"Nice try Festus, but I don't remember telling you my name and let's keep it that way…shall we?"

"Well, my momma always said it ain't polite to call a woman, Hey You, so I think I'll call you Rose, like the prairie rose on the cover of my latest novel." I brushed by him and walked back to the B and B.

Later that evening, he caught up with me at the bed and breakfast.

"Well, well, look who's here. Howdy Rose. You left so abruptly I didn't get the chance to properly introduce myself, the name's Montana Joe, but you can call me Joe – just like in the coffee I'd like to buy you. Meet me tomorrow morning around nine o'clock at that small café next to the gift shop. I'll be there – don't disappoint me."

"Me, disappoint you! Excuse me, I don't know you to disappoint you and if I did know you, you would be more disappointed than you've ever been in your life!"

"Rose, if I understood what you just said I reckon I'd be pretty insulted; however, since I didn't understand it, I'll see you for coffee."

The next morning, I packed my things to make a quick getaway out of Currysville. I had put my bags in the trunk of the car, but my curiosity got the best of me. I drove by the café. Keeping true to his word, he was sitting in the booth by the window drinking coffee. I needed some coffee for the long drive ahead. Unfortunately, this café was the only place to get it. The next town was 80-miles away.

I thought, *You jerk! You got me by the proverbial balls! You probably knew there wasn't another café in close proximity to this shit-stop of a town!*

I entered the café and headed directly to the take-out counter. I tried not to make eye contact with him. Before the waitress could say "good morning", I heard a sarcastic welcome, "Hello Rose, fancy meeting you here . . . coffee?"

"Well if it isn't the Kmart cowboy writer. How the hell are you, Jasper?"

"It's Joe and I'm having another cup of coffee. He motioned to the waitress. "Darlin', would you be so kind as to charge it to this nice lady. Pull up a chair and have a seat Rose."

To myself again, *You are a jerk! Do you come from a long line of jerks or are you the first one in your family?*

"Do you take cream and sugar or do you drink it black? I bet you're an extra cream and sugar gal."

"No, I'm a get-the-hell-out-of-my-way-and-let-me-drink-my-coffee-alone gal!"

"He glanced over at the waitress, "She's really cranky before she has her Joe. Do you want some Joe to go, Rose?"

 "Okay that's it! I'm out of here and don't follow me. I do have a license to carry a gun!" I paid the cashier and walked back to my car.

"Hey, wait a minute, you still haven't told me your name?"

"Just call me 'Rose' since you've grown so fond of the name!" I was so distracted, I bumped into a young boy on a skate board and dropped my wallet. A few things fell out, but the kid helped me pick them up. I apologized and got into my car. I drove off leaving a dust-blurred image of him in my rear-view mirror.

After an hour on road, the coffee kicked in and I needed a quick bathroom break. I pulled into the traveler's rest area and noticed they had internet access. Although I was on vacation, I still felt the need to check my email and text messages.

 I logged into my account and noticed two emails with strange subject titles.

To: Rose
Fr: Montana Joe
*Subject: **"Forsan et haec olim meminisse iuvabit."***

I started to delete them, but being the curious creature I am, I opened them.

Dear Rose,
You thought you got rid of me didn't you . . . Dream on. Actually, I'm headin' out the door, wonderin' what road to take that might lead me to meet up with you again. I'm thinkin' of how many guys you must be annoying right now. Lucky fellows! Hope to see you again, Montana Joe

(P.S. [Unlike me] in case you don't have a highfalutin' degree, the title is Latin translated: Perhaps this will be a pleasure to look back on one day)

(P.S. continued: Ph.D in Communications from Columbia)

Ph.D, Latin . . . the jerk has a doctorates degree from Columbia and speaks Latin – Dr. Jerk to be precise. Who in this day and age speaks Latin! Nobody speaks Latin. I'm being stalked by a Kmart cowboy jerk who speaks Latin. Oh my God he's got me repeating myself like a freaking idiot. And how the hell did he get my email address. I really dislike this guy! Just when I finally find an email service that I like, I've got to change it.

I was about to delete the entire account but decided to read the second email.

To: Rose
Fr: Montana Joe
*Subject: **"The Coming of the Post-Industrial Society"***

Dear Rose,

Seein' that I have your business card (you dropped one in Currysville) I know your name ain't Rose, but I've come to like you as Rose. And, please don't delete this account. Just think how much fun you'll have bitchin' at me every time I write. It's the kind of stuff writers live for. If for no other reason, it'll make great conversation at your next cocktail party . . . your under-caffeinated nuisance, Montana Joe

(P.S. If you're interested, I'll be headin' to Jackson Hole, Wyoming)

Like I'd be interested in following this jackass to Jackson Hole, Wyoming! He's crazy! Not a chance in hell.

Chapter 4

It was late noon when I passed the Welcome to Jackson Hole, Wyoming sign. *Okay, so I'm an idiot. What the hell am I doing? Why did I decide to follow some guy I barely know?*

As I got closer to the center of town I thought, *I've never been to Jackson Hole, how bad can it be? It's a huge tourist town and what are the odds of me running into him.*

I drove around and spotted a hole-in-the-wall restaurant with more than a dozen Wyoming license plates. I love eating at local places, mainly because their food is generally tolerable and cheap. On my way in, I noticed one truck with a Montana plate.

No, I can't be this unlucky. There is no way it's him.

I walked to the bar and ordered a red beer, which is beer du jour mixed with tomato juice. I'd had one on a business trip to Kansas. It was not bad.

I had just taken a sip when I heard, "So I hear Jackson Hole is beautiful this time of the year. Glad you decided to follow me darlin'."

"Follow you, I didn't follow. How did you know I wasn't headed to Wyoming, huh? Maybe I planned to come to Wyoming. Maybe you found out I was going to be here and followed me!"

He leaned back in his chair, "Well darlin' the moment I met you I knew you couldn't pass up an opportunity or a challenge to see if I was going to be here. You're curious that way, did you like my emails . . . coffee?

"No, I don't want any coffee." I turned to the waiter, "This fellow is paying for my drink. Just put it on his tab, I think his name is Joe."

The bartender gave me a puzzled look. "Lady, his name ain't Joe, it's..."
Joe shot him quick look. "So, your name isn't Joe?"

"And your name ain't Rose, what's that have to do with the price of Timothy hay."

"What? What the hell does that mean, and what the hell is Timothy hay!"

He tilted his cowboy hat back on his head, "To tell you the truth Rose, I never understood that comparison either. Now, how about that coffee?"

The people in the bar were laughing so hard I got up and walked out. Joe turned around and said, "Folks, I'm sorry, she's been a little cranky all day . . . not enough coffee I suppose."

I walked back to the car fully expecting Joe to be hot on my heels; however, when I turned around he and his truck were gone.

That's odd, he didn't come after me. Now who's the crazy person? I'm upset because some lunatic didn't come after me. This is insane!

It was getting late. I needed find a place to stay. The only place open was a small hotel. As I drove closer, I noticed the "no vacancies" sign was lit. I started to leave when someone from the hotel ran outside. He had a piece of paper in his hand.

"Is your name Rose?"

"Yes . . . I mean no, why?"

"A gentleman booked a room for you. He also said to make sure there's a coffee pot with a timer in the room?"

"Was he about six-foot-plus with a shit-eating grin?"

"Yes, that's the fellow, and he said you would describe him that way."

"And did he book the room directly next to me?"

"No he didn't, in fact he gave up his room for you. He said you needed the room and coffee more than he did. Here's your keycard."

Hmm, this is too weird even for me. But I'm tired and I'm not going to turn down a free room.

At the end of the hallway was room 8C. I was covered with road dust. It was late, but I needed a shower. The hot water felt good on my road-weary shoulders.

I don't know whether to hate him or thank him. Tonight, I think I'll thank him; I'll have plenty of time in the morning to start hating him again.

I'd forgotten my bathrobe. I'd packed one of my ex-boyfriend's white oxford shirts. I slipped it on and took my laptop out of my case. I sat it on the table near the coffee pot and turned it on. Just habit I guess, but I needed to see how the world was doing without me.

The hot shower relaxed me. I hadn't driven long distance in quite a while. I'd forgotten how stiff you get sitting behind the wheel of a compact car. My email icon was blinking – twenty five emails. I was too exhausted to read them. I shut it down, set the coffee timer for 7:00 AM and went to bed. *I'll read them in the morning.*

The smell of freshly made coffee woke me up. *Thank you Joe!* It was about 8 o'clock in the morning. I opened the curtains. The Wyoming sun appeared brighter. I grabbed a cup and sat down to read my emails. There had to be at least fifteen more. I noticed there was one from Joe. For some reason I opened his first.

To: Rose
Fr: Montana Joe
*Subject: **Smiling Like a Picasso Painting on an early Friday Morning***

Dear Rose,
It's late and I'm here in Jackson Hole, sitting at my computer with you on my mind. I hope the hotel room was to your liking. Writers are rather eccentric, of course. We forget the basic rules of grammar and the basic rules of life (i.e. you should go to bed at night and get 8-hours of sleep). I tend to wake up at all hours of the night with ideas that need writing down. This morning, I woke up at 2:30 AM (hey, that's 4-hours sleep). I had some backache. Did we have these when we were in our twenties? I

bet you do too, with all that driving just to follow me to Wyoming. It's now 7:00 AM and I made a pot of strong coffee but still intend to have coffee with you today if you're up for it. You are one spunky gal Rose. I like spunky. I'll look for you at the coffee shop around 9:00 AM. Still in Jackson Hole, Montana Joe

I didn't bother to read the other emails. For some reason his email made me smile. *I don't know what's going on and I really don't know if I want to know; but I'd better get dressed. I guess I'm having coffee with a Montana cowboy.*

The sign on the coffee shop door said that it opens at 7:00 AM. But there were no customers inside. Everything was set up and the lights were on. I could smell the aroma of freshly brewed coffee, but the shop was empty. I pushed the door and noticed it *WAS* open. I thought, *Oh shit, what's going on?"*

I peeked inside when a voice from the back hollered, "That better be Rose. If not, I've got a .45 Colt pointed at your mountain oysters and I'm not afraid to use it!"

I hollered back, "It's Rose . . . Don't shoot me!"

"Well, well, well, good morning Rose. Glad you could make it. Have a seat at the table with the daffodils – I'll be out in a second."
About a minute later, Joe walked out holding a pot of coffee and a tray of something that smelled like heaven.

"You ever had a good home-cooked cowboy breakfast?" I looked around there was still no one in the shop.

"Where are the customers? You didn't shoot them, did you? Is this my last meal before you chop me up and turn me into the afternoon lunch special?"

He put the tray and the coffee on the table and laughed. "You've got some imagination, Rose. You should be a writer."

He had my card so he *knew* I was a writer. I asked him again why the shop was empty.

"Well Rose, sometimes the only way to get to know someone is to sit and share a meal with them. And I hate being interrupted while I'm eating."

"So you just asked all the customers to leave?"

"Nope, I thought it might be best if no one was around in case you didn't like my cooking. Plates might go flying and it could get ugly . . . coffee? You ever had fresh brewed cowboy coffee, Rose? Ain't nothing like it. Here you go, try some."

It was good. I had to admit it was the best coffee I'd had in a while.

"Where'd you learn to make coffee like this?"

"Rose, you'll just have to be patient. I'll be happy to answer some of your questions after breakfast, now let's eat."

"I must say you cook well, Joe. I haven't eaten like this in year. I'll be on the treadmill for 24-hours trying to work it off."

We closed up the café and headed outside. It was beautiful in Wyoming. There were dozens of craft shops and art galleries where local artisans exhibited their work. We stopped at the bakery. There was a strawberry cheesecake in the window.

"I've got to have a piece; I love cheesecake. It's my secret indulgence."

Joe took out a bandana from his back pocket and pretended to wipe my mouth. "Rose, you need to back away from the window – you're droolin'."

We stopped at a silversmith shop and browsed around. I noticed a beautiful silver and turquoise squash blossom necklace.

"This is gorgeous! I love turquoise and silver. It's a shame I'd have to remortgage my condo to buy it."

He grinned, "Yup, it is beautiful Rose, really beautiful."

We left the store and strolled down the sidewalk. He reached down for my hand. "Nothing like holding a purty gal's hand while walking. You don't mind do you?" I told him no and we continued walking.

We spent the entire day together. I thought it was sort of cool exploring a town with someone who knew every inch of it. It's what I assumed people did when they were on vacation. The time flew by and we noticed it was getting late. The sun was setting. The sky was filled with brilliant hues of violet and orange. We stopped in front of the hotel and he let go of my hand.

"Well, I guess this is where we part ways, Rose. Thanks for having grub and coffee with me. So, I guess I'm not a psycho killer after all." I smiled and he hugged my shoulder.

"Behave yourself girl. You really do need to stop talking to strange men wearing cowboy hats."

Before we said goodbye I asked, "So, how did you get the shop to open just for us?"

"Let's save that conversation for later. Goodnight Rose." He tipped his hat and walked away.

I got back to my room and realized I'd left my laptop on. The email icon was blinking like crazy. I was afraid to check how many emails I had. I clicked on the icon and there were at least 70 unread emails. I scrolled through them and noticed one from Joe. We'd just left each other. How did he write an email so quickly? I clicked his name and started reading.

To: Rose
Fr: Montana Joe
Subject: ***How Post-Impressionists Attempted to Discover the Absolute behind Individual Things***

Dear Rose,

Now, don't that impress the Van Gogh, Cezanne and Gauguin, right out of ya! I know we just left each other, but I have to tell you that was the best time I've had in quite a while, Rose. Now, to answer your question . . . I knew we had to eat, so I thought what better way to get to know each other than eating lots of good food. My good buddy Wyatt owns the

shop. Anyway, back to me waking up thinkin' about you. I daydreamed about us sitting at a table with fresh cut daffodils, breakfast and, of course, hot cowboy . . . coffee, that is. I guess I spend too much time writin' fiction. But novelists are able to put themselves into another scene and live in it vicariously. Thank you, Rose for indulging my fictional account of our first date. Whoa, did you just call that a date? Heck darlin' we just met. An innocent rendezvous at best. Thanks for a great day! Adios, Montana Joe
(P.S. I left something for you with the clerk at the front desk)

I never called it a date! Just when I think he's tolerable he infuriates me to the point of wanting to punch my laptop. And, what could he have left for me at the front desk? I was with him all day. He didn't have a chance to buy anything? Maybe he took something from me while I was in the ladies room. I checked my purse. Cell phone, glasses and credit cards – everything was there. I called the desk clerk and asked if he had something for me.

The clerk said, "Yes, but you must come down to sign for it. The gentleman was very clear about us not taking it to you; he said something about you needing exercise after a huge breakfast?"

I put my shoes back on and walked down to the desk. I thought, *"Needs exercise! What an obnoxious son-of-a bit . . ."* The clerk came over with a gift box.

"Are you Rose?" I nodded. "This is from Joe, Montana Joe. There's a card attached."

I took the gift and card back to my room, almost afraid to open it. But, I thought, *"What the heck."* I ripped the paper off and opened the box. Nestled in Native American print cloth was the squash blossom necklace I had admired along with matching earrings.

The card read, "Two natural beauties . . . you and squash blossoms."

No way! No way did he buy this for me. This thing could pay off my American Express bills for the rest of my life if I hocked it. *I can't keep this!* I put it back in the box and took it back to the clerk.

By the time I got to the desk, the clerk said, "He mentioned you would probably come storming down here to give it back and he said to tell you FAT CHANCE! He also said he'd be checking out of his hotel and needed to get back on the road. He left Jackson Hole an hour ago."

I should have been doing the happy dance because I was finally rid of this guy. But somehow I felt a twinge of sadness. Was I starting to like this jerk? Even worse, I think I actually missed him.

Quit it Rose, you're not looking to meet anybody, stick to the plan and forget about him. Oh my God, did I just call myself Rose?

I checked out of the hotel and left Jackson Hole.

Chapter 5

I continued driving north and kept thinking about Joe. His annoying cowboy voice replayed in my head, I couldn't forget his unnatural obsession with coffee or how he got under my skin so easily. Nonetheless, I couldn't shake the feeling that I would meet up with him again. The question is: *Do I want to? Will he be happy to see me? What am I doing? I'm daydreaming about some jerk I just met. More like a nightmare.*

About five hours later, I reached a little town called, Meeteetse, Wyoming. You know the kind of town that has one stoplight, one church, one restaurant and one liquor store. It was incredibly rustic, right out of an old western novel. It was just the type of place Joe would visit. I followed the signs pointing to lodging.

Maybe I should stay a while, if only to wrap my brain around what was going on with me and Joe. In reality, there is no me and Joe. I need a drink.

I parked in front of the liquor store and walked inside. Not much of a selection but they did have my favorite whiskey. The store manager came over and asked if he could be of assistance. I told him thank you, pointed to the bottle and said "Me and this fine Tennessee gentleman were well acquainted." He chuckled and walked back behind the counter.

I'd just left the store when I heard a familiar voice say, "You know that stuff will kill your brain cells. Did you like the necklace?"

I turned around to see Joe leaning against his truck.

"What the hell are you doing here? I didn't even know I was coming here until I got into my car this morning. You ARE stalking me!"

"Now, why would you think that, Rose? I told you I do research for my western novels and what better place than a town like this so rich in old west culture. And, to be quite frank . . . I think it's YOU stalking me! You need to get a life, girl."

"Me . . . stalking YOU, get a life! Just when I was starting to like you just a teensy bit, you spout all kinds of bullshit!"

He paused, "So you do like me, huh? Now, ain't that a kick in the head. That's another one of those old sayings I never understood. Why on earth would someone enjoy being kicked in the head? I've fallen on my head a few times."

"Well, that explains everything. Maybe that's why you are the way you are . . . and don't change the subject."

"Can you refresh my memory darlin' – what was the subject?"

"I don't remember. You infuriate me so much; it drives me crazy!"

He started to walk away. I had to run to keep up with him. His legs came up to my waist.

"Well, Rose I think I'll be leaving. You enjoy your evening with that Tennessee gentleman in the brown sack. Adios, darlin' and stop stalking me or I'll have the local law enforcement throw you in the hoosegow – that's cowboy lingo for jail.

I finally caught up with him and grabbed his arm.

"What is going on? I'm not going to leave until you explain what's happening."

It wasn't like me to literally chase after a man. *I shocked myself.* He turned around and looked me dead in the eye and said,

"Rose, have you ever heard of fate? Maybe it's just old-fashion fate that brought us together. Ain't this the kind of adventure you said you were looking for? Well, you put it out there darlin' and now you've got it. All of this could just be your destiny. Listen, I'd like to continue this philosophical discourse with you, but I've got a book signing and a radio show to do. If it ain't too late, I'll email you afterwards or maybe in the morning. Okay?"

He turned the corner and was gone.

Back at the lodge, I checked my emails. There was nothing from Joe. I checked off and on – still nothing. I decided I'd have one or two drinks of that Tennessee gentleman and finally fell asleep.

The next morning, I checked my emails. I now had 90 work emails – all of which needed to be answered or deleted. I scrolled the list and there was his name.

To: Rose
Fr: Montana Joe
Subject: **Ludwig Feuerbach and his Philosophy of Materialism**

Dear Rose,
My evening activities went longer than expected. I set the timer on the hotel coffee pot. I want some coffee . . . it's across the room droolin' away like you do when you see a piece of cheesecake. If that machine only knew how close it was to gettin' shot it wouldn't tease me like this. It's like three days of no-sleep is catchin' up with me. I've got to cut back on coffee. But it's my only vice. Zzzzzzzgrmmmmhmmmp . . . maybe it's done, brb.

Okay, that's better. Who snuck in here and wrote that first paragraph... what a grumpy o' cowboy. Last night was nice, Rose. For the first time, I actually felt you were able to tolerate me. I think I even saw a smile, am I right? Anyway, the book signing went well and so did the radio show. Why anybody in their right mind would want to listen to me drone on and on about myself baffles me. Anyway, how's about I take you out to dinner tonight? We can continue our philosophical discourse about the evils of drinking alone. I'll meet you at 6:00 PM in the lobby of the lodge . . . and wear the necklace and earrings. I wanna see how they look on you.

Laying in a lumpy, lonely hotel bed, Montana Joe

I thought, *"Nothing serious, just have dinner with someone, no expectations. Maybe this was my fate. To meet someone, have no attachment and travel to new and exciting places. Maybe Joe knows what he's talking about? Maybe he's full of shit. Or maybe I'm so gullible that I don't know when I'm being played by a tall, handsome fiction writer in a cowboy hat. Oh well, I guess I'll find out because I'm going out to dinner with Montana Joe in Meeteetse. Now that's a phrase I never thought I'd rattle off in million years."*

I walked into the restaurant. The host asked how many were in my party.

"I'm expecting a guest, so there will be two of us tonight."

I sat at the bar and ordered a seltzer with lime. I wanted to stay sober in case I needed to make a mad dash for the door. It also dawned on me that I arrived on time. *I never arrive on time. I hope he doesn't think I'm too eager or desperate. Oh God, I don't want to appear desperate. I'm just having dinner with a friend, and I'm on time. Okay, enough of the stupid self-talk.*

Out of the corner of my eye, I saw this impeccably dressed man wearing a gray cowboy hat. I thought, *"Good Lord, Joe, you clean up well. Much nicer than those tacky cowboy shirts and jeans you usually wear."* He said something to the host. The host laughed and pointed at me. He waved and walked over to the bar.

"Eh, excuse me ma'am, I was suppose to meet a gal named Rose for dinner, but I think I'll ditch her for you." He smiled and kissed me on the cheek. "You look beautiful darlin'. Most gals I've known take forever to get ready so I thought I'd come fashionable late. Have you been waiting long?"

"No, not long at all. In fact, I arrived a few minutes before you. And, I must admit you clean up well too."

"How about we go to our table? I've got so many questions to ask. I want to find out all about you Rose. Why you're traveling alone lookin' for adventure, what made you take this particular trip, how you got to this point in your life. It's a novelist's prerogative."
I took a sip of my seltzer water.

"I don't consider my life interesting. I just had a string of bad relationships and decided to travel, end of story."

"There is never an end to a story Rose. There is always a masterpiece buried beneath the layers of everyone's life just waiting to be told. I know you have one heck of a masterpiece in you Rose."

"I don't know about a masterpiece. My story is nothing special. Lots of women have the same type of issues happening every day. Life goes on. It's sad but true Joe."

"Let me be the judge of that."

Surprisingly, I was beginning to relax and have a good time. We talked and laughed for hours about how we ended up where we were and what circumstances got us to this point. We talked about how we shared the same sense of wit and humor. I was enjoying Joe's company.

How can someone I just met feel so familiar. I've never opened up to anyone like I did with Joe. He has a way of getting me to do and say things I wouldn't ordinarily do or say.

Maybe he was right. Maybe it was some kind of divine intervention that brought us together. Whatever it was, I decided I would go with it. In fact, I think I will email HIM tonight.

We were the last people to leave the restaurant. I told Joe it was the best time I'd had in months.

He grinned and said, "Like they said in the movie, *'Romancing the Stone'*, I've never been anyone's best time before."

I thought back to our first meeting. We could barely tolerate each other; yet, this evening ended with him being a fascinating dinner guest. Besides, how can you dislike someone when you've bonded over prime rib and imported beer?

The walk to my car was awkward. *Do we lock arms, hold hands or do we walk on the opposite sides of the street?* I decided to hold his shirt sleeve.

"Okay, I know I ain't your favorite person *yet* but I don't have trail lice. We can hold hands if you'd like."

We walked hand-in-hand until we got to our cars.

"Rose, dinner with you has been the highlight of my day . . . heck my week! Much more than this old cowboy ever expected. It was a pleasure getting to know you, Ma'am."

"You're not too shabby yourself, Joe. Not too shabby at all."

He brought my hand to his lips and kissed the palm. "Goodnight Rose."

I don't remember the drive back to the lodge. My mind was in a haze. How could a kiss on the hand feel so much like making love to someone you've loved for years? Was I really falling for this western character who sounds and acts like someone straight out of a Louis L'Amour novel?

My laptop was already on. I couldn't wait to see if he sent an email giving a blow-by-blow of dinner. There was nothing in the queue from Montana Joe. That didn't mean I couldn't email him. I clicked on compose.

To: Montana Joe
Fr: Rose
Subject:

I wanted to write a witty subject like Joe but couldn't think of anything. I didn't want him to think I admired his nonsensical subject titles. So I thought it best just to say something simple.

Subject: ***Thanks for Dinner***

Dear Joe,

I just wanted to send you a quick note to thank you for dinner. The steak and conversation were both palatable. More than I'd expected. And the palm kiss was a nice touch. I think maybe you've been reading too many romance novels, Joe. Anyway, I really enjoyed myself. Rose

It was almost 1:00 AM and time to shut down my trusty laptop companion.

I'll check back later tomorrow to find out if he replied.

I'd just turned down the bed when heard a gentle knock on the door. It startled me. I put on my white shirt and answered the door.

"Who the hell is it? I should also warn you that I have a gun!"

"Evenin' Ma'am, I need to speak to a Miss Rose please. I'm Caleb Barnett, Sheriff of Chouteau County, Montana, and we have a situation here that we need your help with."

This voice sounds very familiar. "You wouldn't be related to some guy named Montana Joe would you?"

"No, Ma'am. I'm much better lookin' than him, but it does concern him. You see he's walking around his hotel lobby mumbling about some young lady named Rose. It seems he's quite taken with her and needs to find her ASAP."

I cracked open the door and, of course it was Joe. "And what brings you to my room. Don't you have some other tourists to annoy?"

"I just read your email. I couldn't help but come by and tell you thanks for having dinner with me. Being such a witty subject title, it kept me awake, and I wasn't able to sleep. Rose, you need to learn how to create an interesting subject title that would get an old cowboy out of his comfortable bed at one in the morning and drive over to her lodge room. Sadly, your subject title didn't accomplish that. However, it did charm me into giving you a proper goodnight kiss."

I opened the door. "So, now you want to kiss me?"

"Yeah, I do Rose. Have you ever been kissed in the moonlight in Meeteetse, Wyoming? I must say I've never kissed anyone in Meeteetse. Strange, huh?"

He stooped down, pushed his hat back and kissed me. The strangest thing is . . . I kissed him back.

"I'll be going now. You are sweet, ever so sweet Rose, goodnight again darlin'."

I closed the door dazed by what just happened. My email wasn't that great for such a personal reply. *I honestly believe this man is falling for me and what's stranger. . . I think I'm falling for him.*

I realized I had a week remaining of my vacation. So far, I've visited nothing but podunk towns and met a man who insisted on calling me Rose. I checked my email and there were two from Montana Joe. I opened his reply to my email first.

To: Rose
Reply fr: Montana Joe
Subject: **Thanks for Dinner**

Dear Rose darlin,

Why are you reading this reply when you know I delivered the reply to you in person? I guess you want another reply. That's if you're up for another kiss of course.
Your kissin' cowboy, Montana Joe.

I clicked on the next one.
To: Rose
Fr: Montana Joe
Subject: **The Driftin' Cowboy Band**

Dear Rose,

Are you dreaming about kissing an old cowboy in the moonlight? I used to sleep three to five hours a night. But I think I gave that up when I met you. I don't know. I can't remember. Am I still standing in the hallway of your hotel? Are we still kissing each other? Did I ever leave your room? Maybe that was a dream. Maybe you're a dream. Oh man, I'm tired. I think I'll lie down on the hotel floor and take a nap. Did I tell you I always take naps on the floor? It's an old habit. Cowboys are too dusty and dirty to be allowed on the furniture.

I'm still thinkin' about you and how you've become so special in my life. I know – how can that be true? We've known each other for less than two weeks. I've got to write, but I can't stop thinkin' about our kiss. I need coffee darlin'. The coffee pot in my room is broken. I was going to shoot it but the bastards would probably tack it onto my hotel bill. I need to wake up because I've got a manuscript due in three days. And for some reason I've been preoccupied with some spunky art columnist who keeps running around (wearin' that big old white shirt) in my mind. I need (1) strong coffee (2) I need to finish this book and (3) I need to kiss you again, Rose. I'd be willin' to skip one and two and go directly to number three,

Your crazy busy cowboy,
Montana Joe

I reread his email a few more times. He was falling in love with me. I was so afraid of getting involved again…afraid to find out he's married, terminally single or gay. Not that there's anything wrong with being gay, but I had my quota of gay male friends.

I closed my eyes and replayed the kiss over and over in my head. I remembered the sweet lavender smell of his shirt and hair--how his wind-roughened lips softened on mine. He had soft ears. The lobes were like baby's skin. Leave it to me to get turned on by soft ears.

All my life I'd dreamt of someone like Joe. I guess I'd never envisioned it in the form of an over-educated cowboy novelist with an irritating sense of humor. But his shit-eating-smile and soft blue-green eyes, pardon the cowboy pun, lassoed me in. I had no idea how to get in touch with him other than email. I decided to write him an email worthy of a Montana Joe subject matter. I sat my lap top on the bed and clicked on compose.

To: Montana Joe
Fr: Rose
Subject: **Pierre-Auguste Renoir in the forest of Fontainebleau**

Dear Joe,

Last night was an unexpected pleasure. I wasn't sure what to think of it but I decided to accept it for what it was, a man and a woman sharing a moment after an incredible evening. I don't want to make it anything more than that. I know how you relish your privacy so I promise not to badger you with redundant emails. I just wanted to tell you that it was a pleasant evening and a truly pleasant kiss.

Fondly, Rose

(P.S. I hope this subject title is at least worthy of another dinner and being the curious man that you are, I should tell you I was totally naked underneath that big old white shirt.)

Before I lost my nerve, I clicked send and headed to the shower. The water was steaming hot, and I finally had a hotel room with a decent shower head. The water pulsed through my hair like fingers. I thought about Joe reading my email wondering if I was naked. Knowing him he took it seriously and is probably on his way over right now. I grabbed the mini bottle of hotel shampoo and lathered it into my hair. It smelled just like Joe's hair. I shut my eyes and fantasized about him working his fingers through my hair, leaning into my wet soapy body pulling me towards him. At that very moment the water went cold!

"Holy shit, what the hell just happened?"

I rinsed the rest of the suds out in the sink and wrapped the towel around my head. The hotel phone rang – it was the hotel manager.

"Hello, I'm sorry to disturb you ma'am, but it seems we have a busted water pipe, and we'll need to shut the water off for an hour. I hope this doesn't inconvenience you. Of course, we'll comp you today's stay."

I considered it my karmic punishment for having sexual fantasies about a man I just met. Maybe Joe had something to do with the busted pipe?

Now, I'm blaming this guy for everything. It's raining; it must be JOE'S fault. I broke a nail; that's JOE'S fault too. And, I don't even know where he is. He could be in another state romancing some other woman. Maybe he'll call her Daisy, Petunia or Tulip. Maybe he has a fetish for flowers.

My hair dryer was already packed away. I got dressed, went outside and let the breeze blow it dry. There was something relaxing about the wind blowing through my hair. I could never do this in the city – mainly because of the pollution. But the air here was crisp and clean. I fluffed it and pulled it back into a ponytail.

I headed back to my room and noticed he'd replied to my email. For some reason, I felt anxious, wondering what he'd think about my lame attempt at creative subject titles. I clicked on his email.

Reply To: Rose
Fr: Montana Joe
*Subject: **Pierre-Auguste Renoir in the forest of Fontainebleau***

Dear Rose,

Hmmm, butt naked underneath the shirt, Enjoyed my kiss--did you now? You know all this sex talk isn't helping me get this manuscript finished. It's HARD to edit picturing you butt naked. It's just makes me want to find you and plant another wet kiss on your lips. I hope my lips weren't too rough darlin'. For some reason I got a lot of work done. Today I'm on my way to a little Montana town called Malta. I have a book signing to do at a bookstore and friends to visit. Don't have any idea where I'll spend the night (maybe in a sleeping bag . . . only got one, so if you show up we'll have to scrunch real close). I never had a research travel companion, hmm. Thursday and Friday I'll bum around the Missouri Breaks area of northeastern Montana. I'm thinking about writing a series there. We'll see. I'll be drivin' down dirt roads, talkin' with old timers, and drinkin' coffee in those little cowboy cafés and seein' if there's a story to be told. Just think how much fun it would be if you came with me girl. But then again, you have this unusual habit of showing up wherever I am. Well, I'd better get back to work. I left directions to Malta at the desk, just in case. And this time, dinner is on you. Oh, and dress casual, so butt naked is acceptable. I'm sure I'll see you soon. I'm startin' to miss you already.

On the road to Malta, wearing a shit-eating-smile, Montana Joe

(P.S. Nice title – but I would suggest not quitting your day job)

Now what do I do? Should I go to Malta, do we scrunch into his sleeping bag and screw our brains out – I don't know. I needed to talk to someone. I grabbed my cell phone and called Patrick. I told him I'd check in from time-to-time, but I'd been so preoccupied with Joe I forgot. It went directly to voice mail.

"Hello, this is Daniel and this is Patrick your message went straight to our voice mail which is the only thing 'straight' in our household, so leave us a message."

"Hi Patrick, it's me, I just called to check in. Hope Bill's okay and I just wanted your advice. You see, I met this six-foot-four'ish cowboy novelist jerk and now I think I've fallen for him even though he drives me crazy with his obsessive need for coffee and his infuriating sense of humor. We kissed but that's as far as it went. NOW, he wants me to come on a research trip with him to some cattle town . . . Eh, anyway, I'll try to call you back or call me on my cell. The reception is pretty shitty out here, so if you get my voice mail, leave a message and I'll call you as soon as I can, uh, other than that I'm okay, love ya', bye."

A few seconds later Patrick called.

"Hello, my dear schizophrenic workaholic friend, I just listened to the voice mail you left on our home phone. In fact, I let the entire office listen to it. We all agreed; if you don't want to end up an old woman who hoards cats and watches shows about other old women who hoard cats, then you'd better get your ass to Moldavia or Malta or where ever the hell this delicious, tall, cowboy-drink-of-water is and fast. Three of my male co-workers said they'd screw him just from your description and they're not gay! Honey, you need to get out of that box you've been living in, light it with a match and move on. Follow this Tom Selleck-Sam Elliott-Gary Cooper hunk-o-cowboy and don't call me again until you have a bad case of the post-sexual tremors, okay? Now give Patrick some phone sugar and go after him. Love ya dear, bah-bye."

He didn't give me an opportunity to speak. Maybe that was for the best because I would have talked myself out of following Joe. I don't want to live in a box the rest of my life.

"Damn it, I'm *headin'* to Malta." Oh Lord . . . he's got me droppin' my G.!"

Chapter 6

Thirty-five miles to the Malta exit. I tried to find a radio station to give me some idea of what to expect in this town. Nothing but agricultural news reports, bible-belting stations and country music. All of which I hated. The RFD radio station was talking about the different prices of Timothy hay and Fescue.

So, this is the shit Joe was talking about.

I thought he'd made this stuff up. Oh well, at least I now understand how hay is priced and which hay is better. That'll make a great opening statement at my next staff meeting.

My exit was coming up soon. Welcome to Phillips County. I traveled another ten miles which led me to an off-road, which led me to an unpaved dirt road. I could see an old hotel in the distance. It looked like the kind of place Joe would stay. I drove slowly down the unlevel road trying not to rip the muffler off my car. My gas gauge was almost on empty – I needed to fill up. I also needed to pee like a race horse. Another one of those sayings I didn't understand, however, I'm sure Joe did.

It was a gas station with older pumps that didn't have a credit card swipe. They trusted you to pump and pay. I filled up and walked inside.

"Hello? Is there anyone here? I'd like to pay for my gas and use the restroom, *if you have one.*"

I looked around and there was no one in the station. The back door opened and a young kid who looked about sixteen popped in.

"Howdy ma'am, I'll be with you in a minute – just need to get this grease off my hands."

"Take your time, but I really need to use the, eh, facilities."

He pointed to the back of the station. It was actually nicer than I thought it would be. Fresh cut flowers in a back water town rest room. *Now that was something you don't see in the city. You'd be lucky if they have toilet paper.* I washed my hands and checked my hair the mirror. My complexion was glowing. It was refreshed like I'd been to a weekend spa. *Maybe disliking someone gets the blood pumping and cleanses the skin. Maybe Joe is good for something other than raising my blood pressure.*

The kid came out from the garage with semi-clean hands and stepped behind the register. "That'll be thirty- dollars and two cents – you can take the two cents from the penny jar."

I handed him my credit card. He looked at it and took a deep breath.

"Ma'am, I'm really sorry but, eh, this station only takes cash. He must have noticed the look on my face because he said, "I'd be happy to take a personal check – I'll need your driver's license."

I remember blanking out for a second. *Who doesn't take credit cards? I've driven into the 1950's. Maybe I can borrow some cash from Andy, Aunt Bea and Opie!*

I told him I didn't have any cash because I only carried credit cards when I was traveling. Basically, it was easier to keep financial records. "Is there an ATM close by? I'd be happy to leave my laptop as collateral."

"I trust you ma'am, there's one in town outside the hotel. Just drop it off when you can."

I was so embarrassed but I realized that I wouldn't be in this situation if it weren't for Joe. I asked him if it was the only hotel in the town.

"Yup, the only one, ma'am; don't worry it's got running water and electricity." I thought, *"Even the hicks are smart asses."*

I mumbled under my breath that my life was so much simpler before I met Montana Joe.

"Did you say Joe, Montana, Joe? Okay, you must be Rose. He said you might be following him to Malta. I'll just charge the gas to him."

"Seriously, he said I'd be following him here?"

This is one of the things about him that infuriates me! He is so presumptuous! It could also be one of the things I love about him.

The kid rang up my purchase. "Here's your receipt, have a good'n Miss Rose."

The road to the hotel was unlevel and extremely dusty. A dust cloud billowed behind me in my rear view mirrors, like the entrance into another universe. I guess I had entered a different world. It was simple, laid back and trusting. Nothing like my high-pressure, column-writing world filled with deadlines and meetings. Maybe Joe has a point. Perhaps, I needed to stop and smell the prairie roses. That could be the reason he insisted on calling me Rose. I may need to re-evaluate myself and my life – maybe later.

I arrived at the hotel. It was so much more beautiful than I expected. Its authentic western design was straight out of the old Wild West. It even had a hitching post and watering trough for horses in the front. I checked in and was escorted to my room by a young fellow dressed in western attire. I asked if all of the hotel staff was required to dress like that. "Like what, ma'am?" *Never mind.* I gave him a tip and unpacked.

I was also surprised that the room had an internet connection. I hooked up my laptop and checked my email. As I've come to expect, there was one from Joe.

Fr: Montana Joe
To: Rose
*Subject: **Angel Flyin' to Close to the Ground***

Dear Rose,

*You're in your office . . . busy being the efficient art columnist . . . sailin'
your way through another sea of administrative hassles and editing
problems when . . . an unannounced visitor bursts through your door. .
.you look up startled to see a tall, rustic ol' Montana cowboy, wearing
cowboy boots, wranglers, long-sleeved western shirt, gray Stetson
cowboy hat, dancing blue-green eyes.   You stand to greet him . . . he
tosses a box of beautiful wildflowers on your desk, grabs you up off your
feet . . . plants a soft kiss on your lips (his are warm, willing and slightly
chapped) . . . then exclaims . . . "Rose, you make me feel like the luckiest
man who ever walked the face of the earth!" . . . he kisses you again, this
time like a man with a very urgent need . . . suddenly, there are voices at
the doorway . . . your co-workers are huddled there watching . . . "are
you alright . . . do you know this guy?" "Yes I do, he's my cowboy from
Montana, and he always does things like this." . . . would someone close
the door . . . I definitely do not want to be disturbed for an hour (or is
that a day . . . year . . . lifetime?) . . . End of scene.*

*Hah, didn't know an old western writer could write romance! But on a
serious note, Rose, I feel like an old-time prospector who's just stumbled
by accident onto a claim so rich he can pick off a chunk and make
jewelry without even refining it. I keep slappin' my cheek (the one on my
face of course) to make sure I'm not dreaming all this. I keep running
over things in my mind, to make sure this isn't just another of my fiction
stories.*

*I'm falling for you Rose and from that kiss the other night, I think you
could be falling for me too. Now don't start getting nervous. I promise I
won't pressure you. I'm a fellow who doesn't lie. If I like someone I tell
them, if I like them a lot I tell them, if I'm falling in love [with them] I
show them. I won't hold back unless you want me to Rose. What can I
say, I'm hopeless, I'm helpless and I'm yours if you want me.*

*I know this is a long email but I didn't want to discuss this over dinner
tonight at the eight o'clock Prairie Rose Café. There will be too many
people there and I didn't want to make a scene in case you said, "Yes, I
feel the same!" I think the café management frowns upon lovers having
hot, passionate sex on their dinner tables. And NO I didn't change the
name for you – just a happy coincidence. See you tonight.*

Walking ten feet above the ground, Joe

It took me a minute or two to catch my breath. How did I miss him falling in love with me? Was I too preoccupied protecting my heart that I didn't realize my heart was falling for him? Maybe I will take Patrick's advice. I'll tell Joe how I feel. Even if it's just one night of monogamy it will be well worth it.

It took me three hours to get ready. Most of my social contact with Joe had been lightweight – nothing to primp over. But tonight I wanted to look my best. I wanted his head to turn and do a double take. And I didn't care what people thought if we decided to have hot, unbridled sex during entrees. I put on the necklace and earrings he gave me. I let my hair air-dry again because I wanted him to bury his nose in my neck during our welcome embrace and realize it was the same fragrance of his shampoo. I wanted it to be something familiar. Oh my God, I'm starting to fantasize like one of those cheesy romance writers. I'd better get going.

We arrived at the café at the same time. It was uncharacteristic for me because I'm always running late. I guess we were anxious to see each other, only this time it was for a different reason. This time we wanted to be with each other.

I saw Joe standing by the bar and walked over to him, "Hello Montana Joe. I believe we are having dinner together."

His eyes squinted, "Ma'am, I know I'm good-looking and smellin' like a fine French whore on holiday, but I don't believe I know you. I'm here to meet an angel who has fallen for some ol' manure-crusted, boot wearin', ex-rodeo rider, with a bad back and failing eye sight from sitting at the computer too much. Now if'n you see her would you tell her I'll be waiting over here by the bar. You'll recognize her because she'll be butt naked."

He kissed me on the check and whispered, "Hello Rose, you look beautiful." His arm slipped around my waist as we walked over to our table and sat down. He stared at me through the dim candle light.

"I never realized how young you are Rose. What the heck are you doing with an old guy like me? You could have any guy you wanted. I guess some gals like their guys young and inexperienced. Fortunately, you like them old, horny and desperate – lucky me."

Over dinner, I told him my story about how my relationships seem to always go south before I could give them a chance and that most of the guys I knew were just about their careers and scoring with women. He listened intensely, as though he were taking mental notes of the entire conversation. I knew this because I do the same thing when I'm writing an article. It's the subtle nuances that make the story come to life. Joe had that kind of inquisitive mind.

We decided to have coffee and dessert back at the hotel. I started to walk over to my car, and he reached for my hand.

"I'll be driving us back tonight Rose. Don't worry about your car we'll come get it in the morning, but tonight I'm going to act like a gentleman on a proper date."

My instinct was to resist. I thought, *"How about I drive us back! I'm a big girl and I can drive in the dark just as well as you can."* But tonight I simply said "Okay."

We took a short cut which I later learned was not. However, it did take us by a scenic stretch of prairie land and overhead a sky full of the most beautiful stars I'd ever seen.

"This is why they call it 'Big Sky Country' Rose. It's what I imagine heaven's like. It's what I imagine making love to you would be like."

He took a deep breath then leaned back against the truck. He stared at the sky for a second or two.

Without turning his head said, "It seems I've fallen hopelessly in love with you Rose. My heart skipped a beat the evening you walked into the Currysville library and gave me a wrath of shit at my book signing."

"Wrath of shit . . . Joe, those are the most romantic words you've ever said to me. Hold on I'm beginning to mist over."

My humor broke the sexual tension. We decided it was time to head to the hotel.

The lobby had a huge fireplace that could have been in Citizen Kane.

I asked him if he would like to sit by the fire and have coffee."

"Nope"

"What about dessert?"

"Nope"

"Perhaps some wine?"

"Nope"

He whispered, *"Why are you stalling? Do you want me to seduce you right here in the lobby, because that would be really embarrassing for you."*

Before I could answer he scooped me up in his arms.

"Whoa, Rose you almost fainted, I'd better get you up to your room." I buried my head in his shoulder embarrassed beyond words. "I told you Rose, I'm a man of my word."

He carried me over to the elevators. We got off at the 3rd floor and walked down the hall to Suite 3A. When he opened the door to his suite, I was shocked. The bed was covered in those tin-foil candy kisses. He motioned for me to look in the bathroom. The shower floor was covered in rose petals.

A hand-written note was taped to the bathroom mirror that read, *"If I kiss the ground you walk on and shower you with roses will you love me forever?"*

I leaned against the sink. "When did you do this? No one has ever done anything like this for me." He noticed my eyes were beginning to tear.

"Oh hell, now I've done it, I made her cry. That was not my intention tonight Rose, I wanted you to wrap your arms around me and" . . . before he finished I kissed him. He pulled away for a second.

"Is this what *you* want Rose?"

"Ah, Yep"

"Because I really, really want to make love to you – is that what you want?"

"I nodded and kissed him again"

"Then I'll take that nod and kiss as a yes."

What an incredible night. Rays of sun peeked through a small crack in the curtains. Joe was still sound asleep and had spooned himself so close behind me, I could feel his heart beating. It was as though he wanted to cocoon us from reality. I slipped out of his arms and called room service. I needed coffee. Joe began to stir and so I crept back into bed. His eyes squinted from a single beam of sun piercing his pillow.

He rolled over onto his back.

"Where am I . . . when did I fall asleep . . . I'm still asleep . . . I must be dreaming because I'm in bed with the sexist woman in Montana . . . hell, in the entire North West! That was some night darlin'. Marines on a week's leave haven't had that much action."

"Good morning Joe, coffee should be here in a few minutes."

He rolled over and kissed me. "You read my mind, darlin'. I need it bad . . . coffee that is."

"Rose, was it a dream? Did we really tumble, laugh, ride-me-like-a-wild-bronc, tease and screw the night away until the hotel guests start complaining about the moaning?" I winked at him, "I don't remember anyone complaining."

I sat down on the bed next to him.

"Joe, it was the best night in my entire life. You are the best thing that has ever happened to me. I know it sounds a bit cliché but . . ."

There was a timid knock at the door. The coffee had arrived. The waiter rolled in a cart with coffee, a slice of cheesecake and fresh daffodils.

"Wait, I don't think this is our order. We only ordered coffee."
The waiter looked at the order and said, "This is Suite 3A, correct?"

"Yes it is; however, we didn't order cheesecake or flowers, can you check with the . . . " Before I could finish my sentence Joe put on his jeans and came around the corner with something in his hand and handed it to the waiter.

The waiter stashed it into his vest pocket, "THANK YOU and you have a great day sir!"

"Now where were we darlin, was I kissin' your neck or your breast or . . . . ,"

"You ordered the cheesecake and flowers?"

"Yes I did. Ya' see darlin', you're not the only one who can read minds." I walked up to him and putting my arms around his waist and pulled him toward me. "Okay, what am I thinking right now"?

"Hmm, that these jeans are getting way too tight in a certain area and need to be ripped off as soon as possible, am I right?" I reached down and unzipped them. "Joe, I do believe you are psychic."

The entire morning was spent loving each other. It was late afternoon before we got out of bed. I didn't want my time with Joe to end, but my vacation was coming to a close. In three days it was back to the real world of deadlines and editing. I didn't want to think about it. All I wanted was to be with Joe. We ordered fresh coffee and sat outside on the balcony.

The faint sound of music from our hotel radio filtered onto the balcony. Most were mid-western country songs, then, something caught Joe's attention. He went inside and turned up the volume.
"I love this song Rose, would you dance with me?"

It was one of Faith Hill's songs, *"If I'm Not in Love."*

He took my hand and pulled me close to him. I wrapped my arms around his neck and we swayed to the music. I closed my eyes. Joe whispered the lyrics in my ear, *"Why do I go crazy every time I think about you baby, why else do I want you like I do, if I'm not in love with you."*

I kept my eyes closed until the end of the song. When I opened them – he was smiling. Not his occasional shit-eating-smile, but the smile of man who had just surrendered his heart and soul to someone special.

"Have you been smiling at me the entire time?"

"Yes, I have. You are beautiful with your eyes open or closed. I do love those big brown eyes. They excite me beyond words."

"Rose, if I were to die right now you would be the highlight on my reel of life – a lifetime of moments and memories enjoyed in a single day. You are tough on the outside, soft and sweet like a cupcake on the inside. Hah, maybe I'll call you Cupcake – Cuppy for short."

"And you'll be wearing your testicles as earmuffs – Rose will do."

"Joe, my vacation is just about to end and we need to talk about . . ." he stopped me.

"Rose, let's have this moment without any reality creeping into it. I don't want to be a famous novelist and you don't need to be an art columnist. I just wanna be your old Montana cowboy and for you to be my girl. The real world will have to wait for our attention a little bit longer."

We danced on the balcony, enjoying the sunset and the music. I thought, *"I could learn to love Montana. I've already fallen in love with Joe."*

Chapter 7

We quickly showered and dressed then headed down to the lobby. My car was out front. "While you were in the shower, I had one of the hotel staff bring it over that way we can enjoy the time we have here in Malta and not play valet." I could feel my eyes welling again.

"Oh, here we go again, I made her cry. I'm worthless. Having them bring your car to the hotel wasn't suppose to make you teary eyed, I just thought it would save you time."

"You know that's not why I'm crying Joe. I know that when we leave, this could be the last time I see you." *I could feel my heart breaking already.*"

"Rose, I'm only going to say this once, well maybe twice because I know you won't listen to me the first time. You will never be rid of me. Until my dying day you will always be in my heart, you know my heart Rose and I know yours. No more tears darlin', let's make this our day – a day we'll always remember. No matter what happens, this will be our special time together."

He was right. I wanted to spend these last few moments enjoying myself. He knew my heart and wouldn't crush it like so many had done before. I wiped my face on his shirt sleeve.

"Hey, keep them tears to yourself girl! Today we explore the wonders of Malta, Montana."

Joe gave me what he called the two-bit-tour of Malta. We drove for hours laughing and talking like we'd known each other for years. He plopped his cowboy hat on my head and said, "Girl, you need a real honest-to-goodness cowboy hat, why don't you keep mine. I know it's old like me and it smells of barn sweat and hay but it'll remind you of your old cowboy. Oh, and there's something else in the back seat."

It was a pair of weathered beige chaps with silver Conchos on the sides.

"They belonged to my grandpap, now they're yours – you earned them last night."

We headed back to the hotel and packed up our cars. Joe was right I could read his heart because I knew what he was about to say.

"Well darlin' this is where we part ways again. I'm headed to California. I need to meet with a fella' who says he's got original hand written stories that belonged to some local gunslinger. He thought I could use them in my novels."

I took a breath, "I know, I've got to head home, back to my job." He reached in the back seat and put on another hat.

"Do you always carry a spare?"

He laughed, "Yep, you never know when you'll give your hat or your heart to a purty gal."

I followed him to the interstate. He headed west I headed east toward home. He rolled down his window, "Hey Rose, where exactly do you call home?"

I pretended not to hear him. I wiped the stream of tears from my face, put my sunglasses on and drove off.

I was about a two-day drive from New York. I stopped at a motel for the night. I was physically and emotionally tired. I knew I wouldn't hear from Joe for a while. I kept replaying our time together in my head not wanting to forget a single minute of it. I knew it was something special...something no one could take away from us. But still, I wanted to know how he was doing. He said he would email me when he could but the internet wasn't reliable in the Sierra Nevada mountain range. I checked my email to see if there was an interesting subject title from Montana Joe.

The bed was lumpy and smelled like a wet dog had stayed in the room. But I was tired, it was cheap and I needed internet access. I turned on the television to check the weather. It dawned on me that I hadn't watched television in three weeks. To be honest, I didn't miss it. The national news was on. In between the commercial breaks, they generally give the local news and weather. I'd hate to wake up only to hear reports of a hay truck hitting a cow or a freak tornado coming at the precise time I'm checking out.

I was brushing my teeth when the national news reported a huge brush fire burning near the Sierra Nevada mountain area. "Oh God, that's the same direction Joe was driving!" I checked my email every minute – still nothing. An hour later, my cell phone rang. I didn't recognize the phone number.

"Hello"?

"Hello darlin' I can't talk too long I'm using the Sheriff's cell phone. For some reason mine won't get any reception. I just wanted to let you know that I'm okay. I knew you'd be worried."

I thought, *"Worried? How about panic stricken!"*

"Are you okay, really Joe are you safe?"

"Yes, Rose I'm okay, nothing that a hot bath, hot sexy gal and two or three hours of hot sex wouldn't cure. So . . . what are you wearing?"

"Stop joking Joe, I was worried sick!"

The reception was getting worse.

"Rose, I've got to go, the fires are moving fast and if I'm going to die I want your voice to be the last voice I hear. I'll email you when I get to my hotel, I love you Rose."

"Wait, Joe I lov . . ." The connection ended.

It was a relief to know he was okay and still as horny as ever. In fact, it was the first time I laughed since we'd been apart. It felt good. *But did I not hear him correctly or did he say he loved me?* I wanted him to repeat it but the phone went dead. Was I about to tell him that I loved him too? Can two people fall in love this quickly or was it just a vacation fling? My heart knew it wasn't a fling because I had way too many summer romances, and I knew how they went. You meet, you drink, you screw, you say goodbye in September. My time with Joe wasn't like that at all. Hell, I couldn't stand him. I thought, like most successful novelists, he was a pompous blow-hard loving the sound of his own voice. But he turned out to be a nice guy.

I was about to turn off the lights when I heard my email alert. It was a message from Joe. I flipped the lights back on and grabbed my laptop.

To: Rose
Fr: Montana Joe
Subject: **The Loneliness of the Long Distance Runner**

Dear Rose Darlin'

I just arrived at my hotel. I'm hurtin' from the long drive and for the first time in my life I'm lonely. I need to hear you laugh and tell me that you care about me. I care about you. I don't know whether you heard my last reply before the phone disconnected but I told you that I loved you. I thought I heard you say 'I love you too" or was it just wishful thinkin'?. Do you Rose, do you love me? Being away from you hurts more than my achin' body and that's a hurt I haven't felt in quite a while. I guess because I've never fallen in love with anyone like you before.

I'm sorry to sound depressed, but dadgumit girl I am depressed. I couldn't sleep too well. The hotel bed is too big for this lonesome cowboy with a developing Montana-sized hard on. It woke me up out of a sound sleep. It needs someone . . . It needs you! Maybe this fellow will cancel our appointment, maybe the letters are a fake and we can spend more time together. Now, I'm cynical, horny and depressed. Damn near worthless. I really miss you Rose. I miss everything about you and some things, oh how I miss those things!

The loneliest trip ever and missin' you, Joe

[*1963 British film – "The Loneliness of a Long Distance Runner" A movie that I've never forgotten.]

I immediately relied:

To: Montana Joe
Fr: Rose
Reply Subject: **The Loneliness of the Long Distance Runner**

Dear Joe,
I miss you too, and yes, I did tell you that I love you. It felt good to say
it. You make me crazy and that's what I love about you. I never thought
I'd fall head-over-heels for a cowboy but there's a first time for
everything. I wanted my vacation to be an adventure and it was – a
wonderful unexpected romantic vacation. And the best part, I found you
Montana Joe.
 Love and miss you too, Rose

The closer I got to the New York border, the more my mind started to wander. I felt as though I was dying and going to my own funeral. The lightness I enjoyed when I was with Joe disappeared. I wanted him in my life. I wanted that sexy and maddening cowboy who made me feel like the only woman on the face of the earth – I wanted Joe. Then it struck me . . . *I didn't know his name – I didn't know his real name!*

I reached over to the passenger's side seat and grabbed his cowboy hat. The scent of his shampoo lingered. Reflecting back to the night we spent together made me grin, sort of like the shit-eating grin he flashes when he thinks he's putting one over on me.

I was about to put it on when I noticed three gold initials stamped into the hat band, L.J.M. *I know he writes under the nom de plume of Montana Joe. These must be his initials. I can't go back to New York without knowing the legal name of the man I love. They would lock me up in the psych ward of Eagleville Regional Medical center. He knows my real name because I accidentally dropped my business card. How completely insane is this situation. I've got to go back!*

I pulled off the interstate to call my office. I didn't know how I would explain the need for additional time off, but I didn't care. I needed him to tell me his real name in person not via email or telephone. I loved calling him Joe, and I had to admit I was beginning to love the name, Rose. Or maybe it was because HE calls me Rose. It didn't matter. Either way, I needed to know his true identity if this bizarre relationship was to go any further. I dug through my purse, got my cell phone and called the office.

"Hello Art Columnist Suite, Jannine speaking, how may I direct your call?"

"Jannine, it's me I need a huge favor."

"Well hello ME, where the hell are you? I really miss you! When are you coming back to work?"

"That's why I'm calling; I need another week off. Can you fix it with Rick in Human Resources? I promise I'll answer my own phone calls for a month if you can make this happen. Jannine, I desperately need this time, okay?"

"Hmm, need more time, desperate . . . you met a guy! Oh my God you met some guy, tell me everything, where, when, who!"

"I can't tell you because I know you Jannine. You'll have my wedding invitations printed and mailed before we're off the phone. But I can promise you this. When I get back I'll give you all the lewd and juicy details and I'll even throw in that lavender cashmere sweater I brought back from Spain. You know the one that's, way-too-small-that-I-swear-I'm-going-to-lose-fifty-pounds-to-get-into-but-never-will-sweater. You can have it if you do me this huge favor."

"Wow, I've never heard you beg like this before. He must be hung like a horse!"

"Jeez Jannine, get your mind out of the gutter. Can I count on you, please, I'll be your best friend I'll share my lunch with you."

"You've been using that line on me since I started working here. It's a good thing we're best friends . . . and yes I'll do it."

"You are two-and-a-half complete dudes! Thanks so much Jannine, call me back if there is any problem, love ya' bye."

If anyone could get Rick to approve more vacation time it was Jannine. She was a born manipulator. She could tell the Pope to go to hell and he would. I know I can count on her to work her magic. I'd better send her an email just in case there's a problem.

I found a truck stop with internet connection and sent her the email. Less than fifteen minutes later she said it's done and approved, but I owed her big time because she had to lie and tell him how nice he looked. He's such an obnoxious, overweight prick that it made her head ache. I replied that I'd buy her the largest bottle of Excedrin when I got home. Her reply, *"Only for you girl, now go get your man!"*

My thoughts wandered as I headed west. It would be a three or four day drive back to Montana. I realized I could do with more clothes, shoes and definitely underwear. I also realized my east coast attire wasn't appropriate for the Montana terrain. I had jeans but no sturdy shoes or boots. I made a mental list and kept my eyes open for a big box or sporting goods store. Either one should have hiking or cowboy boots. *Oh God, cowboy boots! Am I actually thinking of wearing them?* I saw a high fashion model wearing them once in a photo shoot. *How uncomfortable can they be?*

I caught a glimpse of a billboard advertising western wear and apparel stores 6-miles ahead. I guess the further west one goes, the more one will find western garb. All I could imagine were those gaudy cowboy shirts with the fringe and those horrible western line dancing skirts. *I won't be caught dead in one of them!* I drove into the parking lot of Jackstones Western and Cowboy Outlet. They had a hitching post outside the store. *Like someone would ride up on a horse. Now, maybe I'd drive up in a Mustang with a bitchin' V-8 underneath the hood.*

I didn't want to spend too much on clothing I probably wouldn't wear again. I rummaged through their sale rack. It wasn't as bad as I thought. Everything was 40% off. I couldn't pass up a sale. I took a few things into the changing room to try on. *Is this a size 5? Maybe I picked up the wrong one. More like a size 15. Must be the big boned store?* I took them off, went back to the rack and picked smaller sizes. *Okay, now that's much better!*

The gal in the shop was a bit peculiar. Before I left she said, "I can't believe you are still wearing regular clothes, when are you due." *Did I misunderstand her, maybe it's the western drawl?*

"Excuse me . . . did you ask when I was due."

"Yes honey, you are glowing like a precious mother-to-be, bless your heart. Congratulations!"

If I wasn't in such a rush, I would have sucker-punched her. She was much larger than me so I politely said thank you and left the store.

I glanced at myself in the store window and she was right. I was glowing but thank God for a different reason. I was not ready for kids!

The strip mall had a gas station-slash-cafe. I needed to refuel the car and my coffee mug. A short trip through the drive-thru and I was back on the road. They also had internet access. I wanted to check my email. There were fewer than I expected. There was one from Jannine and two from Joe. I read Jannine's first.

To: "Rose" ha, ha,
Fr: Jannine
Subject: **Emails from Hell**

Hey girl,

I just wanted to let you know I'm answering all of your work emails so you can concentrate on Joe, you can thank me later!
PS I'm starting to like this Rose character, she's much cooler than you, lol.

I thought, *"Jannine girl you are an angel I owe you!"*
I eagerly clicked on Joe's.

To: Rose
Fr: Montana Joe
Subject: **Roman Art and Architecture and its Influence on Mankind**

Dear Rose darlin'

Sorry I couldn't email you until now. *This barbed-wire mountain internet service is pissing me off!* *Doesn't it know that a desperate woman is waiting to hear from her cowboy! Anyway, I always have trouble separatin' fact from fiction. And my heart is reviewin' my darlin'*

Rose. I believe most ever' word I spoke to you was true from the bottom of my heart. You are beautiful inside and out.
I've never known anyone who lifted me up like you. You are the highlight of my life and the precious memory that I will carry with me always.

I never even knew anyone could make me feel so alive, so loved, so cared for, so adored, so important! You are the sexiest, and most remarkable woman I've ever had the privilege of knowing. You make me wish I could go back in time and live my life over. I've never felt that way before. Come with me on my research trip [to California] and see if what we have for each other is the real deal.

Your head-over-heels in love cowboy, Joe

I read the email twice to make sure it was asking what I thought it was. I was on my way out west at the same time he was asking me to come out west. *Maybe we're both psychic?*

I replied with four words:

To: Montana Joe

Fr: Rose

Reply Subject: **Art and Architecture *and its Influence on Mankind***

"I'm on my way!"

The next day I received another email from Joe. This one was completely different from all the others.

To: Rose
Fr: Montana Joe
Subject: **Dreams that you dare to dream**

Dear Rose darlin',

I HATED having to leave you. So you can imagine my heart skipped a beat seeing your four words! Baby, since I met you I've felt like singin' and dancin' my way through the day. (And if you knew how bad I sing and how lousy I dance, you'd know how crazy I am about you.   I feel like I'm over the rainbow.

That night in Malta was incredible
"Somewhere over the rainbow . . . way up high"
So, I thought we'd forget about everything and just make love all night
"There's a land that I heard of once in a lullaby"
I'd planned to have you moaning until sunrise and then some
"Somewhere over the rainbow . . . skies are blue"
But something unexpected happened
"and the dreams that we dare to dream really do come true"
So what happens? I cuddle you up in my arms
"Someday I'll wish upon a star"
And whisper sweet (very sweet) things in your ear
"and wake up where the clouds are far behind me"
And once again the plans wash away
"Where troubles melt like lemon drops"
The glow on your face and the sparkle in those big beautiful brown eyes
"way above the chimney tops that's where you'll find me"
Made me want to hold you tight and never let you go
"Somewhere over the rainbow . . . bluebirds fly
It was the sweetest night I've experienced in years . . . maybe decades
"birds fly over the rainbow . . . why, oh, why, can't I?"
Baby, I had no idea I was going to say and do all those things.
"If happy little bluebirds fly, beyond the rainbow"
There was no script. I've never said them like that before
"Why, oh why can't I?"
It's just like a deep part of my heart opened and it flowed out.

It was, for me, a totally unexpected and wonderful experience. I don't think I can really explain how wonderful. But . . . I know you know . . . you know my heart.

Darlin', I don't know if I'll have any time today (I've got to review galleys and mail a finished manuscript) . . . but I promise I'll email you tonight.

Your hopeless romantic, Joe
"Dreams really do come true"

 By the time I'd finished reading his email, my cheeks were covered in tears. *How can one man know me so well in such a short period of time?*

Haven't we known each other for years? How does he know my favorite film is, The Wizard of Oz?

The cynical part of me believed he was having me tailed or bugged or maybe did one of those online bio searches on me. But the romantic in me believed in love-at-first-sight, soul mates, and kismet. There was a perfect match uniquely created for everyone. Coupling an over-achieving city art columnist with a laid back, sarcastic, handsome, Montana cowboy was the perfect example. What an unusual pair. But like Joe's special blend of one-half French roast and one half Arbuckles brand, if it worked—it worked. I packed up my laptop and headed back towards the interstate.

I drove non-stop through Kansas and Colorado stopping only for food, gas and an occasional nap or two. I didn't want to waste a single minute sightseeing. The only site I wanted to see was Joe. I was just about to cross the Colorado border into Utah when I needed something to drink. I'd been traveling on coffee with loads of sugar and fast food – both of which add extra pounds to my well maintained figure. I thought it best to have a real meal.

I turned off the interstate for a quick bite and to stock up on bottled water. A small mom-and-pop type restaurant with a packed parking lot was still serving breakfast. I walked in and they knew right away I wasn't from around these parts. I smiled and asked if I could order something to go. A woman came from behind the cash register laughing out loud.

"Honey, we don't eat and run in these parts of the country. Now why don't you sit down and have a good home-cooked breakfast. Lord knows you could stand to gain a pound or two."

"I would love to but I'm trying to get to California by tomorrow night. I really would like to get back on the road."

She shook her head, "Hon', you'll have plenty of time to meet whoever it is that's got your nostrils flarin' like that. I bet doughnuts-to-dollars it's a cowboy. It's always some old saddle bum cowboy that girls feel the need to chase after, am I right?"

I laughed, "Well you are right on the money, but he's no saddle bum. He's the man I plan to love for the rest of my life."

"Come on, you can give me the juicy details over a ham steak, biscuits and gravy. She walked me over to a table where a regular customer was eating and pulled over two empty chairs.

"Randy, go on over there and sit with Milton. Me and this gal got girl stuff to discuss."

He grumbled something under his breath, picked up his half-eaten meal. I mouthed, "I'm sorry." He was not amused, but politely relocated.

"So, tell me about this fella' that's got you running half crazy across the country – I bet he's a rodeo man."

I didn't want to give too much information. Gossip has a tendency to fly like wild fire in small towns. If I told her how we met and that I've only known Joe for three weeks, I'd be run out of town like a cheap whore turning tricks on the steps of a church on Sunday morning.

"He used to rodeo but now he's a writer. I'm also a writer – an art columnist to be precise."

She slowly exhaled, "I guess it's good to have something in common with the man you love. Most folks here get married to the first man that winks at them. Four kids and fifty pounds later you realize you don't know anything about them. And that's why I'm stuck here in this place slinging hash to feed my children. Their no-good daddy left me high and dry."

I could see her eyes tearing. I offered her my napkin.

"You go and don't look back. Go find your guy and live your life the way you want too, not the way people think you should."

I think she was trying to convince herself more than offering me motherly advice. I reached for my wallet to pay the bill.

"Honey, put your money away. Randy's picking up the tab, ain't that right Randy?"

He dropped his coffee cup. Everyone laughed. "Poor Randy, he's so easily rattled."

I gave her a hug and she handed me a sack with hot biscuits and refilled my coffee mug.

"This should keep you fed through Utah. You go on honey, it's on the house. Be safe and take care."

I drove for another three hours and thought I'd better check my email. I stopped at a half dozen rest stops none of which had internet access. Joe had my cell number; however, all I had was his email address. I sat in the car staring at a no-internet-connection error message hoping it would miraculously pick up a signal.

I was about to shut down when a weak signal popped up. An eighteen-wheeler with a satellite dish attached was heading for the truck parking area. I jumped out of my car, stood in front of this huge tractor trailer, waving my arms like a mental patient. The driver hit his air breaks and stopped before I became road kill.

"Oy, what the bloody hell are you trying to do get yourself killed?"

"I need your internet signal for five minutes! I can pay you, please it's an emergency."

The driver backed his rig into one of the "Truck Only" parking spaces. I was fascinated by his ease and skill getting the huge truck into such a small spot. I have trouble parallel parking my compact car.

He stepped out of the cab and walked over to my car.

"So what kind of bloody emergency are we having today, 'ay? Heart attack, seizure, broke a fingernail and need a bloody emery board?"

I noticed a thick British accent, "You're obviously not from these parts are you?"

"Well aren't you the clever carrot, NO I'm not! And stop avoiding the bloody question. What's the emergency that is keeping me from my bed? A bed in which I should be sleeping after driving eleven hours straight."

I didn't want to give this Benny Hill wanna-be any information so I told him I had a family emergency and my blood type was so rare they needed to synchronize their operating time with my arrival.

To which he said, "You are such a horrid liar, girl with more front than Brighton. But whatever it is, it must be terribly important to create such a dreadful tissue of lies. Go on then, you've got five minutes so don't prat about!"

I thanked him even though I wasn't sure whether or not I'd been given permission or been insulted.

He went into the rest area and I hopped up into his cab. It wasn't as bad as I had imagined. It was clean and tidy, equipped with air conditioning, a small refrigerator, a television and more importantly internet access.

I only had five minutes so I got down to the business at hand. I opened my email account and found an email marked IMPORTANT from Joe. No witty subject matter just a blank subject space.

I thought, "Oh God I hope he hasn't changed his mind or maybe something is terribly wrong!"

It took a minute before I had the guts to read it. But I had to no matter what.

To: Rose
Fr: Montana Joe
Subject:

Dear Rose darlin'

I hope you get this email in time. Change of plans, leaving California tonight and heading back home to Montana. You are so much more important than some old letters. Baby, head to Montana and I'll meet up with you at the hotel in Malta. See you soon darlin'.
Your forever cowboy, Joe

(PS I live about 10-miles west in Wagner, so it was no coincidence I knew the place so well.)

I didn't wait to turn off my laptop. I closed it and jumped out of the truck as the driver was walking out of the rest area.

"From the chuffin' big grin of your face, I assume you confirmed you're arrival with the doctors?"

"What . . . chuffin', confirm what, oh yeah I did and he's quite pleased I'm on my way."

He walked me to my car and I handed him my card. "I owe you big time if you ever, I mean EVER need anything let me know. And again thank you . . . "

"Paul, the name's Paul and I'm from England as if you haven't already figured it out"

"Thank you so much Paul from England. You are a darling man for helping me. Remember . . . I owe you!"

I sped out of the rest area heading north to Montana. Paul watched until my vehicle was out of view and tucked the card in his jacket pocket thinking, *I might just take you up on that someday girly.*

Driving to Montana gave me the time to reflect on this whirlwind romance I was experiencing with Joe. Less than a month ago, I was ready to swear off men completely. And the worst part was it didn't bother me in the least. Men were time wasters, pure entertainment between career plans and deadlines. I never wanted to get too involved.

My last relationship was about sex and once the sex fizzled out, there was nothing left but a stale routine of polite conversation. It took years for me to let the relationship go. There were no signs of marriage in our future. When I was ready, he wasn't and he never seemed to be ready.

Maybe I never gave them a chance. I didn't want to give my heart to someone who, in a few months, would leave me heartbroken. It was easier to keep it sexual with no strings attached. My biological clock was ticking. Even though I wasn't ready to have kids, I always thought about having a family of my own, a husband and a house with a big backyard – sort of a happily ever after story. Childish dreams, perhaps, but I was determined to hold on to them.

The sun was about to set when I decided to call it a night. I didn't know the roads and thought it best to head for a motel. I looked for a sign that offered internet access and found a small group of cabins for rent. I went into the office knowing full-well I didn't need to rent one but was hoping he had rooms or knew of a local bed and breakfast.

An older gentleman came from the back. He looked to be of Native American decent.

"Hello there, you must be lost. Our tourist season isn't for another month."

"No, I am not lost. I need a room. Do you know a place where I could stay the night? I'm on my way to Malta and its getting dark."

He laughed, "There are no places to stay between here and Malta, well at least with running water and indoor plumbing. You don't look like a camper."

"You're right I'm not a camper, just a very tired gal trying to get to Malta"

He sat down on the stool behind the counter. "What brings you to Malta?"

He seemed so sincere I felt comfortable telling him my situation. I told him about the man I was going to visit and how we met.

We talked for about an hour when he said, "Would you like a cup of coffee?"

"I would love a cup, thank you so much!"

He came back with two big coffee mugs and a plate of cookies. "I was about to have my evening snack when you drove up. It's nice to share it with someone. My name is Raymond Winterbee…nice to meet you."

I thought for a minute and said, "My name is Rose and very nice to meet you too Raymond."

He winked, "Rose, you are so beautiful you need only one name."

"You said you needed a place to stay. I would be happy to let you stay in one of the cabins for the night. It may be a bit stuffy. I'll open the windows before you go in. It's smart to stay the night. These roads are tricky to navigate in the dark especially when you're not familiar with them."

I was humbled by this gentleman's generosity. No one in the city would do anything this thoughtful for a stranger. I'd accepted the fact that urban life was rude and self-centered. It was expected. But his kindness touched me in a way I'd never experienced before – almost mystical.

He had a necklace of sorts around his neck. I admired it and asked the nature of the symbols. He told me they were representative of things his tribe honored.

"We call them fetish necklaces. My grandfather made this for me when I was born. I wear it to honor his spirit."

He reached behind the counter and handed me something. "Here this is for you. I made it this morning. It was a beaded bracelet with a firebird imbedded in the bead work.

"The Firebird is the sacred bearer of happiness. You have Cherokee blood in you, don't you Rose? You are fiery but quick to calm. The Firebird is your symbol."

I was completely taken aback by his gift. It was absolutely beautiful. "I will always cherish this and your kindness – again thank you for everything."

Raymond's observation amazed me. My grandfather was half-Cherokee. I never pursued his background but Raymond knew right away. We finished our coffee. The long drive was catching up with me. I needed sleep. Raymond said he would show me to my cabin.

"Please feel free to use the internet access. I never use it. I'm not smart when it comes to computers. I prefer writing letters. But you young people seem to rely on it. Good night Rose."

There was no shower in the cabin just a large claw foot tub. I hadn't taken a good hot bath in years. I never seem to sit still long enough to enjoy a bath, but tonight it felt like a soothing slice of heaven. I could feel my entire body relax. My tension drifted away with the steam.

For a minute I thought I heard Joe say, *"I wish I could join you darlin'."*

I toweled off and got ready for bed. *Maybe I should check my email just in case Joe had a change in plans.* I clicked on the email icon. There was one from Joe.

To: Rose
Fr: Montana Joe
*Subject: **The Angst and Iconography Inherent in Joyce's Ulysses***

Darlin' Rose,

I'm about a 120 miles from Malta. I'm gettin' by imagin' how good it will be to hold you again. To say I miss you is like lookin' at the ocean and sayin' "water." Darlin' I can't even see the edges let alone describe how I miss you.

I was lookin' a bit shabby around the collar so I got a haircut. I had the gal trim it light (speakin' of whom, heavy-set ladies should never, ever wear stretch stirrup paints!!!) Somehow, the gray is still there. Nothin' I can do about that darlin'. I spent the afternoon finishing the manuscripts and mailed them off to the editors. Now I have as much time as I want to be with my Rose. You know my heart.

Baby, our hearts are united forever. You know that. So do I. I can't imagine how in the world I could love you more than I do. This cowboy is crazy about you, Rose. Of course, some would argue, this cowboy is just plain crazy.

Your crazy (in love) cowboy, Joe

His email eased my body more than the hot bath. I drifted off to sleep knowing that in less than a day's drive we would be together again.

The sun was coming up through the trees when I heard voice outside the cabin door.

"Morning Rose, its Raymond, there's hot coffee and fresh muffins in the office kitchen. Help yourself."

I got my things together and went outside on the cabin porch. It felt good to breathe in clean Montana air. I felt more rested than I had in days. I put my things in the porch and walked over to the office.

Raymond hollered from the kitchen, "Come on back Rose, I've got your coffee ready."

I sat down at the small wooden table. "Raymond, how can I ever repay you for your kindness? I'll make sure Montana Joe knows how well you've treated me."

He paused for a moment then asked, "Montana Joe, you know Joe. We are good friends. He comes here when he needs a quiet place to write. In fact, he usually stays in the cabin you were in last night. I thought, *No wonder I felt his presence.*

Raymond went on to tell me how Joe was a man true to his word.

"He has good spirits watching over him. And now he has you Rose. I can tell that you are good for him. He is lucky to have you." He walked me to my car.

I was about to get into the car when I realized I hadn't paid Raymond. "How much do I owe you for the night?"

"You've already paid me with your company Rose. I hope we meet again. Tell Montana, Raymond says hello and he owes me an autograph copy of his latest novel." He waved goodbye and headed back to the office.

Chapter 8

I'd been on the road for about six hours when my cell phone rang. The number didn't register with me.

"H-h-hello?"

"Well don't sound so happy darlin' – it's me, Joe. How far away from Malta are you . . . and what are you wearing, hopefully just a smile."

"Joe, I didn't recognize the number. Where are you and whose phone are you using?"

"You want the long or short version?

I paused and took a deep breath ready for the worst.

"Well, I was bettin' this fella that he couldn't dismount from a horse going full gallop. He said he could and, of course, I said he couldn't. Anyway, he lost the bet. I was laughin' so hard my phone slipped out of my jacket pocket into a pile of horse shit. Needless to say, I had to get a new phone and I thought it was about time I got a new number. Don't want any of my old cowgirl pals callin' me anymore. You're the only girl in this cowboy's life. I wouldn't want you to punch 'em in the nostrils."

"You are insane, what am I going to do with you."

"Yup, that's me your insane totally crazy about you cowboy. And, I know lots of things you can do with me most involve less clothing and more lovin'."

"I'm about 40-miles from Malta so let me get my hands back on the wheel and concentrate on the road. You can be quite distracting cowboy."

"Okay, but I have to admit I'm a bit jealous of that steering wheel. I'd love to feel your hands around my . . . ."

We lost reception. It was a good thing because the phone call was quickly becoming x-rated. *We'll have plenty of time for that Joe, plenty of time!*

When I finally passed the Malta city limit sign, my excitement overwhelmed me. I was also nervous about spending more than a day or two with this man, who in reality, I barely knew. I didn't want to start doubting my judgment, but I needed to look at this objectively. *Do I trust my heart and go with it, or do I analyze the situation to death until I find something wrong with it?* I decided to love this man with all my heart and let conventional judgment be damned.

For once in my life, I wanted to do something completely out of the ordinary, well at least for me. I could see the hotel coming up on the horizon. *Finally, I'll be with my Joe. Hmm, my Joe I like the sound of that.*

I saw his truck parked near the hotel. It was muddy and needed a wash. *What the hell has he been doing?* There was a parking spot beside him. I pulled into it. I peeked in his driver's side window. *Hmm, junk food wrappers and coffee cups. This man is in desperate needs of a home cooked meal.*

I walked toward the hotel when I saw Joe waiting outside. *Hair a little bit shorter, but I like it.* He saw me and picked up his pace. I ran into his arms and hugged him.

"Excuse me, ma'am, do I know you? You better high-tail it out of here because I'm waiting for my Rose darlin' and . . . "

Before he could say another word, I kissed him and didn't stop until someone walked by told us to get a room.

"Hello baby! My Lord, I can't tell you how much I've missed those kisses. I daydreamed about them all the way to Malta, except you were wearin' fewer clothes."

I looked at his face. It was covered in scratches. "What the hell happened to you? Where did you get all those scratches?"

"Long story, I'll tell you after we've had a hot shower and about five hours of sex or a five-hour shower and hot sex. Either way you're gonna be naked girl and there will be sex involved.

"Goodness Joe! Is sex all you think about? Don't you think about anything else?"

"Sorry darlin' I wasn't paying attention. I was imagining you butt-naked on my lap . . . what was the questions again?"

"I shook my head, "Joe what am I going to do with you."

"Just love me baby, just love me. Oh, by the way, I brought you a little surprise. It's up in the room – hope you like it."

He opened the hotel door and covered my eyes. I kept walking until he said stop.

"Now open your eyes."

It was a beautiful saddle. I'd never owned my own saddle. I used to ride a lot as a kid but we always had hand-me-down saddles from the summer camp.

"I love it Joe! I didn't know you owned horses."

"I don't. I figured you rode me so hard last time that you might like a proper saddle."

I didn't know whether or not he was joking about not owning horses, but when I saw his crooked shit-eating smiles spread across his face I punched his arm.

"Whoa, that ain't any way to treat a fella that just brought you a two thousand dollar saddle. It's even got your initials on it."

It had the letter 'R' branded between two linked hearts.

"I hope you like it because I don't plan on fallin' in love with anyone else, unless their name begins with R – and just for the record, I own eight horses so you'll have your pick. I think we'll start you off on Daisy, the plug horse. She's only got two speeds slow and slower, but she's a sweetie and real gentle."

I thanked Joe and remembered, "Oh before I forget I ran into a friend of yours named Raymond. He spoke very highly of you."

He smiled, "Raymond Winterbee, now he's one interesting fella'. Knows more about the old west than any historian I've ever met. He helps me with my stories. You know he's full-blooded Blackfoot."

I told Joe he knew just from looking at me that I had Cherokee blood in me.

"Raymond is very observant. Did he also know that you were hot for an old cowboy who drove non-stop to get back home to see you?"

"No, however he did happen to mention that I stayed in the same cabin as you do when you go on your research trips. I felt your presences there."

He sat at the bottom of the bed and sighed.

"Well, to be honest darlin' you were weighin' heavy on my mind all day and all night – mostly at night. I was really tired so I traipsed off to bed about 10:30 PM and stretched one of the hotel pillows lengthwise and pretended it was you. I had my arms wrapped around that pillow the entire night. I woke up with a achin' hard on expecting to see a cute gal with big brown eyes and a hot body willing to pleasure me. But all I found was a slightly startled and indignant pillow. I was a little saddened not to wake up in your arms. But I'm not sad now – glancing down at the bulge begging to show in his jeans"

"Joe, just when I think you've reached your maximum level of bullshit, you come up with even more shit than a herd of cattle with diarrhea."

He winked, "Right now I'm full of something, but it ain't shit. You're teasin' a desperate man darlin' so why don't we end this conversation and let me take you to bed. I've miss you somethin' awful Rose."

Mid morning we checked out of the hotel and headed to his place. He tail-hitched my car to his truck, and I hopped into the passenger side. His truck was larger than my car. Joe was much taller than me and needed more leg room. He jokingly asked if I needed a booster seat. I flipped him the bird and buckled my seat belt. It was fun being a passenger for a change. I loved the majestic beauty of Montana. The drive was pleasant and uneventful, but for some reason I felt extremely anxious. Until now it was all fun and games, but he was taking me to his home, his private place. I pretended to be engrossed in the scenery; however, my heart was racing a mile a minute.

He noticed that I was more quiet than usual and asked what was wrong.

"Joe this is a big step for me. I hope I don't screw it up by doing something stupid."

"And just what kind of stupid thing do you plan on doing – redecorate my home to look like a New York boutique or even worse . . . use instant coffee. That'll get you horse whipped." We both laughed out loud.

"Darlin' I know your heart, always remember that, now scoot over here and give me your hand."

He put it over his heart. I could feel it beating.

"Every beat is a reminder of how much I love you Rose." He raised it to his lips and kissed my palm. I did the same with his.

"Rose, every day I want to fill your hand with kisses. If I'm away all you'll need to do is raise your hand to those beautiful lips of yours, and it'll be me kissin' you.

We held hands until we reached the entrance to his property. His driveway was longer than my city street. It cut through a thicket of trees to a rustic ranch house. To the left was a barn with stables attached. A small pond was on the far side of a gated pasture. I'd never been any place like this before.

He parked the truck beside of the barn and came around to the passenger side door.

"Welcome home Rose. Mi Casa, Su Casa."

"It's beautiful Joe. I've never seen this much land. Does it have its own zip code?"

"Heck, darlin' you ain't seen nothin' yet. Once I get you settled I'll take you on the two-bit tour of the property. But for now let me show you around the place."

His living room/dining area was sunken with a big fireplace in the middle of the room. Two steps up to the right led to a kitchen large enough to put my entire house in. Two steps up to the left were the bedrooms. Each bed room had its own bathroom and attached deck with a panoramic view of Montana.

"Okay Joe, I've died and gone to heaven. Why didn't you tell me Montana was actually heaven in disguise?"

"You are my piece of heaven Rose wrapped in one beautiful sexy body. A body I would love to hold for the rest of my life. But right now baby I'm starvin' how about we have something to eat and then I'll take you to the barn to meet the rest of the family."

To my surprise, Joe knew his way around the kitchen. He made western omelets that were unbelievably good.

"I usually whip up a mess of biscuits to go with them but I thought toast would be quicker."

We finished eating and I put the plates in the dishwasher. He looked over at me and laughed.

"Darlin' around here we use the dishwasher when I've got a corral of people over for dinner. I do most of the dishes myself. But don't worry. I use that dish washing liquid that leaves my hands soft and smooth."

He left the dishes in the sink and tossed me an old Carhartt jacket. "It's time to head out to the barn. You'd better put on a pair of barn boots. You do have boots don't you Rose?"

"Yes, I've got these." I showed him the new boots I brought from Jackstones. He tried not to laugh at my choice of so-called work boots.

"Hmm, those are nice but why don't we leave them in the box, you can wear a pair of Cecilia's work boots." I guess he saw my expression, trying to figure out who Cecilia was?"

"Don't worry, she's is my housekeeper darlin' – no need to get jealous."

Who said I was jealous, curious at best, but not jealous.

As we walked past the fireplace, I noticed a photograph of a young man standing with Joe. He looked like a younger version of Joe. I didn't say anything but tucked the question away in my mind for later.

The barn was much bigger than it looked. It had a hay loft, ten stables and a walk-in tack room. The stables were empty of horses but full of horse shit.

"Now you see why I didn't want you to wear your new fancy city boots. It can get pretty messy out here."

I thought, *Yes, I can SMELL that.*

Joe stood at the barn door leading to the pasture and whistled. "I'd move away from the door . . . here comes the family."

Out of nowhere came eight horses in full gallop running right towards the door. Joe whistled again and they slowed down. He made a clicking sound with his mouth and they walked into the barn like well mannered children.

"Howdy boys, come over here; I want you to meet someone very special. Her name is Rose, don't eat her."

I hadn't been around horses in years. I must admit I was a little nervous. They were so large and powerful I thought I was going to be trampled. But they were just as gentle as my cat.

"The palomino is Daisy. You'll be riding her tomorrow. Daisy this is Rose. Now, she ain't too good at holding onto things, unless it's her cowboy, so don't buck her off, okay."

"Tomorrow I'll bring your saddle out and get it ready for you. It's new and a little stiff – nothin' a little neatsfoot oil won't fix."

While he was giving me the tour of the barn, we talked--mostly small talk about how everything in Montana seemed fresh and clear, how quiet and still things were in comparison to the big city. We wanted to enjoy every bit of our new relationship. It was also the first time I used the word relationship. I helped Joe muck out the stalls and get the horses watered and fed.

Walking back to the house, we had some serious talk about how our lives were so different and how fate brought us together. We left our boots outside and finished our conversation with coffee by the fireplace.

Joe showed me how to make his special cowboy brew. I had to admit I preferred it over the expensive lattes I'd been drinking.

"Not bad for a city gal. Before you know it you'll be drinkin' day-old coffee and fixin' beans and bacon over a campfire. I'll make a cowgirl out of you yet."

"And how do you intend to do that? Dress me up like Dale Evans and teach me to sing Happy Trails."

"Nope, I'll teach you how to tie a half-hooey. I'll practice on you tonight."

He caught me staring at the photo of him and the young man. I tried to turn away but he said, "That's my son Morgan, he'll be twenty-five in September. His momma never told me about him. She passed away fourteen years ago. He'd been living with his aunt in Santa Fe and about ten years ago turned up on my doorstep with a letter from her and the clothes on his back. I couldn't deny him. He's the spittin' image of me when I was his age."

"Yes he is Joe. He's got your eyes. He's a very handsome young man – you should be proud."

"I am proud. He came in second in the statewide semi-professional calf roping competition this year."

I had to admit I didn't know much about Joe's world, and I'm sure he felt the same about mine. But I wanted to know everything about him. I felt as though I already did.

"How about you Rose, anything important I should know about you? Do you prefer the right or left side of the bed, sunny-side up or scrambled, do you snore? I know you drool."

"Very funny Joe, but sadly my life is rather dull and mundane. I work 12-hours a day, eat out every night, no kids, I own a cat and some plants. The cat is still alive and healthy, which is more than I can say about the plants."

Joe walked over to the fireplace and put some logs onto it. I wondered why being the end of April. He said it gets pretty cold at night and if we decided to make out in the living room, he didn't want me to catch a chill.

We sat by the fire and talked for hours. I'd never opened up to a man like this before. I guess I never trusted anyone as much as I trust Joe.

"Well darlin' I think it's time we hit the hay. Morning comes early at Montana's place. Horses need fed, fences need checked and I promised you an authentic cowboy breakfast."

I winked at him and in my best western drawl, "Okay boss man, I reckon we'd better mosey off to the bunkhouse and git some shut eye"

Without blinking he said, "That was the worst imitation of a western drawl I've ever heard, but keep tryin' baby. Now, let's go to bed. We'll see if your hooey skills are any better."

I woke up at 3:00 AM and couldn't go back to sleep. I thought all the excitement from the day before was still swirling around in my brain. It was a lot to take in. Joe was still sleeping and I hadn't checked my email in two days. I put on his shirt and took my laptop to the living room. I was surprised Joe had internet access, but then again, how else would he get his manuscripts and galley changes to his editor.

I logged in and closed my eye. I was nervous to see how many unanswered emails would be in the queue. Strangely, there were not as many as I expected. *Bless you Jannine.* However, there was one directly from Rick marked urgent.

"What the hell does he want? My week isn't over yet and I'm not expected back for three days. "

URGENT- It seems you don't have any more vacation time left. I was in error to approve your additional time and got a stern warning from my boss about it. It looks as though you won't be paid for your extra week and they are docking ME a day for my part in it. Jannine seems to think me being docked is humorous, but I just wanted to let you know about your time. Please respond to this email ASAP for further instructions of how to make up the extra week. And the boss wants you back in the office by the end of the week

Rick

End of the week . . . how the hell am I going to be back by the end of the week and more importantly how will I pay my rent without that check! This sucks big time. Oh God, I can't believe I put Jannine in the middle of all this. What am I going to do and even worst I've got to leave Joe and go back to fix all of this.

I started pacing, my mind racing a million miles a minute. I didn't hear Joe come up behind me.

"You're gonna wear a hole in my rug darlin'. What's got you up so early in the morning and so pissed off?"

I didn't know whether to tell him or lie. But I didn't want to start our new relationship off with a lie. I explained my dilemma. He seemed way too calm. At first it annoyed me and then he explained.

"Okay, so what I'm hearin' is, you don't have any more time left for vacation, right? And because I made you come to Montana they're docking you a week's pay, correct? Well it seems to me that would be MY dilemma, not yours. We can resolve this in the morning but for now, turn off your laptop and come back to bed."

He wrapped his arm around my shoulder and we walked back to the bedroom.

The sun came up at 6:00 AM and I rolled over to an empty bed and the smell of bacon waffling down the hallway. I could smell fresh coffee. I put his shirt on and followed the smell.

"Morning Rose, I was just about to bring you breakfast. Looks like you were in a rush because you left your pants in the bedroom."

He leaned down and kissed me, "Good morning baby. I hope you slept well after all the unnecessary upset over that email." *I didn't think it was unnecessary upset. In reality I could be out of a job.*

I was still upset. I'd always been in control, able to solve my own problems and make my own decisions. I was never one to ask for help even when it was in my best interest to do so. I didn't know how to let go of that kind of control and allow someone to be there for me. I pushed my breakfast around staring at the plate.

Joe frowned. "What did those eggs and that bacon ever do to you to deserve that kind of treatment? You're still upset aren't you baby?"

"Yes I am Joe and I've never had to ask any one for help or assistance and I hate the fact that I have to ask you AND you've only known me three weeks."

He slid over next to me on the kitchen bench. "Rose look at me, I know we've just met and you've got no good reason to trust me and if you haven't noticed I've come to care a lot about you. You should know by now that I would do anything for you, I love you darlin' and bein' six-foot plus, to quote Led Zeppelin, that's a whole lotta' love."

He hugged me for what seemed like eternity – it felt good.

"Now let's dry those tears and get those horses fed. I seem to have an uncanny ability to make you weepy Rose. Maybe you're allergic to me?"

"Okay, you got me smiling again. We'd better get going. Them horses ain't gonna feed themselves."

"Rose I'm impressed. Nice cowboy presentation . . . next, I'll teach ya' how to drop your G's!"

I got dressed and headed out to the horse paddock. He came out with my saddle. I was excited about riding. I hadn't ridden in years and was a little intimidated knowing that Joe was an expert rider.

We saddled up Daisy and Bailey, Joe's chestnut brown quarter horse. Daisy looked a life-size replica of *My Little Pony* with a long blond mane and tail.

Joe let me ride in his round pen to get me used to the saddle. It was a perfect fit. Once I felt comfortable, we left the paddock area and went for a ride. I'd forgotten how free horseback riding made me feel, loping along with nothing holding me back. I think I surprised Joe with my riding ability.

"Whoa, you got Daisy into a lope. She must trust you."

We dismounted by his pond to let the horses cool down. "You know something Rose, I think I've resolved your problem. Just tell them I said you can't leave Montana. Problem solved."

"And you think that will convince them not to fire me?"

"Okay, well maybe I need to work on my delivery, but yes, that's my proposal, speaking of which – there's something inside my saddle bag."

Joe got up and walked over to his saddle and retrieved something out his the bag. He helped me up and smiled. I thought, *"Oh no, it's his shit-eating-grin. Maybe it's a note to take back to my boss saying I won't be back due to saddle-sores or something silly.*

"Rose, you know I'm a man who doesn't mince words or hold back what I think, feel or want. And darlin' I want you. I knew it the first moment I saw you in Currysville library. Even after that wrath of shit you gave me, which by the way was quite eloquent; I said to myself, 'Joe, go after her because she is a once in a life time dream come true' and here we are."

I was so nervous I didn't know whether to run or faint. *He's going to ask me to move in with him – I can feel it.* I kept breathing and waited for him to finish.

"Rose, if you haven't guessed by now . . . I'm askin' you to marry me."

I know I stopped breathing for at least five seconds. He took my hand and placed something on my finger. *I couldn't feel my body. It felt as though I was floating.* I stared at this unbelievably beautiful ring – two gold lassos linked around the heart-shaped diamond.

"I'd like to be your cowboy forever if you'll have me."

And here I thought he was going to ask me to move in with him. Never in a million years did I expect this. This is crazy and I'm crazy because I love him and of course, I'll marry you Joe!

I barely remember saying yes, but I must have because Joe was smiling from ear-to-ear. A few seconds later I shouted, "YES, yes I will marry you. I'm insane, you're crazy. We should have our heads examined, but YES, my answer is yes Joe."

"I love you, darlin'. You are and will always be my heart. Never, ever forget that. Let's get the horses back to the barn; the wind's pickin' up a bit – looks like we're in for some rain." We started to mount up when I stopped.

"Just hold on a minute partner, don't you think I have the right to know your true name? You don't have some weirdo name like Seymour Butts, do you? I'd like to know before the wedding. It's a small concern but I want to know what name to write on the invitations – unless you want to put 'Montana Joe is marrying the-women-currently-known-as-Rose."

He squinted and pushed his hat back on his head. "Darlin', you have such a way of obliterating a tender moment. I'll tell you tonight over dinner. And now that you're gonna be my wife how about we call your office and tell them you won't be back for a while. We've got some celebratin' to do."

We made it back to the paddock area just as the sky opened up. The rain was coming down in buckets. I thought we'd try to make it back to the house. Joe had other plans.

"Come over here baby and snuggle up beside me. He pulled one of the horse blankets over our shoulders. Close your eyes and listen. I closed my eyes. Joe leaned over and kissed me. I love rain. It's like a lullaby for the soul. It makes me smile almost as much as you do Rose. I always wondered how folks could live their entire lives in the city listening to police sirens and people hollering for cabs and such. It ain't healthy and it certainly ain't natural."

He was right. It was no way to live. There was so much more to see and experience in the world, so much beauty I had no idea existed until I met Joe. For the first time in my life I felt at peace with myself. No deadlines, no office drama, no compromises.

I asked Joe if he ever had any regrets in his life.

"Can't say that I have, Rose. You see, life is to be lived to the fullest; every moment is a precious gift – like you Rose. You are my precious gift. Like that rainbow that just appeared over the pasture. Some folks say rainbows are God's way of smiling at us." I smiled and kissed him on the cheek.

"Joe I need you to do me a huge favor."

"And what would you like me to do?"

"Please don't let me talk myself out of happiness. Don't let me convince myself what we have is too perfect. I don't want to screw it up like I've done so many times in my life."

He turned toward me and winked, "That is one favor I will be obliged to honor . . . for the rest of my life."

The rain stopped. Everything felt cleansed including my negative self thoughts.

We'd just entered the front door when the phone rang. It was Joe's cell phone. He took the call in the bedroom. A few minutes later he came back to the living room.

"Is everything okay?"

"Yup, it was heaven calling and asking me to send their sexy angel back. I told them they'd better not try to take my Rose or I'd lasso them and drag them through a cactus patch behind old Daisy. Nothing to worry about darlin'. It was my editor. Seems he likes my new writing style. I told him I had a new muse or should I say my future Mrs. Muse."

I decided it was time for me to earn my keep. I prepared dinner for Joe, nothing special but I hadn't cooked for a man in a while. Cecilia had a well-stocked pantry and refrigerator. It had all the ingredients for my famous lasagna.

Joe set the table on the deck. I'd never seen such a beautiful sunset. Maybe it was an ordinary sunset but I was seeing things through an entirely different frame of mind. We ate too much, laughed too much and definitely drank too much. I asked Joe if he thought a person can love too much. He said he didn't think anyone could love too much, unless they were a hooker.

"I've interviewed some saloon gals down in Abilene, Texas that said they weren't loved enough and asked if I'd like to love them, for a modest fee of course." I laughed until my sides hurt. Something I hadn't done in ages.

We talked about our travels or in my case, lack of travel. Joe mentioned the places he'd visited on his research trips. He asked if I'd ever been to Olympic peninsula rain forest in Washington State, Brownsville, Mexico or South Padre Island. I said I hadn't.

"Neither have I. We need to get out more darlin'. Maybe we should plan a trip." I admired his child-like honesty.

"The wine seems to be going to our heads. I think I'll jump in the shower – would you like to join me?"

"Rose, are you trying to seduce me, 'cause I haven't been that type of fella in quite a while and I'm out of practice."

I took off my top, my bra, and my jeans leaving a trail of clothing to the bathroom.

"But I reckon practice makes perfect – you've convinced me girl."

I was drying my hair when Joe walked over and toweled off my back. "Rose, I've got to admit I'm no young man and I've taken plenty of showers, but I NEVER knew a human being could do all THAT in a shower. You must work part-time for Cirque du Soleil."

I gave him a coy smile, "It's all in the water temperature – the hotter the water, the hotter the action."

He shook his head and walked into the bedroom. I turned to follow him and he stopped me. "Wait a few minutes. I've got to do something."

What could he need to do that we didn't do in the shower?

He reopened the door and motioned for me to enter. The entire room was aglow with candlelight, wine and two plates of strawberry cheesecake were sitting beside the bed. There was something else I hadn't noticed when he gave me the tour of his bedroom. The ceiling had a screened-in retractable skylight.

"I love to look at the sky before I go to sleep. It makes me feel closer to heaven. But now I have you Rose. You are my piece of heaven right here on earth.

The starry sky looked magical, like the Vincent van Gogh painting. Maybe it was the wine, maybe it was everything but it didn't matter. My eyes began to tear like someone who'd just won the lottery. I guess in some way I did win the lottery and Joe was the jackpot.

"Oh boy, I've gone and done it again. Every time I try to do something nice for this gal she starts bawling her eyes out. That's it, no more surprises for you crybaby!"

I pretended to punch him when he wrestled me to the bed flipping me over onto my back. "Now if'n you can stop cryin' for a minute I'll point out some of the constellations for you. I know you wouldn't recognize them on your own – the poor, under-educated, city girl that you are."

He pointed out the Big and Little Dipper, Ursa Major, Great Bear and a few others. It was like Joe opened up a whole new world just for me. We fell asleep watching the night sky.

It was still dark outside when I woke up with a smile on my face and a throbbing headache. *Damn you red wine!* I remembered seeing some aspirin in the small hallway powder room. I was heading down the hall when I caught a glimpse of him from behind standing nude in the living room. *My Lord he looks good front and back. I can't believe he's older than me.*

He was on the phone speaking in a whisper. The only thing I could hear was, *". . . okay, yes . . . me too, love you . . . see you soon, bye."* I continued into the powder room picked up aspirin bottle, went back in the bedroom and brought out his jeans.

"That better not be another woman on the phone,"

"No, it wasn't another gal Rose. It was my son Morgan. I called him and told him about us getting hitched. He was very happy for us and is planning to come to Montana to meet you." *Meet me, oh no, suppose he hates me?*

"Don't worry Rose, he'll love you just as much as I do." *Damn it, he is psychic.*

"I suppose you'll need to call your office too." He handed me the phone. "Go on, call 'em and let them know that you will be busy for the rest of your life."

He sat beside me smiling while I placed the call. With the time zone difference I knew Jannine would be up and heading to work. *She is going to have a fit.*

Chapter 9

"Okay, one more time . . . I want a Grande Mocha Latte, NO foam, a shake of cinnamon and an extra shot of espresso, to go!"

Jannine turned to the guy behind her. "Am I speaking another language or am I just under caffeinated because the new barista can't seem to get my order correct?" The sleepy customer shrugs his shoulders.

Now my cell is ringing! "Hello and this had better be more important than my morning Latte."

"Hi Jannine, it's Rose eh, I mean, Amelia, how are you?"

"Hello Rose, eh, Amelia, I'm trying to get this new coffee shop barista to get my order correct before lunch!"

"Jannine Paris Westone, sweetie, I need your full attention . . . forget about the latte for a second!"

Jannine pulled the phone away from her ear and stared at it for a second then replied.

"Is this really Amelia, because I thought I heard you say forget about coffee. And it must be extremely important because you called me by my full name."

"Jannine you remember when I said I met this guy who I kind of liked, well, actually like a lot. It seems he likes me a lot too. We really enjoy each other and I enjoy him as much as . . ."

"Honey, how long is this conversation going to last because if it's going to be one of those 'Once Upon a Time' stories, I'm going to need my LATTE which is STILL not ready! Please for Christ sake, give me the shortened version."

I took a deep breath and blurted, "Jannine, I'm getting married."

Complete silence on the other end. "Okay, I'm back. I had to pay for my latte now . . . what did you say?"

Joe grabbed the phone and in his best western cowboy drawl said,

"Howdy Jannine this is Montana Joe, Rose's soon-to-be husband. We wanted you to know about our upcoming nuptials. So get some fancy duds and be my lovely soon-to-be-bride's maid of honor."

Joe put the phone on speaker just in time to hear Jannine saying, "You are shitting me, No way! Are you really getting married to this guy you've only known a day! Oh shit, I just dropped my coffee. I'm in shock and I'm happy for you if this is what you want."

Joe laughed, "Well darlin' I can tell you this is what WE want and she's known me longer than that, mostly in the biblical sense of course, but I plan on getting to know her a lot better after we're married."

"Jannine, Joe makes me happier than anyone I've known in my life and he ain't too bad on the eyes either. I guess I could do a lot worse – winking at Joe."

"So, Amelia what are you going to do? HR is really pissed that you've taken so much time off. Aren't you worried about being fired?"

I looked over at Joe and said, *"Nope."*

"I've never heard you so confident and relaxed. Normally something like this would set you off like a bottle rocket. You love your job and we love you. Now, the more important question . . . how is this going to affect ME, did you ever stop to think about that? What am I going to do without you?"

I could hear Jannine sniffling which started me crying.

Joe mumbled, "Lord, I've got two women cryin' at the same time. I'm goin' to hell for sure!"

"Listen Jannine, I will need to come back to get my things and we can talk then."

"Are you bringing the cowboy with you so I can give him a piece of my mind for stealing the best friend I've ever had?"

I wiped my eyes. "You mean the best friend you have! You are my best and dearest friend Jannine – I love you."

"But seriously let me know what you want and I can get it packed and send it to you. Don't you dare leave that man –do you hear me."

"Yes, Jannine I hear you and you are way too good to me, thank you I would truly appreciate it!"

"You are welcome honey. Now I've got to run and spread the news our Amelia is getting hitched, love you, ciao!"

Joe brought over a couple of badly needed tissues. "That went well don't you think. And you thought there would be a big commotion with lots of drama."

It was dark when we got up. The first light of the day was about to break. We watched the sun rise.

"Ain't that beautiful Rose, there's nothin' a beautiful sunrise can't fix."

He was right. A new day is a gift; an opportunity to start life over again. I was starting a new life with Joe. In a few weeks I would be his wife. *This is crazy. I must be crazy maybe this time crazy is a good thing.*

Morgan packed his clothing, made preparations for his mail and loaded his car for the drive to his father's place. He was excited to see his dad again, however, nervous about meeting Rose for the first time. *What if she doesn't like ME? I'm sure she didn't plan on starting a new marriage with a bouncing baby 24-year old boy.*

While driving he thought about how cool it was to have the last name Montana and live in Montana. His mother was from Mexico. She would tell him stories about the blue mountains of Mexico and how his father loved taking her there. She believed that's where he was conceived. She also told him that his name was almost 'Blue' but decided to name him Morgan after her father.

It was a three hour drive from Billings to Malta and Joe's place was about another thirty minutes away. He twisted his mouth to one side like his dad did when he's thinking about something serious. *I don't want to arrive empty handed; maybe I should stop and buy some wine or flowers.*

He spotted a small town outside of Billings and got off at the exit. A small gift shop owned by the local folks had handmade jewelry and crafts. I don't know anything about Rose except she seems to cry a lot when she's happy. Maybe I could get her handkerchiefs or a box of tissues. He chuckled to himself and continued browsing.

The store's owner walked up to him and asked if he needed help.

"Yes, I reckon I do ma'am. I'm looking for something for my soon-to-be stepmother. She'd marrying my dad and I'm goin' to meet her for the first time. What would you suggest?"

She smiled, "Well dear I wouldn't get her what you're holding in your hand."

Morgan had picked up a large decorative tomahawk. He pretended to chop something then placed it back on the display counter.

The woman asked him to follow her to the next aisle. "This may be more appropriate." It was a lovely silver squash blossom bracelet with turquoise inlay.

"Oh yeah, this looks like something she would like – now something for dad."

He noticed they had homemade buffalo jerky. *He'd love this.*

He paid the woman and thanked her for her help. She smiled, "Glad to help. You know she will love you whether or not you bring gifts." He asked how she knew this.

"You have good spirit I sense it. She has good spirit too and so does your father. It shows in you, dear. Now go and welcome your new mother; she will be excited to meet you"

Morgan got to into his car and thought, *this is the weirdest place I've ever been. How does she know I have good spirit just by looking at me? I'll ask dad if he know about this good spirit stuff.*

Up ahead he could see the signs for Malta. Another twenty minutes to go. He felt a flood of anxiety wash over him as he got closer to Joe's place. *Stop it Morgan you've never been this nervous in your life why now? Plus you're bringing gifts . . . women love gifts, right?*

His dad's place was coming up on the horizon. He took a deep breath, "Okay Morgan, It's show time – there's no turning back now."

He drove slowly to the front of the house. Joe was the first to hear his car. "Rose darlin' it's time to meet someone."

I ran from the kitchen. "He's here . . . already? I'm so nervous – how do I look?"

Joe twisted his mouth to one side.

"He'll love you as much as I do, now come on outside with me and meet the only other man who is as handsome as I am."

Joe opened the door as Morgan was about to knock.

"Hello, Son it's good to see you." They hugged and slapped each other on the back.

"Hi Dad, wow you look younger than I remember. Must be this new woman in your life, where is she?"

I walked from behind the door and said, "That would be me, I'm eh, Amelia but you can call me Rose. It's so good to finally meet you." I extended my hand.

Morgan leaned into me and gave me a gentler hug.

"We are about to become family Rose. In Montana a handshake is for people who are sealing a land deal. It's good to meet you too. Oh, I almost forgot I have gifts for both of you."

He ran back to his car and brought in two gift bags. "This one is for you Rose and this is for you Dad, hope you like them.

Joe opened his first. "Jerky now that's my kind of gift, thank you Son!" Joe quickly opened it and chewed off a piece.

I reached into the bag and took out the small blue box inside. I opened it to find a delicate squash blossom bracelet almost identical to the necklace and earrings Joe gave me. I turned around so they wouldn't notice my eyes tearing.

"Damn it Morgan, it's bad enough I make her cry whenever I give her gifts and now here you go doin' the same." They both laughed.

Morgan chuckled, "I knew I should have gotten her those laced handkerchiefs."

I turned around and hollered, "Both of you, stop laughing at me or I'll kick your asses into the next state."

Morgan leaned over to Joe and whispered, "You told me she was feisty; I like her already."

I told them I was heading back into the kitchen to check on tonight's dinner. "Hope you like roast beef Morgan."

"Yes ma'am, I don't do much cookin' so anything that doesn't involve hot water and noodles is fine by me."

Joe motioned for Morgan to follow him to the barn. It seemed that 'man-talk' was to ensue.

He pulled over two bales of hay, sat down and handed Morgan a piece of jerky. "Son, I'm glad you came. I wasn't sure whether or not you would."

"Why wouldn't I Dad? From what I've seen so far you and Rose love each other. She's also incredibly beautiful. You didn't tell me she was black."

Joe frowned, "Is that a problem for you, son?

"God, NO Dad, she is really attractive – like Halle Berry hot! If she were any hotter . . . you'd be dead. Hell, I'm half Mexican myself. Who am I to judge anyone? But, I can totally see why you fell in love with her so quickly. She's intelligent, fiery and gorgeous – great combination."

Joe continued, "You know that I don't have a prejudiced bone in my body. In fact I believe folks like that should be horsewhipped. I've found geniuses and jerks are equally distributed among all races. I can assure you there's no prejudice in this old cowboy!"

Morgan smiled. "I just have one question, Dad . . . does she have a younger sister?"

Joe laughed and shook his head. "Yes she does, but they don't get along, however, she does have a cute little administrative assistant named Jannine that you might find interesting. I should warn you son, she's one hell cat on wheels – feisty just like Rose."

Morgan grinned, "Sounds like she could be fun and dangerous. But hey I'm always up for a challenge."

They walked back to the house and straight into the kitchen. Rose was singing along to the radio and swaying to the music. They stood quietly by the door watching her performance. When the song ended Morgan and Joe applauded. She swung around beet red and embarrassed.

"You know the last person who snuck up on me like this got shot."

Morgan looked at Joe as if to say, *Is she serious?* Joe nodded, "It must have been a mercy killin' so they didn't have to listen to her lousy singin'."

I rolled my eyes and started setting the table.

Joe excused himself and headed to the bedroom. He was covered in hay dust and it seemed he had a tickle in his throat for a few days that he couldn't seem to get rid of. It was probably allergy related. I know the weather was affecting my sinuses too.

Morgan sat down at the table. He talked about school and I told him about my career. But it was obvious that he was more interested in talking about Jannine. I told him she was on her way out to bring me a few things for the wedding. He'd get to meet her then.

"In fact, she will be my maid of honor. You are going to be your dad's best man, right?"

You two will make a cute couple . . . at the wedding of course. I didn't mean 'a couple'."

Joe came back into the kitchen smelling fresh and clean.

"You took a shower without me."

Joe kissed me on my cheek. "Yup, but there were some parts I could have used your help with girl."

Morgan blushed. "Whoa, TMI folks, I think I'll go do the same, I smell like a barn."

I mentioned that there were fresh towels in the hall closet next to his room and to help himself.

I huddled close to Joe and asked him what Morgan thought about me. Was there anything he didn't like, was he happy for us, did he think I was fat?

Joe stared at me as if I'd lost my mind. "Excuse me, I've seemed to have misplaced my future wife, you know the super confident one that doesn't care what people think. Would you please find her and tell her I want her back."

"I'm serious Joe, what did he say about me. "

"Rose, I'm going to tell you this, and I never want you to ask me anything this crazy again. First, he thinks you are gorgeous; in fact, he says and I quote, 'Halle Berry hot.' Now listen carefully. He thinks you are the best thing that has happened to me in quite a while. He's happy we found each other darlin'.''

I let out a sigh of relief. I didn't know what I would have done if his only son didn't approve of me.

"Can we finally eat – I'm starved and horny. You get me so hot when you're in the kitchen cookin'. We'll deal with the horny part later tonight." We kissed and nibbled each other until we hear Morgan coming.

"Hey, is it okay to come in? I don't want to intrude on your make-out session."

All three of us sat at the dinner table and had a great dinner and wonderful time talking about our lives, school, work and a pleasant variety of other subjects. It was something I'd only dreamt about. Then it dawned on me – this was the family I've always wanted. I was finally happy. Nothing could ruin my bliss and I was marrying the man of my dreams. I was about to become Joe's wife.

Our wedding was less than two weeks away. Jannine and I had picked out the perfect wedding dress online and it was being shipped today. Jannine thought I should wear something that would accent my golden skin tone and the beautiful silver jewelry Joe and Morgan bought me. I also decided to carry two daffodils. Joe said that I should carry a rose, like the nickname he'd bestowed on me. I told him I was highly allergic to roses. He thought it amusing calling me Rose when I was so allergic to them. I suggested daffodils instead.

"It would be a symbolic reminder of the first flowers I gave to you. Daffodils will do just fine."

Jannine was on her way to the airport when she called me. She wanted to know if there was anything else I needed. I assured her that I had everything and all I needed was for her to keep ME calm. I laughed to myself because Jannine was naturally hyper. She was like a cyclone of energy. Something I always admired about her.

Joe had requested Raymond Winterbee who was also an ordained minister to perform the ceremony. It would bring our journey full circle. Raymond asked us if we wanted to write our vows. I hadn't thought about it, but it seemed logical that both of us being writers composed something to join our lives together on our special day.

I thought it would be interesting to review some of Joe's and my old emails. They were filled with such wonderful memories. Maybe I could find something in them we could use. As I scrolled though dozens of emails I drifted back to our first meeting in the Currysville library, the horrible library coffee and his insisting I meet him for good coffee. I feel like I've known Joe all my life. Maybe I have? Maybe this was the fate Joe was talking about – who knows.

I stood in front of our bedroom's full-length mirror looking at myself. I never saw myself as beautiful, but today I felt like the most beautiful and the luckiest woman in the world. Maybe I didn't see what Joe saw, but I was glad he liked what he saw. I started playing with my hair – sweeping it up trying to decide how I would wear it on our wedding day.

I saw Joe's reflection in the mirror. "Do you always spy on me while I'm doing dumb things?"

He walked behind me and put his arms around my waist.

"You've never done a dumb thing in your life darlin' well, except for not marrying me sooner."

He turned me around, "Do you Rose take this man . . . and if I do say so myself, this handsome man to be your cowboy – don't start cryin' just nod your head yes."

I laughed and said absolutely. "What am I going to do with you Mister Montana?"

"I don't know Mrs. Montana what would you like to do with me, 'cause I know what I'd like to do with you, how about we test drive our honeymoon."

I heard Cecilia chuckle from the hallway, "Maybe I should take the rest of the afternoon off."

We both thought it would be a good idea. Besides Morgan and Jannine would be here in four hours and we wouldn't have any private time.

Morgan left mid-morning for the airport. He offered to pick up Jannine. He'd never seen her before so he hand-printed a sign with her name on it. Her flight was due to arrive on time. He paced around the arrival area unconsciously fidgeting with the edges of the sign until they were creased.

There was a commotion coming from the arrival area. He heard a woman yelling. He thought, *"What the hell's got her so pissed off?"* It was a cute, sexy girl carrying a red purse large enough to house a family of five. The airport attendant was noticeably annoyed but kept his professional smile.

"I'm sorry Ma'am, but anything over 40 pounds is considered luggage and needs to be put on a luggage carrier. We don't want to be held liable if you drop it on yourself or on other travelers."

Morgan moved back letting this crazy lady pass then noticed the purse had the initials JPW on the side. *Oh God in heaven, is THIS Jannine? Please don't let this be her!*

Morgan took a deep breath and said, "I'm here for a Jannine Westone, would that be you ma'am?" Jannine whipped around and said yeah who the hell wants to know? Are you airport security?

"No ma'am, my name is Morgan I'm Lash's son. Miss Rose sent me to pick you up. I'll be driving you to our ranch."

Jannine yanked her purse away from the airport attendant and handed it to Morgan.

"Oh my God you must be Amelia's Morgan! Hi I'm Jannine her Administrative Assistant and bridesmaid very nice to meet someone who's not a JERK like the workers at this airport!" She frowned at the airport worker while Morgan retrieved the last of her luggage.

He loaded her things into his vehicle and ran around to open her door. Jannine smiled as she slid into the seat.

"You are such a gentleman, Morgan. Not like the city assholes I meet. They'd knock a woman over just to steal her cab." Morgan smiled timidly and put the key into the ignition.

The first half hour was quiet. Jannine was in awe of the Montana landscape. Every five or six miles she would gasp saying, "Oh look such beautiful mountains and trees and horses and flowers."

Morgan nodded saying, "Yes, it's really beautiful here in Montana."

He was afraid to say anything more. He didn't know Jannine but knew she could hold her own and wasn't afraid to speak her mind. They were about half way back to the ranch when she relaxed enough to ask him about Joe and Rose. The conversation was short and polite. Morgan started to relax. He pointed out some of the local attractions, landmarks and wildlife. By the time they reached the ranch driveway they were chatting like long lost friends. Rose could see the cloud of dust from Morgan's car and ran to the door. Joe walked up from the barn covered in hay dust and horse shit.

He met Rose by the porch door. "I hope she don't mine a bit of horse shit on my boots. I don't want to make a bad impression."

Rose laughed and said, "You . . . make a bad impression, no way! You would need to steal her business card and write her endless, annoying, emails to do that."

He kissed my palm. "That's what I love about you Rose; you are such a quiet and retiring gal. Never a cynical word comes from those luscious lips of yours. Speaking of luscious, are you wearing any panties?" He slipped his hand down the back of my jeans. I rolled my eyes and smacked his hand.

"Try to behave yourself, okay?"

Joe shrugged, "And where exactly is the fun in that?"

We walked over to the car and before I could introduce Joe, Jannine jumped out and bear hugged him.

"You must be the famous Montana Joe, the only man who can get this overworked, type-A personality to slow down. You deserve a medal."

Joe gave her his infamous shit-eating-grin, "And who might you be, wait-- don't tell me. You must be Rose's Victoria's Secret model friend or are you her baby sister – either way it's mighty nice to meet you darlin'."

"Hello, how about a big hug for your not-that-much-older-than-you best friend." Jannine grinned and ran over to me. We hugged each other and started crying. In unison we said, "I've missed you so much – how are you!"

Joe shook his head, "Oh Lord, now they're both cryin' what am I gonna do with the two of them bawlin' their eyes out every time they see a cute puppy or baby or me dressed in my cowboy wedding tux."

Joe looked at himself in the mirror and ran his fingers through his hair, "You are a handsome devil even if I do say it myself."

I nudged Joe and told him to go out to the car and grab a few of her bags. We walked into the house still squealing and excited to see each other. Morgan brought the rest of Jannine's things in and headed to the guest room. He thought, *"She must be moving in. Nobody in the world travels with this much luggage."*

Jannine and I went into the kitchen. A fresh pot of coffee was brewing. Jannine seem to be intoxicated by the aroma.

"Oh my God it smells so good in here. When did you start brewing your own coffee?"

"Ever since I met this over-worked, caffeine obsessed cowboy writer."

I poured two cups and we went out on the deck to catch up on the big city life. It seems that nothing had changed. Jannine was telling me about some old rich bitch who donated a huge sum of cash to a new state-of-the-art digital photography gallery. She thinks she must be sleeping with someone and they must be good in bed for her to fork over seven-figures without blinking an eye. Jannine also told me that Rick was demoted because of my vacation fiasco.

"Jannine I feel absolutely terrible. You did this as a favor to me and Rick gets demoted. I'll call HR and tell them it was my fault and . . . " Jannine bristled, "You will do no such thing girl! Rick's been screwing up things in HR for years. Your vacation error was just the tip of the iceberg. He's such a putz – it was just a matter of time before he got caught."

We changed the subject and talked about Joe. I told her when I first met him how I couldn't stand him. He was so overconfident and persistent. But things quickly changed – he started to grow on me. I fell in love with his honesty and his western drawl habit of 'dropping his G's'. We'd finished our coffee. I took the cups into the kitchen for a refill when I noticed the house was unusually quiet.

I heard whispers coming from the bedroom. Morgan and Joe were talking. They looked serious then smiled and laughed. Joe patted him on the shoulder and handed him two small boxes. Even from the door I could see two beautiful gold wedding bands with diamond inlay. I rushed back to the deck.

"Well that took you long enough . . . where is the coffee?"

"Jannine I just saw our wedding bands! Joe handed them to Morgan to keep until the wedding. Oh my God . . . I'm really doing this – I'm getting married!"

I dropped the chair like a sack of cement. Jannine reassured me, "Yes, you are honey. That's why I'm here."

"Am I doing the right thing?"

She stepped back and held my hands.

"If you could see the way you light up when he walks into a room you would know you are doing the right thing. My God woman, if I didn't love you so much I would be trying to steal him away from you. I don't even like cowboys, well, I didn't until I met Joe; he's gorgeous! And you never answered my question – is he hung like a stallion?"

"JANNINE, sometimes you are too much for me to wrap my brain around. That is private information between me and my husband-to-be." *Hmm, my husband-to-be, I liked the sound of that.*

I went back into the kitchen and rinsed out our cups. Joe and Morgan were sitting at the table finishing off the pot of coffee. Joe whispered something to Morgan and he laughed out loud.

"What are you two lying about now? When your dad gets that shit-eating-grin I know he's up to no good."

Morgan looked over at his dad. "He just wanted me to ask you if you, eh, plan on wearing something, eh, naughty for the honeymoon. "

I rolled my eyes and walked back outside. We were already acting like a family. This is what I'd wanted all my life; people I could love and rely on through thick and thin. For the first time I felt at peace with myself and ready to marry the man I love.

It was a sleepless night for me. I turned over only to see Joe was sleeping the sleep of angels. He looked so peaceful. I thought it best to let him sleep. We had a long day ahead of us. I got up, made coffee and sat outside to watch the sun rise. It seemed brighter than usual. Maybe it was because in a few short hours I would be married.

I could hear the stirrings of the house waking up; the sound of running water, drawers opening and closing and yawns ending with good morning. When you live alone it's the rude blare of the alarm clock, the grinding of the electric can opener opening the cat's food, combined with the slamming of the door as you rush out the house. All of which reminded me of just how lonely my life was.

The smell of fresh brewed coffee brought them one-by-one into the kitchen. Morgan walked in first giving me a tender side-hug wishing me an early congratulation and Jannine wiping her eyes trying to focus without her contacts. I thought, *Where's Joe? Coffee usually wakes him up.* I poured a cup and brought it into the bedroom. I saw him shut his eyes pretending to be sleep.

"It's a shame I'll have to drink another cup of hot delicious coffee seeing that my husband-to-be is still sleeping and snoring."

Without opening his eyes he said, "First, let me make one thing perfectly clear . . . I do not snore and second, that better be my beautiful bride-to-be holdin' that cup."

I put the cup down and crawled under the covers.

"Good morning good-looking, I was waiting for you to come back to bed so we could have wild passionate sex or at least to bring me some coffee. You know that both are considered your wifely duties."

"Wifely duties, sex and coffee are part of my wifely duties. I wasn't aware of that particular clause in the marriage contract."

"Yep, I made certain the Padre added it. Now roll over and spread em' before the kids wake up."

Things were just about to get hot and heavy when I heard footsteps outside of the door. Jannine and Morgan barged in – both covering their eyes. Jannine suggested that we save our energy for the wedding night. Morgan just laughed. I guess my wifely duties will have to wait. I kissed Joe on his forehead and hopped out of bed.

"Now if'n you youngin's wouldn't mind, I'm butt-naked under here and I'd like to get up and get dressed. In case you've forgotten, I'm gettin' married today."

Morgan put his hands over Jannine's eyes.

"That's way too much information for morning conversation dad."

He grabbed Jannine's arm and escorted her out the door. She slowly leaned back and peeked inside.

"No peekin' girl! I'm gettin' up to take a shower. And no matter what Rose has told you I'm not hung like a horse."

Dead silence . . . then a string of giggles. Joe laughed and started his shower.

Morgan headed out to the barn to feed and water the horses while Jannine and I went into the kitchen. We sat down at the table nibbling on the blueberry muffins I'd baked the night before.

I picked at the berries and muffin crumbs. She noticed I was nervous.

"Honey, you need to calm yourself. You are one of the luckiest women I know. You've actually found your soul mate. How freakin' fantastic is that!"

"God Jannine, I hope you're right. Am I doing the right thing by getting married so soon? I love Joe so much. I hope I can make him happy."

She leaned forward and hugged me. "Honey, this is the *rightest* thing you've ever done in your life, if there is such a word as rightest. And if you haven't noticed the man is over-the-moon happy!"

I said, "I don't think *rightest* is a word, but Joe sure makes me happy."

Jannine smiled, "Now then, let's get you ready to marry your man."

Chapter 10

It was 11:00 AM. Jannine and Morgan headed over to the church to help set up the flowers. They made a handsome couple. I thought about how well they were getting along. Jannine seemed so relaxed around Morgan. Her whole demeanor was different. I've always thought of her as a daughter. Her happiness was important to me and Morgan seems to enjoy her company.

The ride to the church was quiet – almost surreal. The Montanan sky was so blue against the green grass and the air smelled sweet. I was about to become Mrs. Montana. The name Montana seemed so majestic. *I smiled thinking how appropriate his name was for him.*

I thought back to the time when he knew me only as Rose and knew him as Montana Joe. Now there's an idea for a novel. Maybe Joe could write our love story. Then again, I'd have to write it because knowing Joe it would turn out to be a pornographic, blow-by-blow account of our sexual escapades.

Joe reached over, caressed my hand and kissed my palm.

"I hope you're thinking about all the wild moves I'm gonna make on you during our wedding night."

I asked him, "Are there any wild moves left?"

"I've got plenty of wild moves darlin'. You won't be disappointed, I promise."

We arrived at the church. It was beautifully decorated with all types of prairie flowers inside and out. Jannine and Morgan did a wonderful job. I noticed Bailey and Daisy hitched outside. *What does Joe have planned?* I was too nervous to dwell on it. Joe put his arm around my waist.

"Well darlin' this is it. If you're gonna run, now would be the time to do it. Otherwise, I do believe you and I are gonna get hitched today. And by the way, I know I've mentioned this at least a thousand times today – you look absolutely, drop dead gorgeous. I swear I don't know what you see in this old cowboy, but whatever it is, I'm glad you do. I love you Rose. Are you ready?"

I couldn't speak because I knew I'd start to cry and I didn't want him to see me cry on our wedding day. I nodded yes and we walked down the aisle to the altar.

Raymond was dressed in his tribal formal wear. Jannine and Morgan were standing beside him. A handful of Joe's friends were there. His housekeeper Cecilia was the only one I knew, however, all appeared very happy for us.

Raymond asked everyone to join hands as he read a very special Cherokee Prayer Blessing. I gave Jannine my two daffodils to hold.

"May the warm winds of Heaven
blow softly upon your house
May the Great Spirit
bless all who enter there.
May your moccasins
make happy tracks in many snows,
and may the Rainbow
Always touch your shoulder."

Raymond whispered to me, "That was in honor of your new found Cherokee heritage - blessings to you both." Joe looked at me as if to say, *"Please don't start bawlin' we've got to get through the rest of the ceremony."*

It took every ounce of concentration for me to stay focused and present. I didn't want to zone out on the, I do's. I glanced over of Joe. I'd never seen him so happy and relaxed. There were a few beads of sweat forming on his brow. It relaxed me knowing that he was not as calm as he appeared to be. He glanced over giving me his this- cowboy-loves-you look and winked.

It came time for us to say our vows. I looked at Joe in disbelief. We forget to compose wedding vows. Raymond asked if we wanted the traditional vows read. We said no because there was nothing traditional about our nuptials. Joe and I decided to wing it. He cleared his voice as we faced each other and joined hands.

"An old friend once told me if you live a good and honorable life when you look back, you'll enjoy it a second time. He also said if you meet a woman that makes you forget your name, don't wait to show her how you feel. Tell her you love her and if she'll have you, ask her to marry you. Well, that's exactly what I did that day in the Currysville library. I met the woman of my dreams and asked her to marry me. Of course she thought I was a nut bein' the first time I'd ever set eyes on her. But I knew right then and there she was the one and only woman for me.

Darlin' I never in my life thought I'd get the opportunity to live my dream. You read between the lines into my heart and soul. I don't know how you learned to do that so quickly. I never had anyone in my life do that. You are my special dream come true . . . it is as if I am writing a wonderful romantic scene and I suddenly find myself in it and you are the beautiful lady I'm writing about. Loving you is like sweetness and heat. The heat melts my body and the sweetness melts my heart. And I'm honored to stand here in front of everyone and say I love you and I'm blessed that you've finally come to your senses and accepted my proposal to become my wife."

He smiled as the guests chuckled at his closing statement. Raymond turned to me and said, "You may now say your vows."

"When I was a little girl I was taught to be tough; to stand my ground and never back down from a challenge. If I thought I was right, I would stick up for myself. I never backed down. I thought I was right to run from you. I thought I was right to ignore your advances. My good

friend's father used to say, "You're right . . . so what!" Joe, I think you are persistent, annoying, obsessed with coffee and sarcastic beyond belief. And, I was right. You are all of those things and more. However, being right doesn't seem to matter anymore.

I was wrong. I have never been so wrong about someone. I was wrong about you. I was wrong to doubt how much you love me, I was wrong about your kindness, your strength, and your ability to make me feel like the only woman on the face of the earth. You are an amazing fiction writer, a great dad and my best friend. Your smile warms my heart and your touch ignites my body and soul. And that Mr. Montana feels so incredibly right. I love you Joe – forever and always.

Raymond motioned for us to turn toward him. "It's time to exchange the rings."

Morgan dug into his left pocket and handed the rings to Raymond.

"These rings are a symbol of the eternal circle of marriage – a never ending journey."

He handed one ring to me and one to Joe. Raymond whispered, "You do want to use your given names, right?"

I looked at Joe, he looked at me – we nodded yes. Joe took hold of my hand, placed the ring on my finger.

"I, Lash Jackson Montana, yes my mother loved the cowboy star, Lash LaRue, hence my first name, take you, Amelia Kristen Matthews to be my beautiful wife, through sickness and in health, the good times and bad times, the lean times and rich times, to have and to hold, until we ride off into the sunset at the end of our life together, forever and always."

I was overwhelmed. I couldn't see or feel my hands. However, I did hear him whisper, "Baby, I love you so much," as he kissed my palm. "That kiss is for eternity, so hold on to it."

My hands were shaking as I placed the ring on his finger.

"I, Amelia Kristen Matthews take you Lash Jackson Montana to be my handsome husband, through sickness and in health, the good times and bad times, the lean times and rich times, to have and to hold, until we

ride off into the sunset at the end of our lives together, forever and always, until death parts us – and hopefully that will be decades from now – forever and always."

Raymond then brought our hands together holding them close to his heart.

"I bring these two together as husband and wife. Let the spirits of our ancestors who live on in my heart watch over and smile on them always. You are now one eternal. Congratulations, you may now seal this bond with a kiss – and knowing Joe the way I do it'll be two or three.

Joe smiled, took my hand, kissing my palm and placed it over his own heart. He said, "This heart is forever yours." He leaned down and tenderly kissed my cheek, then my lips. I told him, "As is mine. Forever and always you have my heart – I love you." We were officially married.

We thanked Raymond for performing the ceremony. I told him I didn't know how we would ever repay him for his kindness. He smiled and said we did. Seeing us happy and together was payment enough.

He patted us on our back and said, "It's a good feeling to bring two soul mates together. I must admit you two traveled an extraordinary journey to get where you are. I'm honored to be the one who brought you together for your new life adventure."

Jannine trotted over and kissed me on my cheek. I asked her to hold on to the two daffodils. I wanted to keep them as a reminder of our special day. She wrapped them in cloth napkin and tucked them away in her purse. She then hugged Joe and whispered something in his ear. He let out a laugh that could be heard outside the church. I was afraid to ask what she'd said but I couldn't resist. Joe whispered what she'd said to me. I let out a shriek like something possessed. For the first time since I've known Joe I saw him blush. He wiped is forehead with his sleeve.

I turned red as a cherry, "Oh my God, I can't believe she asked you that!"

Joe laughed and said, "OH MY LORD, I swear Rose, that gal is a firecracker!"

Morgan came over asking what the ruckus was about. I couldn't repeat what she'd said because it was too raunchy, even for me. Morgan assumed it was something insanely inappropriate and thought it best not knowing.

The last of the wedding guests left the church and headed to the outdoor reception area. Just the family remained. Jannine had already started celebrating hoisting a champagne bottle and glass over her head singing, Ozzie Osborne's, Crazy Train, breaking in an off-key rendition of Chris Ledoux's, Life is a Highway. I asked her how she got so drunk so quickly. She said, "Who's drunk? I'm always like this at weddings."

Morgan handed us our honeymoon clothes. We went into the back room and changed into riding attire. I watched my new husband undressing and smiled.

"Quit your gawkin'! I've got something planned and we're burnin' daylight. It's a two hour ride and we need to be there before sunset."

"Well excuse me for admiring my husband's tight ass."

"Buckle bunnies call it a wrangler butt from years of ridin' bronc and bulls. Yours ain't half bad either. Hmm, what have you been ridin'? Never mind, we'll discuss that later but for now let's get a move on."

We hugged Morgan and Jannine, thanked them for their help and told them we'd see them in a week.

Joe walked Morgan to the car. "Son, thank you for being my best man, it meant more to me than you'll ever know. I love you, Son."

"You're welcome Dad – I love you too. Now get going; your bride is waiting." They hugged and said their goodbyes.

Jannine promised me that she would hold down the fort until our return. At first, I was worried that there wouldn't be a fort left to come home to, but she assured me she would be responsible. Plus Morgan would be staying there too. Between the two of them I felt a sense of relief.

Joe brought over Daisy and Bailey – it was time to go.

"Are you ready for the ride of your life darlin'?"

I mounted Daisy and said, "Yup."

"Okay, let's head out Mrs. Montana."

Mrs. Montana, it was official I was now Mrs. Lash Jackson Montana. However, we continued to call each other by our nom de plums. I'd grown to love the name Rose and I enjoyed calling him Joe. Joe was the man I fell in love with and Lash is the man I married. He loped up next to Daisy and took hold of my hand. I love you Rose. We kissed and began our adventure as husband and wife.

About forty minutes into our ride we stopped to rest the horses. Joe pointed out some Montana landmarks, native flowers and birds. I was still in a daze from the wedding and reception. I pretended to be engrossed in what he was saying but couldn't help thinking about how we ended up together--how our relationship began with my despising everything about him and later emerging into an epic love story. I've learned that fiction writers are unusual individuals. They tend to live their lives in a totally different dimension and constantly blur reality. Maybe we were acting out one of his stories? Maybe we were creating a new story – I don't know and to be honest, I didn't care. We were blissfully happy and that's all that mattered.

When Joe realized I wasn't listening, he said, "You know many pink ships carrying loony birds have sailed to Montana on the invisible orange lakes that flow through the Mars prairielands."

Unconsciously I said, "Yes, that is so true."

"Rose, you're haven't heard a word I've said."

I should have been embarrassed but I laughed and said no.

"Good, because it was absolute bullshit. I was just trying to impress my new bride. I couldn't tell you the difference between a swallow and buzzard . . . jerky?"

I ripped off a piece and popped it into my mouth. "Okay Joe, if you're finished your pseudo botany and zoology lessons I think we'd better get going."

We mounted up and continued riding headed west. The wind and sun felt good on my face. I remember reading cowboy stories about folks traveling west. I never would have guessed I'd be riding the range with my very own cowboy. It's funny how life puts you in situations and locations you never thought you'd be. For Joe this was his element. He was at home riding, camping and writing about the Wild West. He was a natural in the saddle. I was getting really sore. I guess he noticed me squirming.

"We're almost there darlin', just hold on."

I saw a small structure in the distance. It looked like a campsite. As we rode closer I could make out the outline of a large tent, a table setting and chairs.

"Welcome to Motel Montana! I thought you'd enjoy a night under the stars rather than a comfortable hotel room with room service. Was I right?"

I could barely dismount. *Soaking in a hot tub is more of what I had in mind.*

"Now I understand why cowboys walk the way they do. It's like straddling a barrel for two hours!" I stretched out my legs and back.

Joe laughed, "Don't you worry. I'll rub that sexy back and cute little butt with some horse liniment tonight and you'll be fine come morning; but not until we make this union official.

The view was spectacular. I'd never seen such a beautiful sky. Maybe it was the fact that I was gazing at it with my husband. It all seemed so surreal. I stopped trying to analyze my happiness and enjoy the present.

We walked over to the tent. I thought we'd be sleeping in sleeping bags. But to my surprise, there was a full-sized bed with fresh linen. He hugged me from behind. "Bet you didn't plan on this did you. Are you surprised?"

I was beyond surprised. For once in my adult life I was totally speechless. I knew not to cry because I'd be teased the entire night – well, maybe not the entire night. I, too, had big honeymoon plans for us.

"Yes, I'm very surprised. You never cease to amaze me Mr. Montana. What am I going to do with you?"

He pressed his body against mine, "I know what you can do to me later, but let's eat first. I've got more surprises coming tonight."

Dinner was amazing. We dined on lobster he had flown in from New England, California champagne and of course, for dessert strawberry cheesecake. It was perfect. The whole day was perfect. The sun was about to set when Joe retrieved two blankets from the tent and took hold of my hand. We walked to a spot near the edge of a small canyon.

"This is God's country darlin'. One of a few places I feel small and insignificant." I told him that he could never be insignificant.

"I didn't say I WAS insignificant I said I FELT insignificant. See there you go not paying attention to your husband again."

"And that's one of the reasons I love you. You know how to make me laugh."

We gathered some wood and started a campfire. The sun set quickly and the sky lit up with more stars than I could have ever imagined. "Is this one of my surprises? Did you name a star after me?"

He scratched his chin, "Nope, not a bad idea though. Anyway, I can't name a star after you because if I'm correct I believe the name Sun is already taken. All the other stars would pale in comparison. Just keep your eye on that patch of sky to your left."

He wrapped a blanket around our shoulders and we sat quietly for about ten minutes when something streaked over our heads. It was a shooting star. I'd never seen a shooting star before.

Joe explained it was an old folklore when you see a shooting star that you make a wish.

"Now go on and make a wish. If I'm still sittin' here I know your wish didn't come true."

"Hah, very funny Mister Montana."

He started to say something when I placed my finger over his lips, closed my eyes and made my wish. I opened my eyes and snuggled next to him.

I whispered, "Aren't you wondering what I wished for?"

"Nope"

"Aren't you curious?"

"Nope"

He linked my arm with his, "Rose, I don't need to know what you wished for because nothing you could wish can change the way I feel right now. You *are* my star Rose, my brilliant and beautiful star. How did I get so lucky? I guess being persistent paid off after all."

About a minute later, there was another, then another. The sky was filled with shooting stars.

"Wow, we're in the middle of a shooting star fest!"

Joe just shook his head. "You poor, urban, city girl, I do believe it's called a meteor shower. Remind me to sign you up for an online astronomy class."

We drank the last of our champagne and watched the night sky come to life. It was the most magnificent event I'd ever seen. Joe further explained this particular meteor shower happened every fifty years and we wouldn't see it again until we were old and gray. I jokingly told him that we should make plans to see it again – trading in our horses for them fancy electric wheelchairs.

It was getting late. We decided to head back to the tent. Joe remembered to pack his old Coleman lamps. As we walked back to the campsite I thought about how just a few months ago I considered camping sacking out on the sofa bed of the Holiday Inn. And now I'm married to an honest to goodness cowboy. Funny how life changes even when you are hell bent to keep things the way they are. Joe noticed I'd gone silent.

"A nickel for your thoughts – why so quiet darlin'? We've only been married nine hours. Have I gone and done something to upset you already?"

"Nope"

"Is there anything I've said to offend you?"

"Nope"

"So I'm still getting laid tonight, right."

"Yes you're gonna' get laid, however, that's not the reason I'm quiet. I was thinking about how life can change in the blink of an eye…how making plans can lead folks away from what they truly want. I'm happy my plans were mislaid and brought us together. I love you Joe."

He smiled and said I love you too Rose.

"And more importantly, I like you. Baby, our hearts are united forever. You know that and so do I. I can't imagine how in the world I could like you more than I do. This cowboy is crazy about you Rose. Of course, some would still argue this cowboy is just plain crazy."

Back at the campsite the fire was smoldering just enough to cast a candlelight glow over the tent. I was about to doused the ashes when Joe gently took hold of my hand.

"Let it be Rose, I want you now. I want all of you from your toes to those big, beautiful brown eyes and everything in between."

He walked me backwards guiding me down onto the bed. I never thought in a million years that my wedding night would be consummated in a tent underneath the stars, on the plains of Montana. He stripped off my clothes then he lowered himself on top of me. I whispered, *"My wish is about to come true."*

The sound of rain woke me up. I was wrapped in Joe arms so tight I couldn't move. I didn't want to wake him but the tent flap needed to be closed.

I tried to wiggle free when I heard him mumble, *"Are you trying to leave me already? Stay put I'll get it."* His nude silhouette outlined the physique of a much younger man. He was in amazing physical shape for a man of his age.

He slipped back into bed. "I must admit I did get awful excited thinkin' about you traipsing around the tent naked. It's not often that a man of my age gets that kind of an opportunity."

He reached over and tweaked my nipple. "I think I'll take that puppy with the cute tan nose."

"And here I thought I married a sophisticated, mature man. I didn't realize I'd married a horny teenager, I don't believe you!" He slid back the sheet exposing a well developed erection. "Is this sophisticated enough for you?"

It took me completely by surprise. "Look at me, I'm beet red. Oh my God Joe you are too much."

He gave me a wicked smile. "That ain't what you said to me last night and the night before that, and . . ."

I pulled him on top of me and we made love until we were drenched in sweat. The rain had blown the tent flap open again and we didn't care. We were already soaked and weren't about to stop.

Sex with Joe was so unlike anything I'd ever experienced. Our bodies fit flawlessly together. His rhythm was slow, gentle and passionate; rising and falling like the motion he used to break a green horse – not too rough, not too fast. I got lost in his movement causing my body to arch matching him stroke-for-stroke until we exploded into one massive rolling orgasm.

Exhausted and completely breathless, we lay motionless for a few minutes to recoup. Joe rolled off me off onto his back.

"Now that darlin' is what we call foreplay in Montana. Are you ready for some real lovemakin'?" The expression on my face caused him to laugh out loud.

"I think I'll save some for tomorrow let's get some sleep cowboy." We kissed goodnight and drifted off in each other's arms.

By daybreak the rain had stopped. Joe got up and started the fire for coffee – old fashioned cowboy coffee perked over a low fire.

Getting dressed I thought, *How amazing was last night. The day before I went to bed Miss Matthews and this morning I awake as Mrs. Montana. I still couldn't fully comprehend that I was now married to Joe. We are united as husband and wife, forever and always. At least I hope we'll be together forever. I don't plan on doing this again.*

The coffee had just finished brewing. I finished packing our things while Joe tended to the horses. They were a little wet but our saddles and horse blankets were dry. Joe must have brought them into the tent while I was sleeping. I asked about the rest of the things. He said everything was all taken care of and to enjoy my coffee.

About an hour later the horses were dry enough to saddle and head back home. Home, now that was something else I had to get used to. I had a new home with my new husband. I liked the sound of that.

We arrived back at the ranch mid afternoon. As much as I loved our incredible honeymoon tent extravaganza, it was good to be home. I missed being in the kitchen, eating breakfast on the porch and my daily morning daffodil delivered by my favorite cowboy.

I noticed Jannine and Morgan's packed bags sitting in the living room. I hollered for Jannine when Morgan walked out of the bedroom with two more bags.

"Hey there, welcome back. Hope you and dad had a fun time camping Montana-style."

I was surprised Joe had told Morgan about our honeymoon plans.

"When did your dad tell you?"

Morgan said, "It wasn't his idea it was mine. I thought you'd enjoy experiencing old western camping, under the stars, with a bit of modern conveniences. Was the bed comfortable?"

I thought, *If you only knew just how comfortable that bed was you would turn as red as a cherry.*

"The bed was very comfortable thank you."

Jannine came running out from the bathroom still wrapped in her towel. She hugged me as if I'd been gone for a year.

"Amelia or should I continue calling you Rose, either way . . . welcome home! You've got to tell me all the juicy details when we get back."

I was totally confused. "Back, back from where? What's going on, where are you two going?"

"I thought it would be a good idea to give you newlyweds some privacy, so I invited Morgan to New York. He'd never been to the Big Apple and I thought it would be exciting to show him around. Can we stay at your place? It's much larger than mine and you have cable. I'll even take care of your cat and you know how much I hate cats. Please . . . Rose?"

Joe walked in during our begging session. "Okay what did I miss?"

"Your son and my assistant decided it would be a good thing to let us newlyweds have a few weeks together. Jannine had offered to take care of my cat and condo and has offered Morgan a trip to New York."

Joe chuckled, "Now ain't that sweet of you youngins. It wouldn't by any chance have to do with the fact that you don't want to hear me moanin' and groanin' while I'm pouncin' on my new wife, hmm."

I rolled my eyes, "My God Joe, sex again, really?"

In unison, Morgan and Joe said, "Sorry, we didn't hear you we were too busy thinkin' about sex."

I flipped them the bird and walked into the bedroom.

They gave each other a high-five then Joe told Morgan to have a great time. He offered some fatherly advice telling him to be careful and keep an eye on Jannine, the genteel flower that she is. Morgan grinned and told him he would.

It was time for them to leave for the airport. I was sad to see Jannine go. I'd forgotten what it felt like to be that young. She was just a few years younger than Morgan. Joe was already doting over her like a father; telling her to be careful and keep an eye on his son.

Joe and I walked them to the car, said our goodbyes and watched them drive off. The house felt empty but it was good to be alone. I wanted to enjoy our first day in our house as a married couple. Neither of us wanted to join the real world but we needed to check our neglected e-correspondence. Joe headed to his office to check his email. I turned on my laptop and clicked open my account. Six hundred and twenty-five emails waiting in the queue. Normally, it would have sent me over-the-edge, but somehow it didn't matter. I felt a sense of complacency knowing something else was much more important- my love for Joe.

I briefly scanned them expecting to find the usual stuff. Museums requesting a review of their latest exhibition, galleries wanting write ups about an aspiring new artist.

However, there were two marked urgent; one from my editor and the other from the corporate office.

To: Amelia K Matthews, Art Critic and Columnist

Fr: Bernard Pollintino, Executive Director

*Subject: **Company Policy and Termination***

Dear Miss Matthews,

In review of your recent prolonged absence and in violation of company policy, I regret to inform you that your services are no longer required as Freelance Art Critic for our New York office. Please know that we regret losing you as your work (till now) has been exemplary and your column well received.

It also concerns me that you may be experiencing personal issues causing this unexpected behavior. We value your tenure with our company and would be willing to suggest a list of our employee counseling services.

Again, please call my office to set up a time to meet with said services if you choose to do so.

"WHAT THE FUCK? Who in the hell is this asshole? And who does he think he is suggesting I have mental problems!" I seldom use the "F" word but I was furious. My ranting was so loud that Joe rushed into the room.

"Whoa, what's got my new bride so fired up? What the heck is going on?"

I was too pissed to speak. I pointed to the email. Joe grabbed his glasses. *I didn't know he wore reading glasses? He looks so cute with them sitting on the end of his nose. For a brief moment it made me smile.* He took off his glasses and hugged me.

"Lord have mercy darlin', you had me worried. I thought someone had asked you to pose naked for Hustler or told you there was a world shortage of chocolate."

I was a taken aback by his lighthearted response. This was my career, one in which I was well respected. It was a huge deal to be let go via email.

I went outside to cool off. Joe instinctively knew not to follow me. As angry as I was I admired his decision not to interfere when I was having a melt-down. He knew I needed to seethe before choosing to respond to this inappropriate termination letter. I would have preferred a phone call. At least I could have cursed him a blue streak before telling him to kiss my tan and beautiful ass.

I heard the deck door open with Joe waving a white napkin while holding a plate with sliced cheesecake in the other.

"Is is safe to come out? I don't want to wear this cheesecake if you're still fumin'."

I motioned it was okay. He put the cake on the table and sat next to me.

"Rose you know I would never, ever belittle your career or your dedication to it. It breaks my heart to see you get this worked up over anything. Would you like me to go with you to New York? You can tell him in person where to shove his email? 'Cause baby, I would do anything to make you happy. Plus, I'd like to see you in action rippin' this poor unsuspecting corporate fella' a new one! Hah, now that would just be the bee's knees – yet another nonsensical sayin' I've never understood."

I thought, *Okay, now you've got me laughing. How do you do it?*

He smiled, lifted me up out of the chair and sat me onto his lap.

"Amelia, you know you do not need to work, but if you want to work I will support you in whatever you want to do. I'll respect your choice darlin'. Personally, I would hope you choose to stay home and work with me. I'm always lookin' for a good research assistant. I hear the pay ain't too bad but the fringe benefits are well worth it."

"What kind of fringe benefits are we talking about, sir?"

"The kind that won't get you fired if you sleep with the boss."

He scooped up a fork full of cheesecake and slipped it into my mouth. I put a mound on my finger and let him suck it off. I could feel his rock hard erection throbbing beneath me as he licked the remaining cake off my finger.

"Mister Montana, I believe you are allergic to cheesecake because your jeans seem to get extremely tight whenever we eat it."

"Yep, Mrs. Montana, that seems to be an ongoing condition for me. Dreadful isn't it."

We abandoned the cake and moved the conversation to the bedroom. An hour or so later we jumped in the shower. Joe had reservations for dinner at a local restaurant, known for their bison steak. I've never had bison before. But I was up for an adventure with my new husband.

I was toweling off when the phone rang. It was for Joe. His agent called to remind him of a speaking engagement he had booked in Seattle. I could hear him trying to reschedule. He came back looking disappointed.

"Well darlin' how would you like to see Seattle. I hear it's beautiful when it ain't rainin'. I've got a lecture I'm contracted to do and can't reschedule."

As much as I'd miss him, I didn't want to travel. I'd been on a whirlwind adventure already and wanted to settle in my new surroundings. He said it would only be for two days. I asked if it would be okay if I took a rain check.

Joe cracked up, "A rain check, for Seattle. That's almost funny Rose. And, I'll repeat, don't quit your day job."

"But I don't have a day job anymore. Now what do I do."

You're day and night job is to love me darlin. I'll be home before you know it and we can pick up where we left off in bed."

I asked when he would be leaving.

"I need to leave tomorrow afternoon. Now, before you pick up something and throw it at me, just know that if I could get out of doing this I would have in a heartbeat. But unfortunately this lecture has been scheduled for over a year. It's the life of a novelist darlin'."

I helped him pack his travel bag, keys and laptop by the door. I thought it would be fun to receive those legendary Montana Joe emails again. I still feel like a love-struck teenager when I see his name in my email queue.

The next morning I drove him to the airport departure terminal. He looked tired, but that was to be expected after the week we had. I'm surprised we're able to walk. I hadn't had that much sex in years, maybe decades. We embraced saying our goodbyes and I made him promise to call and write as soon as he arrived. He said he would because he knew I'd drive out there just to give him hell if he didn't. I waited until he entered the terminal.

Airport security strolled over to my car and asked me to leave the drop off area. I thought, *I'll leave when I'm damn ready pal, that's my husband I'm saying goodbye to – so back the hell off!* I didn't want to cause a scene so I kindly smiled and drove away.

On the drive home I reminisced about living in Montana with no expectations accept enjoying my new life with Joe. I've never had memories like this before. More often than not I wanted to forget my past relationships. The memories were usually painful and upsetting.

I got home about four o'clock in the afternoon and changed into my barn clothing. *I must remember to feed the horses while he's away.* He said even though they have plenty of grass they need some grain to keep them full. I have never owned horses so everything was very new to me. Yet another thing I never expected I'd be doing. I fed them, brushed the dust and hay off of Bailey and Daisy then walked back to the house. I stopped to let the sun shine on my face. It felt warm and soothing like Joe's hands cupping my cheeks. I looked at the sky and whispered,

"Thank you God for allowing this man to be in life."

There was some of Joe's over-brewed coffee left in the pot. I poured a cup and heated it in the microwave. He would have a fit if he saw me doing this.

I could hear him saying, "You can boil it, drink it cold, heat it over a brandin' iron fire but never nuke good coffee, it just ain't civilized!"

I laughed as the microwave timer beeped and took my cup out to the deck with my laptop. He should be in Seattle by now. Maybe he had time to write. I opened my email surprised to find two emails from him.

To: Rose
Fr: Montana Joe
*Subject: **Benedict de Spinoza and Why Every Substance is Infinite***

Hello sexy, is it seven o'clock? Isn't the lecture over yet? This is the world's slowest day . . . this is one desperate, needy cowboy!!! I'm pushing myself to compile my notes for the 8 o'clock program but your sweet kisses and your nibblin' of my ears lobes is ruining my

concentration! What am I goin' to do with you? I know what I want to do with you. Quit that nibblin' . . . git out of my daydreams . . . go sit in the corner [of my mind] for a while . . . and for goodness sake put some clothes on! . . . Your hopeless cowboy husband, Joe

I hadn't realized how much I'd missed his emails. His scholastic and out of the ordinary choice of subject titles never ceases to amaze me. I opened up the other one,

To Rose
Fr: Montana Joe
Subject: **Nude Descending a Staircase by Marcel Duchamp**

Baby, the only nude I want to see descending a staircase is you. Some chicks really dig the cool, sophisticated cowboy types, then there's my Rose darlin', she likes her cowboys aging, horny and desperate . . . lucky me. Hold on girl, I'll be home soon! Goodnight baby.

Your lonely cowboy husband stuck in a lousy hotel room
I couldn't help but to respond if only to make him appreciate being away.

To: Montana Joe
Fr: Rose
Re: Subject: **Nude Descending a Staircase by Marcel Duchamp**

Joe darlin' if you could only see me with my hair in a mess, drinkin' day-old nuked coffee, smellin' of horse manure you might think otherwise about seein' me naked. It's a beautiful Montana evening and I miss you. Love, Amelia

A few second later I received his reply,

To: Rose
Fr: Montana Joe
Re: re: Subject: **Nude Descending a Staircase by Marcel Duchamp**

Darlin' you couldn't look bad if you tried. Other than your horrible obsession with nuked coffee I couldn't love you more than I already do. Now, go into our bedroom, strip naked and jump in the shower. That fantasy will keep me happy until I get home and . . . sorry, I just realized I was typing with "one" hand. Baby, you get me excited beyond words.

Gotta' go before things get too heated and I miss my lecture. Behave yourself and I'll see you soon.

Love, Lash
I shut down my laptop and headed to the shower. *I love you too Lash.*

Chapter 11

I noticed the phone blinking indicating a missed voice message. Morgan must have called while I was in the shower. He and Jannine arrived safely in New York. I returned their call to make sure everything was okay. Jannine said that they had picked up my cat from Daniel and Patrick and she filled them in on my new life with Joe. Jannine said Patrick started crying like a baby saying our neurotic, self-absorbed, workaholic little girl has finally grown up. Daniel was more upset he wasn't at the wedding, but told me to say how happy he is for you both.

She also said that Daniel has a small man-crush on Morgan telling me that I should watch my beautiful, over-exercised, well-toned back because he might have to steal him from me. Jannine said that she'd bitch slap him if he laid one of his overly manicured hands on him.

Jannine explained how our wedding took place in a small western-style chapel, with a tribal elder performing the ceremony.

"Afterwards, they rode on horseback to their honeymoon location and camped out under the stars."

She said Patrick sarcastically rolled his eyes and placed his hand over his heart.

I could hear him in the background, "Oh, thank God, because I thought it was going to be tacky. Anyway, I'm allergic to horses. However, if it made our girl Amelia happy, I'm happy for her. Just tell me she didn't wear that gaudy cowboy wedding attire, ugh. That would be a wardrobe faux pas worst than wearing silk in mid-summer. Or even more atrocious – seersucker shorts with last year's sandals, oy vey!"

I laughed out loud knowing that this was Patrick's way of saying how happy he was for me. I told Jannine to thank them, send them lots of love and I would call again soon.

She put Morgan on the phone. He was in awe by the scope of New York. It was much bigger and busier than he imagined. He asked about his dad. I told him he was in Seattle at a lecture for two days.

"I'm surprised you didn't go with him, being newlyweds and all."
Oddly, I didn't feel like a newlywed. I felt like I'd known Joe for years. I didn't feel alone or abandoned anymore. There was a quiet comfort – I finally felt at peace.

I told Jannine if she needed me she could call anytime. They both promised they would and hung up.

A few minutes later the phone it rang again. I didn't recognize the phone number.

"Hello."

"Funny thing about lectures, they never seem to start on time. Thank goodness there's a phone in my dressing room, so I thought I call and have phone sex – unhook that bra baby and get naked."

I laughed, "How do you know I'm not naked and lying spread-eagle on the bed?"

Total silence, then, ". . . sorry, I was thinkin' about baseball. It's a wonderful sport, baseball. Lots of runnin' and slidin' and runnin' and if you haven't noticed, I'm tryin' not develop a hard on."

"Don't you want to hear the rest of my fantasy?"

". . . we'll it's been nice talkin' to you ma'am, we should do this again sometime, but don't let the wife know. Gotta' go darlin', I love you."

"I love you too Joe."

"Good night baby."

I picked up some magazines and brought them into the bedroom. I wasn't sleepy and reading usually helps to relax me. I thumbed through the articles most of which were about horses and horse care. Then it dawned on me that I'd never read any of Joe's books. Some of his novels were sitting in his desk. One entitled, *Lost Trails of Sweet Grass Canyon* and his latest novel, *Chase Down the Wind*.

I thought I'd start with Sweet Grass Canyon first. The book was based on one of Joe's poems and also the book's introduction.

I sat atop a mountain ridge with the sun upon my face
It took me three days journey to travel to this place

I spoke my heartfelt dreams aloud, to the canyon down below
They echoed back a dozen times
In a voice I'd come to know
It was my cowboy story my, haunting destiny
To sit by Sweet Grass Canyon
With echoed memories

I didn't know my husband was also a poet – cowboy poetry mostly. There were a stack of poems scattered about his office. I shuffled through them pausing every now and then to read a few. They were beautiful. One in particular caught my attention. It was called, *A Porch in Wyoming*. When we first met I made a bet with Joe that he couldn't write a poem using the town's name of Meeteetse. Obviously, he proved me wrong but didn't want to tell me. The poem read,

An old driftin' cowboy, Meeteetse bound
Needed some rest and a place to lie down
Many a folk saw him early that day
They walked by his soogan
without much to say

'Cept one lil' gal with a right purty smile
Said, "Come up on my porch and rest here for a while"
She cooked him a meal and let him clean up
And brought him fresh coffee in a blue floral cup

She listened for hours to his tales and stories
Of bronc ridin' mishaps and gold buckle glories
Of rustlers and gun fights and old battle scars
Of nights in the desert camped under the stars

She knew by his tone that his tales were quite true
That his "seen-it-all" eyes confirmed all he'd been through
She told him she'd never been out of this town
She gazed at the sunset...then down at the ground

He tilted his hat back...took hold of her hand
Then turned towards each other just like it were planned
He knew in a moment his driftin' was done
Holding on to each other till moon became sun

He said if I'm welcome . . . I'll stay for a while
She told him he was . . . with that right purty smile
As they stood in the doorway he blessed God above
For that porch in Wyoming where he'd found his true love

I had to admit I was impressed. There was so much I didn't know about my new husband. Then again there were lots of things he didn't know about me like the fact I could juggle or throw my voice and like many children I wanted to join the circus. I begged my mom to buy me a ventriloquist's doll. I practiced every day, entertaining my friends and family members until I was good enough to enter a talent show. I was a dismal failure. Another friend taught me how to juggle. I made money in college teaching other students this useless skill.

I took a few of his books into the bedroom and started reading *Sweet Grass Canyon* until I fell asleep. The next morning, I awoke to the phone ringing – It was Joe. He was on his way home. His voice sounds a little hoarse like he was catching a cold. I'm sure it's from the lecture. *I remember it sounding rough last week – nothing a little bit of TLC won't fix.*

Heading out to the barn, I stumbled over what I thought was a rock. It was an empty bottle of throat spray. It must have fallen from his truck. I'll ask him about it later. If it persists I'll call his doctor. I stuck the bottle in my jean pocket. We hadn't had much rain and the paddock near the pasture was dusty. I put on Joe's barn jacket, fed the horses and put out new salt licks.

Who would have believed a city girl like me would be doing these things? I giggled to myself because the most outdoorsy thing I ever did was jog through Central Park. Now I'm feeding horses, cleaning out stalls and scraping the crap from the horse's hooves. I even know what a half-hooey is. I smiled knowing that Joe would be amused at my new found cowgirl abilities.

Back at the house, I noticed my email icon was blinking. Joe's plane was about to land. I jumped into the shower, got cleaned up and headed to the airport. I decided to drive his truck. That should impress the *dog tar* out of him. I thought, *"What the hell does that mean – dog tar?"* I rolled the windows down allowing the wind blow dry my hair. *This is truly Big Sky Country.*

Flipping through the radio stations, I found a local country western channel. I could identify some of the singers like Dolly Parton, Brooks and Dunn, Alan Jackson, and George Strait. I always liked Dolly even though I never listened to much country music. But I loved her version of, *I Will Always Love You.* George Strait was quickly becoming one of my favorites. I turned up the radio when Brooks and Dunn's, *Neon Moon* came on. I sang along at the top of my lungs until a guy in a pick-up hollered, "For Christ sake darlin', have some mercy on us!" Normally this would have upset me. I just smiled and kept singing.

The airport exit was coming up soon. It was very busy for a week day. I circled the arrival area five times before I saw Joe standing by the door. *God, he's a good looking man and more importantly he's my man.* I'd know him anywhere. Nobody else has a sexy shit-eating-smile like his.

He looked surprised to see me in his truck. I put it in park and ran up to him wrapping my arms around his neck.

"Lady, what did you do with my wife? You see, she drives a crappy little 4-cylinder import. Only a real cowgirl would have the balls to drive this big V-8. His hug lifted me off my feet. "I missed you baby, it's good to be home."

Joe motioned for me to move over into the passenger seat. He said it would be easier for him to slide his hand underneath my tee shirt if he got the urge to unhook my bra. On the ride back to the house, his agent called. It was a short conversation ending with Joe saying he was sure and wasn't going to change his mind. I waited for him to fill me in. He didn't seem too interested about letting me know what transpired.

I asked, "Okay, so what the hell is going on?"

He parroted back, "What's going on?"

I said, "YES, are you going to tell me what's going on?"

"Hmm, well . . . let me see, what's going on. Alfalfa hay is down a dollar."

He could tell I was not amused.

"Okay darlin' as you already know that was my agent. I told him I would be taking the next six months off to spend time with my bride. I know how much you love me being underfoot, leaving my clothes on the floor and tripping over my boots. What better way to start a new marriage."

"Really . . . you'd stay home with me, just the two of us, alone?"

"Hmm, maybe you didn't comprehend the expression being underfoot. Yes, I've decided after twenty years of writing to take a much deserved break. And who better to spend it with than my Rose a.k.a. the woman formerly known as Amelia."

I was speechless. No one had ever done anything like this for me. I turned my head toward the window.

"Don't even think I can't see you tearin' up. Remind me when we get home to call the tissue company and buy a thousand shares of their stock. And since you're already cryin' I have another surprise for you. We'll not be sittin' home, we're gonna travel. I hear-tell Italy is beautiful this time of the year. Reach in my inside jacket pocket"

There were two tickets to Italy.

"This is unbelievable! One of my dreams is to visit the wine country in Tuscany!" I slid over and kissed him.

"You really know my heart don't you Joe."

"Yes baby I do. And you know mine. I still think it's crazy that you love me. It's too crazy for me to comprehend. We're both crazy and what's even crazier is why you don't wear bras that unhook from the front."

We continued talking about the places we'd visit and the interesting people we'd meet along the way. I love listening to him tell stories. He spoke with a slow and sexy western twang. It was deep enough to make me shiver and sweet enough melt my heart. I suggested he adapt some of his books to audio.

"Who in their right mind would pay good money to listen to my gravelly old voice?" I said, "Even if it's just for me it would be worth it." To appease me he said he'd think about it.

We arrived home to a herd of anxious horses waiting for their evening feed. They were happy to see Joe neighing as he walked out to the barn. I grabbed his carry-on and brought his jacket inside. I felt something in his outer pocket. It was a new bottle of throat spray. *What's going on?*

About ten minutes after we walked into the house, he started coughing.

"Are you okay? You've had a bout of hoarseness lately." I handed him the empty bottle of spray I found by his truck.

"So you're rummaging through my pockets lookin' for loose change, are ya'?"

"Stop joking around Joe. What's the matter?"

He took a deep breath and said, "I've had some hoarseness and the doc seems to think its exhaustion, hence the six months off. He also found a small polyp on my vocal cord, nothin' to be worried about. I have to go back in four months to see if it's changed. The spray helps when I do speaking engagements, radio shows and such."

"And when were you going to tell me this?"

"Well seein' we've been married less than two months I thought I'd hold off on all the borin' stuff until our three month anniversary. Anyway, we've got tickets to Italy. If you'd like, we can continue this conversation while we're sitting in the Tuscan sun, drinking wine and eating fine food. Now, should we continue fussin' or hit the shower to do down and dirty things to each other?"

Sex in the shower with Joe was exhilarating. His combined use of tongue and the detachable shower head rivaled men half his age. I asked him where he learned to do all this stuff.

"Darlin' we do have cable in Montana."

Fifteen minutes later, Joe was fast asleep. I wondered if he would miss writing. It was in his blood. He decided to write in his late twenties, mostly about his experiences working with his uncles on New Mexico cattle ranches. It was then he developed his passion for western fiction. I read a little more of Sweet Grass Canyon then drifted off to sleep.

I awoke to the smell of fresh coffee and nutmeg. The aroma waffled through the house. Joe was up and making breakfast pancakes. He put a teaspoon of nutmeg in his batter sayin' it was the way cowboy's made them. I couldn't imagine wranglers carrying a gourmet container of nutmeg on the cattle trail but Joe insisted it was true.

I put his blue cowboy shirt on and tiptoed down the hallway, only to find him butt naked except for his boots. I let out a laugh that could be heard in the next county.

"Excuse me ma'am but loud screams like that will not get these pancakes cooked any faster. Besides I was gonna bring you breakfast in bed. Now you've gone and ruined my surprise." *Like seeing him with nothing on but boots wasn't a big enough surprising?"*

He continued, "Now you may have noticed that I'm . . . eh, without apparel – let me explain. I figured we were gonna get naked after breakfast so I thought we'd cut out the middleman."

"Okay, I know I'm going to regret this but I have to ask . . . so, what's with the boots?

Without cracking a smile he said, "My feet were cold."

"Now come over here and kiss the cook. There seems to be a draft coming from the deck and I don't want any other part of my body to catch a chill."

"You are by far the most deranged man I've ever known."

"Well you know what they say darlin', if priests can be defrocked and lawyers can be debarred it only makes sense that cowboys can be deranged."

I laughed so hard I snorted. I never snorted while laughing before. Not only does this man have me dropping my G's, now I'm snorting – totally destroying my cosmopolitan persona.

"I swear Joe, you are unbelievable."

"Yes I am . . . that's me alright, the unbelievable, deranged cowboy without apparel. Now if you're finished snortin' and laughin' at my choice in morning attire let's eat before my hotcakes get cold and I ain't talkin' about breakfast."

Breakfast was delicious. Joe put on his jeans and took the empty plates and coffee cups to the kitchen. He refilled our cups and got back into bed. He noticed I was distracted.

"What ya' thinkin' about baby. Did you not enjoy my cookin'? Are you highly allergic to nutmeg?"

"No, I love your cooking and I'm not allergic to nutmeg. I want you to tell me the truth. Are you taking this time off because of us or is there another reason. Be honest with me Joe; is everything okay?"

"You worry too much Rose, nothing is wrong. Besides, you look like a chipmunk when you worry. It would be cute if I liked chipmunks – I'm more of a squirrel man myself."

"No joking Joe, if something were wrong you would tell me, right?"

He took hold of my hand and kissed my palm. "Yes, I would tell you Rose, I swear on my favorite pair of spurs and you know how much I love them spurs. I got 'em from an old man in Mexico who said he was the cousin or was it the uncle of Pancho Villa – I can't remember. But they mean a lot to me, so yes, I swear I would tell you."

I frowned for a second. He held my face in his hands and smiled, "You are by far the most beautiful woman I've ever seen. Do you know how beautiful you are – even when you're poutin' you look like an angel." He tilted my face up and gave me a long and sexy kiss.

"That was nice. I'll have another, please."

"Nope"

"Please, I'll be your best friend; I'll even share my lunch with you."

"Nope"

"Darlin', I'm impervious to your beggin' you'll not get a rise out of me."

I looked down, "Eh, that's not what it looks like to me."

"That's beside the point; we can take care of that part of my body later, but for now we've got things to do like prepare for a much needed vacation slash honeymoon – a real honeymoon. Now behave yourself and get dressed there is some place I want to take you. And put your boots on."

Joe loaded the truck with a blanket and some flowers. About an hour later, we stopped at a small cemetery. He drove a few yards and parked. I thought it was odd we were visiting a cemetery on such a beautiful day. I didn't remember Joe telling me about anyone close to him that had recently died. We walked through the damp grass, over to a beautiful headstone.

"It's lovely Joe; who is she?"

He took off his hat and tucked it underneath his arm and knelt down placing the flowers onto the grave. He noticed prairie roses growing next to her headstone. He said he hadn't noticed them until now. They were his mother's favorite flower.

"Rose, this is Charlotte Simone Montana; Mother, this is my lovely bride Amelia who I affectionately call Rose."

It took me by surprise because Joe never mentioned anything about his parents or that they had passed away. I was looking forward to meeting my new in-laws. I wanted to know all about the people who raised this unbelievably annoying and incredibly brilliant man.

I knelt down next to Joe and said hello to his mother. He went on to tell me that today was her birthday and how every year he comes to have lunch with her. It was something they'd do once a month until she died. From the dates on her headstone, I could see she would have been 74-years-old today. I asked Joe to tell me about her. He said she was a beautiful and ornery woman who would give us a run for our money if we misbehaved. I notice he said 'us' when recollecting his childhood.

"You said us – do you have siblings?"

"Yes I do. I have a sister who lives in Texas and another sister who lives in New Mexico. Both are beautiful ladies who have families with full and happy lives. My sister Trish, her partner Bree and their little girl Sophie own a natural food café in Taos. They insist on trying to get me to eat Tofu but that's something I've never acquired a taste for – never will I suppose."

I was so impressed at his ease and acceptance of his sister's life choice. Living in New York, it's no big deal. Gay couples are well received and respected just like any other married couple. I told him about Patrick and Daniel.

"Rose if you haven't noticed there ain't one drop of prejudiced blood runnin' through this cowboy's veins. People are people, there are good people and there are bad people and the bad people are just good people who ain't had enough learnin' on how to be good people. Now please don't make me repeat that because I don't think I could."

I laughed at his lengthy statement and knew it was genuine. Joe had a way of saying things – shooting straight from the hip. No mixed signals, no fluff or double meaning. He spoke his mind.
He continued to tell me about his baby sister Kathleen and her husband Jesse who owned a cattle ranch in South Texas. Three years after their marriage Kathleen discovered she couldn't have children. They thought

about adoption but wanted to wait hoping science might catch up and possibly have one of their own.

"You'd love both of my sisters Rose. They are just as strong-willed and hard-headed as you."

I asked about this father. He didn't have much to say about him other than he was a lousy dad.

"K.T. Montana never had much time for us kids or our mother. Odd thing is I never knew what the K.T. stood for. He was a saddlebum who tried his hand at rodeo then ranchin' and when that didn't work, he left us flat. He was a very secretive man who never shared anything with us. Mother never remarried. She raised us not to be quitters and to accept folks for who they are, not what they are. Good lessons to live by."

I hesitated for a moment then asked him why he never married until now. He said, "Well, I guess it's because I'd never met a woman who was crazy enough to put up with me and my lifestyle. Like I keep tellin' you Rose, novelists are strange creatures who live in another dimension; never knowing the difference between reality and fiction. And, for some reason unknown to mankind, I found this feisty, opinionated, sweet gal who stole my heart the minute I saw her. Why some city guys hadn't scooped her up is still a mystery to me."

He paused for a moment, "I guess some things are just are meant to be – like us."

He's never opened up to me this way. Maybe it was the fact that I'd never asked him about his past. He'd been so open about everything else.

We finished our lunch said goodbye to Charlotte and wished her a happy birthday. On the drive back to the house, I jokingly said it's a good thing Charlotte had two girls. I don't know if the world is ready for three Montana bothers. Joe laughed saying thank goodness because one of him was enough to last a life time, but thought it would have been cool to have a brother. Growing up with younger sisters was challenging to say the least.

About thirty minutes later, we arrived home. I noticed Joe's cell phone vibrated on the console. I picked it up – it was a message from the travel agent. It seems the place we wanted to stay was booked for the season. He continued his nebulous conversation ending with, "Yes, that will be fine – thanks."

"Well, there go our plans to stay in one of them fancy hotels in Tuscany. I was hopin' to get you drunk on all that wine and take advantage of you. Sorry darlin'. Have you ever been to Fiji? Maybe we can go there."

"Fiji could be fun. Never been to either place."

Joe said, "I hear tell if you're fat in Fiji, you're considered a God and Goddess."

I laughed, "Then that rules both of us out because there's not an ounce of fat on either of us."

I told him it didn't matter where we went as long as we were together and happy. I loved listening to him talk about his rodeo life, how his novels help to carry on the spirit of the Old West.

He stopped abruptly, "Hey, enough talkin' we've gotta' start packin' for our honeymoon!"

I was completely confused. *I thought he'd just said the place we wanted to stay was booked for the season?* I was ready to research other locations.

"Pack light darlin', I don't plan on wearin' much, after all it is our honeymoon. Now stop your lollygaggin' and get goin'!"

I gave him a limp-handed salute. "Yes sir! And that will be the last time you order me around. I don't care if it is our honeymoon."

"Hah, like I could ever order you to do anything. Okay, Amelia would you please go into our bedroom and pack a few things then take them out to the truck or we'll miss our flight."

"But . . . we just got home I thought we'd rest tonight and leave tomorrow?"

"Nope, we're leaving tonight. We can sleep on the plane."

"The plane – to WHERE?"

"Italy, we're goin' to Italy – my Lord, girl haven't you been payin' any attention?"

I was still confused. He held me by my shoulders. "Rose if you haven't noticed I'm a loony sort of guy – an occupational hazard of being a fiction writer. The quicker you understand that aspect of your new husband the better off we'll be. Now run along and get packin."

I was excited about going to Italy. I'd never been there. It was on my things-to-do-before-I'm-too-old-to-do-them list. I threw a couple pairs of shorts, tanks and tees, sandals and flats and two swim suits. I asked Joe if I'd need anything fancy. He said to pack the necklace and earrings he brought me and the little white dress he liked.

"Silver and white look so beautiful against your already golden skin. And seein' you'll have no tan lines it'll look even better."

Oh God please, I hope we're not staying at a nudist resort. That's a surprise I could do without.

Joe was waiting by the door with his bag packed. He'd already let Cecilia know we would be out of town for a few weeks and his rancher buddy would take care of the horses. There was nothing for us to do but to enjoy our new found freedom. At the moment, I had no job to worry about and Joe was overdue for a much needed vacation.

We parked the truck in long-term parking, giving the instructions that it be watered and hayed for two weeks. The parking attendant didn't get the joke. Joe chuckled and tipped him anyway. We arrived at our gate and noticed the gift shop had his books on display.

"You really are a celeb aren't you? I wonder if anyone will recognize y—"

Before I could finish my sentence, the clerk came from behind the register and gasped.

"Wow, you're Montana Joe, the western novelist!" She grabbed one of his books and asked him to autograph it for her.

"I love your books! They're so romantic and rustic. It's like you were really there and wrote about it. I love the way you portray cowboys and Indians!"

Joe smiled and asked her name. "Mona, just sign it to Mona Moon-Rae from Montana Joe. I can't believe this!" He quickly signed his name and asked, "Hmm, Moon-Rae, Native American are ya' Mona?

She gave him a blank stared and said, "No why?"

Joe sighed, "Never mind darlin' enjoy the book."

He turned and whispered to me, "Sometime I think my fans are wackier than me, bless their hearts."

I stood in the background watching other fans gather around him asking for autographs and photos. It was an entirely different world living with him. He had a well-established fan base that I had to adjust to. My career as an art columnist paled in comparison. A few minutes later he realized I was standing by the door alone waiting for the crowd to subside. He thanked his fans and excused himself.

"I'm really, really sorry darlin' I didn't expect that nor did I mean to leave you standin' here."

I told him not to worry because it was something I'd have to get use to. He said, "Rose . . . no . . . Amelia, you will NEVER get use to it, because this will be the last time I EVER leave you standing alone anywhere, is that understood Mrs. Montana!"

I nodded yes. He put on his sunglasses and removed his signature gray Stetson cowboy hat plopping it on top of my head.

"Now we can travel incognito. Maybe they'll mistake you for me, seein' that we look so much alike. Come on we've got a plane to catch."

I enjoyed the luxury of first-class. Most of my travel was for business. I was all too familiar with economy coach and cramped seating. First-class accommodations were never an option. The flight was amazingly uneventful. The weather was beautiful; the food and wine both delicious.

I'd never felt so privileged in my life. Two hours into the flight we were so exhausted we fell asleep.

The voice of the captain woke me up saying we would be arriving in Milan in forty five minutes. The last thing I remembered was eating my tiramisu and now I'm waking up in Italy! *Not such a bad place to wake up.* It could have been worse, we could have been redirected to Antarctica, with nothing but summer clothes or our luggage lost with nothing to wear at all – which still leaves me wondering about nude beaches. *He wouldn't dare!*

Our captain advised us to buckle our seatbelts and remain in our seats until we landed. I looked out of the window in awe of the crystal blue water and lush green country side.

Joe opened one-eye and mumbled, "Are we there yet? Lord knows I could use some coffee. Hah, maybe I'll try one of them there espressos. I wonder if an old cowboy like me could get used to them tiny little cups. I'd have to drink at least ten of 'em to get the same kick as Arbuckles."

I said, "If you drank ten espressos we wouldn't need a plane, we'd just hold on to your belt loops."

"Why Rose, I do believe that was an attempt at humor – a lousy attempt I might add, but an attempt nonetheless. But I must warn you, you're dancin' on thin pasta teasin' a man who hasn't had a cup of coffee in eight hours!"

He winked and kissed my palm, "Benevento in Italia, Bella."

"Okay, now I'm impressed – you speak Italian?"

"Darlin', when will you realize that I'm a man of many talents? Yes, I speak a little Italian because my books are translated into more than six languages."

We thanked the pilot and crew for a wonderful flight and headed to another gate to catch a smaller plane to take us to Tuscany. We headed to the boarding area. I noticed it was filled with American tourists waiting for the same flight. Sadly, they were your stereotypical tourists talking as loud as the obnoxious shirts they were wearing. I took hold of Joe's hand and thought, *This is going to be one hell of a flight.*

Joe walked pass the gate.

"Whoa, isn't this our flight? Are you really going to risk missing it for a cup of coffee?"

"Nope"

"Is there someplace else you need to go in such a hurry – maybe the rest room?"

"Nope"

I stopped walking. "Joe, what the hell is going on? Where the hell are we going and who is that man standing at the door holding a sign with our names on it?

He let out a huge sigh, "Lord have mercy darlin', you sure do know how to spoil a moment! If you must know he's our driver or as you fancy city folks say . . . a chauffeur. We're not flying to Tuscany, we're drivin' or rather he's drivin'. Because if the mood hits us to rip each other's clothes off and pounce on each other, we won't embarrass ourselves on an airplane full of strangers."

I have to admit I was surprised. He told me from the start he was a man of many surprises. The driver had already retrieved our luggage. We were on our way to Tuscany.

The drive was beautiful. The fragrance from the flowers and vineyards filled the air. I felt so happy and relaxed I almost felt guilty. Why I don't know. I guess I'd never allowed myself to feel anything remotely close to complete happiness. Maybe it was the fear of being disappointed. Either way, I decided to let all of those negative feelings go and enjoy my adventure with my husband. I loved saying that word – husband. Joe was indeed my husband and for the first time since the wedding I felt married – blissfully married, head-over-heels in love.

About four hours later, we arrived at the coast where a boat was waiting to take us to a small island off the coast to Elba Island. Joe said he'd called in a favor and was able to get us a private villa with a garden balcony close to the ocean. I grabbed Joe's arm and bit it.

"Ouch! What was that for? I thought this would make you happy and you bite me! I reckon I should be glad you're not cryin'. That would be a lousy way to start our honeymoon vacation."

"I wanted to see if I was dreaming all of this. Obviously, from your wimpy yelp we really are here in Italy and about to board the ferry to Ebla Island."

Joe frowned and rubbed his arm. "I swear girl sometimes I do question your sanity then again I question mine for not finding you sooner. And if you wanted to know if you were dreaming why didn't you just bite your own arm! Now if you're done using my arm as a T-bone steak let's get goin'."

It was a short ride to the island and even shorter walk to our villa on the beach. The driver said he would have someone bring our luggage later. Joe leaned down and removed my sandals.

"Doesn't that feel good, the sand between your toes."

We rolled up our jeans and strolled along the water's edge. Even though I knew I wasn't dreaming, I couldn't believe we were staying in such a beautiful Italian paradise. Joe unbuttoned his shirt letting it flow in the sea breeze.

"You know an old cowboy could get used to this lifestyle."

He reached in his shirt pocket pulling out a hunk of beef jerky. He broke off a piece for me. I agreed with him. I could easily get use to this. He stopped for a moment taking off his shirt laying it down on the damp sand.

"Have a seat Rose. I want to tell you a little secret."

I always get nervous when his conversations begin with a serious tone.

"Ever since I was a kid, the girl of my dreams has had olive/brown-skinned, brown-eyed, gorgeous, with a great sense of humor who would love me unconditionally. I always reckoned it was just a fantasy…that she was somebody I created in my head. Never in a million years would I have believed she existed until now. Not only do I love you darlin', I like you. You are my best friend and confidant. Not to mention hot and sexy. You know me and you know my heart."

I was relieved it wasn't something earth shattering.

I smiled and sarcastically said, "Oh, so you do like me after all."

"Do I like you? I like you as much as I love you and I love you as much as I need you . . . and it's embarrassingly obvious how much I need you."

He pulled me up off the sand and kissed me.

"Let finish this tongue-in-mouth conversation at the villa and afterwards and maybe go skinny dippin' in the moonlight."

The villa was indescribably beautiful. There was a bowl of fresh fruits with cheeses on the counter, loaves of Italian bread and bottles of wine. I felt like a celebrity. He pulled me away from the counter area.

"All this can wait darlin'. Let's finish what we started on the beach."

I dropped the bread back on the counter. Joe lifted me onto the counter top and took off my jeans. The sound of the ocean and the floral laden evening air was intoxicating. His thrusts were so fierce it knocked over the bowl of fruit. For a second it startled me.

He moaned, "Rose, please don't stop, I'll pay for the damn bowl, the cheese and fruit later, just don't stop baby."

His orgasm shook my entire body. I grabbed onto his hips as tight as I could and in a couple of minutes I reached my climax. I was exhausted, covered with sweat, fruit and cheese from the broken fruit bowl. He picked a few pieces of kiwi from my thighs and popped them into his mouth.

"Well, that was a nice meal. Maybe I'll order the same thing for breakfast."

Joe picked up the broken bowl and left it by the front door. We took a shower then went to bed jet lagged but satisfied. Morning came much too soon. Outside our bedroom window, the screeching cry of sea gulls pierced the air. The sun seemed brighter in Italy. Maybe it was the fact we were on our honeymoon. Everything seemed sweeter, softer and gentler – more so than the western ruggedness of Montana. I had to admit I missed getting up feeding Daisy, Bailey and the others, but for the first time I slept like a proverbial baby. No thoughts of deadlines running around my brain or redundant meetings to attend. I felt wonderful! Joe woke me up once. He still had that nagging cough. I made a mental note to keep an eye on it.

I put on my robe and walked to the balcony. The ocean was a vibrant blue. A new bowl of fruit was sitting outside the door. I had to grin. *Wow, that was some performance yesterday.* I heard footsteps walking up behind me.

"Well, good morning beautiful."

I leaned back into him and said, "Good morning handsome."

He brushed my hair to the side and kissed my neck. "Actually I was talkin' about the ocean – but you ain't too bad yourself Mrs. Montana. I trust you slept well."

"Yes, I did. I haven't felt so relaxed in a long time. Paradise agrees with me."

Joe said we should come back every year on our anniversary. I totally agreed. There was no better way to keep a marriage alive than a return trip to Italy.

We sat on the balcony drinking espresso and nibbling on fresh baked biscotti. I noticed the two daffodils in a vase.

"Did you order them for me?"

He took a deep breath, "Darlin' I promised when we first met that I would always have fresh cut daffodils for you in the morning no matter where I am or where you are. It's my way of showing you I'll always be here with you."

If I start bawling he'll just make fun of me. I held back my tears and told him what a lovely and thoughtful tradition. I wrapped my arms around his waist and kissed his chest."

"And that is for you. Hold on to it and always know that no matter where I am or where you are, my kisses are just a heartbeat away."

He leaned down and held my chin in his hand. "I don't know how in God's green earth I got so lucky to find you Rose. It's a mystery I'll never solve. I guess I'm blessed in more ways than one."

I asked him in what other way he was blessed. I thought he would give me a sermon on how his success came as a surprise or how his life had been so rich. He grinned and opened his robe. I laughed thinking, *Jannine, if you only knew – he IS hung like a horse.*

Our time on Elba flew by much too quickly. We ate too much, drank too much, laughed too much, tanned without apparel on our private beach and thought about how much we truly deserved this getaway. However, our days in paradise were about to end. It was back to Montana reality. Our driver was scheduled to pick us up at one o'clock tomorrow afternoon. We wanted to spend our last night in Italy on the ocean.

To my surprise, Joe had chartered a sail boat. We packed a few things and headed to the pier. The captain was local – born and raised on the island. He told us once we anchored the boat, he would take the dinghy back to the island to give us privacy. Joe thanked him for his thoughtfulness.

Joe helped me onto the boat. While he and the captain were chatting, I reached into my purse to see if I remembered the throat spray. His cough was going on way too long and its reoccurrence concerned me. I didn't want him to know I was worried. They were headed toward me. I quickly tucked the spray back in my purse.

Mental note number two: have it checked by a doctor when we return to the states.

The captain set sail to a small lagoon on the other side of the island. He said it was secluded to ensure marital privacy. Joe whispered, "That means they won't hear us moanin' and groanin' baby."

The boat ride was amazing. We held onto each other, laughing and talking on deck, watching the waves lap the sides of the boat spraying us with salty sea foam. A few minutes into our trip, the captain hoisted the sails and it was like the boat came to life. They billowed in the warm summer breeze. The captain had a CD player on board. Joe reached into his pocket pulling out what looked like a blank silver CD. He popped it into the player.

"I made this for us darlin'. It's got all of our songs on it."

The first song was, *Now and Forever* followed by *I Will Remember You*, *I Will Always Love You* and of course, *If I'm Not in Love with You* by Faith Hill.

Joe pulled me close, "Nice and slow baby, I want you   close enough to hear my heart beat."

The water was still as glass. It was as if it calmed so that the only movement we felt was our bodies moving together. The entire night was a dream, a lovely dream I never wanted to end. But I knew in a few hours we'd be leaving Italy. I closed my eyes pretending there was no one else in the world except me and Joe.

Joe smiled and said, "I could live forever in your arms darlin'. You make me happier than I deserve to be."

I whispered, "Do you know how much I love you?"

He stopped dancing for a second and said, "I hope I do."

We sat on the deck as the sun set and watched the moon peek from the dark blue evening sky.

Joe held me tight in his arms. We watched the moonlight race across the water, right up to our boat as if we were in the center of the universe and nothing else in the world matters – just me and my Montana cowboy.

We hadn't noticed that the captain had dropped anchor and headed back to shore. The ocean was calm, the night air was warm and that night our love for each other took a magical turn. It was the moment I remembered giving my eternal love, heart and soul to Joe.

The motor of the dinghy woke me. The captain had returned to sail us back to Elba. We'd fallen asleep on deck.

Joe stretched and rubbed his eyes. "I have never slept so well in my life. It must have been the motion-of-the-ocean darlin'."

I smiled knowing it was his exhaustion that allowed him to sleep so well. And not one coughing spell. *Maybe this would be a better place to live.* The wind was with us so the ride back was a lot shorter. We arrived at our villa and it had been cleaned and the villa staff had packed our bags. Not that there was much to pack. We spent most of our time at the beach or in bed – both requiring minimal clothing.

Our walk back to the ferry dock was intentionally slow. Neither of us wanted to leave but we smiled knowing that every year we'd return on our anniversary. We had lots of pictures and memories to take with us.

The drive to Milan was quiet. Joe was more exhausted than he admitted – he was snoring. *I'd never heard him snore like this before.* I gently nudged him and he stopped. He looked so peaceful sleeping. *I love the way his lip curls when he sleeps. It resembles his shit-eating-grin only more angelic.*

He woke up thirty minutes before we reached the airport.

"Well, thank you darlin' for that stimulating conversation. We must do it again sometime. Why in the name of Hector did you let me sleep that long. Are we there yet? And more importantly . . . I've got to piss like a race horse."

I shook my head, "And hello to you too. It was quite an exciting ride. While you were sleeping you missed the parade of cymbals and cherry bombs. You were out like a light cowboy!"

Our driver stopped at a local café. Joe headed to the restroom, and I sat at one of the outdoor tables enjoying the sun. An older Italian gentleman who spoke little English asked if he could join me. I said of course. He kissed my hand and said *molto bella.* He was very sweet and continued chatting even though I could barely understand his delicate attempt to woo me. Joe returned from the restroom and sat next to him.

"I'm gone for one minute, and I find you flirtin' with another guy!"

I introduced my new friend to Joe. He and the gentleman rattled off a half dozen sentences in Italian then looked at me and laughed.

"Okay boys what's going on – what's so funny?"

"Well, Rose if you must know he was tellin' me about the difference between Italian Timothy hay and fescue. He prefers fescue for its ability to withstand rot and I told him I pre . . . "

I got up and walked away. Joe came running behind me laughing and waving goodbye to the old man. I got back into the car and crossed my arms. Joe got in and slid next to me. I slid to the other side.

"Okay now you're pouting. I'm sorry but you make such an easy target when it comes to pokin' fun. He was just telling me what a lucky man I must be to have such an extraordinarily beautiful woman in my life. And that I should never leave you alone, you might get kidnapped by someone who admires your beauty and whisks you away for himself – at least that how I translated it."

I pretended to be annoyed but couldn't keep it up. I smiled a polite smile and said, "You know you can be so infuriating! There are times I want to ki . . . ." He leaned over and kissed me.

"Oh, I thought you were going to say kiss me."

"That's nowhere near what I was going to say. But the kiss was nice, thank you."

"So what I'm hearin' is I'm forgiven, correct?"

"Yes, you are forgiven. Now let's enjoy the rest of the ride without strangling each other. I'd hate to be a widow before I get the chance to be a wife."

Chapter 12

As much as we enjoyed being in Italy, it was good to be home. I missed our breakfasts on the deck watching the horses graze under the big blue Montana sky. Joe couldn't wait to saddle up and take a long overdue ride. He was truly one hundred percent cowboy. I'd never been much for men in chaps until I met Joe. He was a natural in the saddle. Riding cleared his thoughts and helped him write. He always said that a cluttered mind creates lousy characters and stories. No one wants to read anything written by a neurotic, unless you're Woody Allen. And in Woody's case, he made a successful career out of it.

I walked to the barn to find Daisy already saddled. I wasn't dressed for riding but hopped into the saddle and headed to the other side of the pasture hoping to meet up with Joe. I saw him with Bailey sitting under a tree with his hat pulled down over his eyes.

Without lifting his hat he said, "I was wondering how long it would take you to meet up with me. Come sit beside me darlin'." I dismounted Daisy and sat down beside him.

He lifted his hat, "Ain't that the prettiest sky you've ever seen? There ain't anything on this earth that looks more beautiful than the blue in a Montana sky. It's almost as if God said let's gather up all the blue in the world and put it right here in front of us."

Joe stood up and putting his hands in his back pockets; staring out at what he called, "The Great Wide Open." It's funny how cowboys have such nice asses. I remember Joe telling me that buckle bunnies called them wrangler butts. I asked Joe what is a buckle bunny.

"They're rodeo groupies, most wanting to be the girlfriend of a rodeo man. They think rodeo is a glamorous life – it ain't. It's sad because most of the rodeo guys just take advantage of them and move on to the next town and next group of bunnies. If you don't mind lets change the subject." His tone of voice took a serious turn.

"You know Rose when I die this is where I want my ashes to be spread – on the winds of Montana. A quick toss and let the ashes soar."

"And what would you like me to say?"

He thought for a second then said, "How about, Adios Joe – short and sweet."

"That's great because by the time you're ready to kick the bucket, I'll be so senile I won't be able to remember anything more complex than that."

I initially laughed at his request then thought how strange a subject it was to broach so early in our marriage. To be honest it upset me. I never wanted to spend a day without Joe. I didn't want to think about him or me dying until we were in our nineties and too old to pounce on each other.

He explained that he'd never much thought about his mortality until he found out he had a son and now a wife.

"Makes a man think about his future is all. Not that I plan on goin' anytime soon. You ain't getting' rid of me that quickly darlin', but I do need to make some legal changes like adding you and Morgan to my will. I know it ain't somethin' you want to think about but I want to make sure you're both taken care of – in case anything was to happen to me."

I understood his rationale regarding his will and assets. Unlike Joe, I'd never thought about my mortality. All of my responsibilities included my condo, cat and a folder full of unpaid bills. Thinking about the future wasn't something I dwelled on. I lived for the moment. However, now that I'm a married woman I need to start thinking about these things – but not today. Today I wanted to enjoy myself with the man I love.

We weren't that far from the house and decided to walk back. Joe grabbed the lead ropes while I stooped down to pick a bouquet of wild flowers for the bedroom. I loved waking up to fresh flowers in our bedroom.

Joe smiled when I held the flowers to my nose.

"You do know those yellow ones are poisonous?"

I threw them in the air, wiping my hands on his jeans. He laughed, "My goodness girl you are way too easy to tease." He helped me pick them up and said they were just prairie buttercups and quite innocuous.

As much as his wicked sense of humor aggravated me I wouldn't trade it for the world. It kept me on my toes. We unsaddled the horses and let them out to pasture.

A few minutes later, Joe felt his phone vibrating in his pocket. It was a message from his editor. It seems while we were enjoying our honeymoon, he forgot to send in his revised galleys. He excused himself and headed into his office. I could hear him coughing and clearing his throat from the kitchen.

While he was chatting with his editor, I grabbed the house phone and called his doctor to make an appointment. At first, the doctor didn't know who I was and kept calling me Kathleen. I told him I wasn't his sister but his new bride Amelia. He congratulated me and asked if his cough had cleared. I was puzzled because I didn't know he was aware of it. I went along with him saying it seems better; however, I was concerned about it and his frequent need to use the throat spray.

The doctor looked at his chart and said he was scheduled to see him a week from today. Joe hadn't told me about any doctor's appointment. I told the doctor if it was okay if I came along with him.

"If it's okay with Lash then it's okay with me. And please tell him I said congratulations and I can't wait read his newest novel and to meet you, Mrs. Montana."

"Please call me Amelia or as Lash loves to call me, Rose."
I wrote the date and time down in my day planner and tucked it back into my pocketbook.

Joe had finished his conversation. I asked him if everything was okay. He said the book was on schedule and they just needed my okay on the revised galleys. He asked who called on the house phone. I told him it was his doctor's office reminding him of his appointment next week.

Joe thought, *He usually calls on my cell. It was probably the doctor who called while I was on with the editor.* He tried to brush it off and changed the subject.

"Lash, you didn't tell me you'd been seeing a doctor about this cough. Is everything okay?"

He gave me his typical shit-eating-grin, "Now, what kind of honeymoon would it have been if it began with, oh darlin', that reminds me, I've got a doctor's visit next week for this dang-blasted cough I can't seem to shake. Now that's a lousy opening line for a novel. Even worse than, *it was a dark and stormy night!*"

"Joe, this isn't funny. I need to know if this is something I should be worried about."

"Darlin', I'm okay, when you lecture as much as I do you tend to get a tickly throat every now and then. Consider it an occupational nuisance as best."

"Okay, but you do understand I'm going to the doctor's with you. Is that clear Mr. Montana?"

For a brief moment, he looked worried then mustered a polite smiled.

"Now, Rose I don't need you comin' to the doc's office getting all railed up over nothin', but if you insist on accompanying me I guess I can't tell you not to come, 'cause no matter what I say, you'll come anyway . . . am I right?"

"That's right so don't try to stop me. I'm going whether you like it or not."

"Yes, ma'am Mrs. Montana, whatever you say Mrs. Montana . . . Lord help me."

It was one of those lazy mornings we decided to sleep in. Joe was tired and the day was overcast. It was later that afternoon when I checked my email and saw Jannine had sent two. She wanted to update me on a few work changes and a private one from her home account. I'd never met anyone as efficient as Jannine. I suppose that's why she is the only person who outlasted all my other administrative assistants. She anticipated what I needed and when. She knew to have all of my New York mail forwarded to Montana, cancelled my paper subscription to the New York Times and had it sent to me online. I sorted through the pile, most of which was junk mail.

It also dawned on me that I didn't need my condo. Joe said he would never want to live in New York City. "It would be like wearin' a pair of cheap cowboy boots – they cramp a man's toes and style."

I told Joe I was going to put it up for sale and needed to go back to New York for a few days. I wrote Jannine informing her of my plans. A few seconds after I send the email I got her response.

To: Amelia aka Rose
Fr: Jannine
*Subject: **Coming To NYC Re: Coming To NYC***

Just like I thought, you always need to be in control and do everything yourself. There are times I ask myself why you need an assistant when you think you can conquer the world single-handedly. But that's also what I love about you Amelia! I miss you so much and I want to make a deal with you. Morgan and I have grown close. So close that we are thinking of living together. And since you no longer need your condo, we would like to buy it. I didn't think you would mind so I've already taken steps to start the mortgage paperwork. All we need is your signature and it's off your hands. Of course, we'll pay you the asking price. Stay in Montana with your cowboy and we'll take care of everything.

Love, Jannine and Morgan

P.S. Don't bother reading the other email it's about terminating of your benefits, information about continuing your 401k plan, blah, blah, blah, the standard bullshit. And, Morgan and I decided we're keeping your cat and I promise we won't eat him, ha, ha!

I motioned for Joe to come over and read her email. "Now doesn't that just beat all, our boy Morgan is sweet on Jannine." I was surprised how fast they fell for each other. Maybe it has something to do with the air in Montana. Who knows? I do know that I couldn't be happier for two people than I am for Jannine and Morgan. My biological clock is ticking and they were the closest I'll ever come to having kids of my own. I wrote back saying, as always, you've anticipated my needs and of course it's okay to keep the cat. At the moment, I've got my hands full taking care of horses. They're sort of like cats except there's more poop to clean.

I called New York and explained my situation and they were more than happy to trim back the paperwork to get the condo sold. Joe agreed he would co-sign if needed. And to my surprise, the condo representative was a fan of Joe's novels. He said "Throw in an autographed copy of his latest book, and you have a deal."

Joe had gone into the living room to read the newspaper – more like staring at it. He looked lost in thought. I sat down beside him and put my hand on his lap. I said everything had been settled. The condo is taken care of, and I'm free to go with you to your doctor's appointment.

He cleared his throat, "That's nice Rose, I'm glad everything's been handled. I know the kids will enjoy living in New York City."

"Is everything okay Joe? You seem awfully quiet today. Are you worried about the kids buying the condo or that the price of Timothy hay went up a nickel or maybe the alien zombies want me to breed blue babies in the Amazon River?

He nodded, "Yep, that's right Rose."

I turned toward him, "You haven't heard a word I've said! What going on Joe. Don't go silent on me – you know that really drives me nuts!"

He threw the paper down and stormed off into the kitchen. I could hear him coughing. It was getting worse. He tried to stifle it but couldn't.

I followed him, "I'm going to ask you one more time Lash, ARE YOU OKAY!"

He hollered, "God damn it Rose, YES I am, now quit your goddamn motherin'. I'm a grown man. I can take care of myself and did quite well before I met you – so please stop it!"

I was shocked. He'd never blown up at me, ever. Something was terribly wrong, and he didn't want to tell me. I didn't know whether to cry or curse. I turned and walked out on the deck. Whatever he was hiding must be serious. I'd never seen him get this angry over anything.

About twenty minutes later, he came out and sat beside me. I ignored him because I was still angry and hurt. But, I was more upset about not knowing what was going on.

"Nice day ain't it? It's a shame some asshole had to screw it up by hollering at the most wonderful, beautiful, sexy hot woman on the face of the earth he's ever known. Now my question is, can this beautiful lady forgive him, because right now, he really, really needs her to understand how anxious he is about this doctor's appointment."

I glanced over at him. He was holding two daffodils and two cups of tea.

He must be ill, he hates tea.

I went from angry, to scared, to panic stricken. I thought, *What could be wrong that he's so nervous. Oh my God, whatever it is I don't want to lose him, I can't lose him!*

He told me about three year ago the doctor found two abnormal polyps on his vocal cords. One was larger than the other. They removed them – both were benign. He was on medication to ensure they would not grow back. Six months ago, he noticed that his throat started hurting and the coughing returned. He was afraid more polyps had grown and said once his latest novel is published, he would have it checked out.

"Then I met this incredibly smart and sexy woman who stole my heart and soul. She made me forget about everything. I never wanted to leave her side so I married her and until a few minutes ago she loved me like no other woman ever has. I hope that's still true? Can you find it in that big beautiful heart of yours to forgive this crazy-asshole-of-a-cowboy?"

He reached over, took my hand and kissed my palm.

"Baby, I'm so sorry I hollered at you. I'll never do it again, mainly because if I have to have surgery I won't be able to talk or holler… lucky you."

I tried not to laugh, but he caught me smiling.

"Yes I forgive you and yes it will be nice not listening to you yammer on-and-on about overpriced Timothy hay."

He leaned over and kissed me, "I love you Rose."

"I love you too Joe." I hugged him as tight as I could. "We'll get through this together I promise. When is your appointment?"

He looked at his notepad, "It's this Friday at 9:00 AM at Montana Medical. They want to do a biopsy."

His appointment was two days from today. I put on my brave face and told Joe no sweat. Everything will be fine. And afterwards, we can go spend the night in town – maybe go dancing.

"Dancing, now that's the worst idea you've ever come up with Rose. It's painfully obvious you've never had your toes repeatedly stepped on by a terrible cowboy dancer."

I said it was worth the risk.

"Then it's dancing in the Montana moonlight with my best gal and maybe I'll get laid."

I slapped him on his ass I said, "That's right cowboy. Now let's not talk about hospitals, polyps or anything else that we can't control. It's a nice evening how about we go skinny dipping in the pond. He perked up.

"Now that's a great idea. Nothing takes the worry out of a man like seeing a naked woman swimming at sunset and of course getting laid afterwards."

I slowly stripped off my clothing in front of him and headed toward the bedroom, "How about we just forget the skinny dipping."

The two days flew by. The ride to the Montana Medical Center was quiet. I decided to drive so that Joe wouldn't have to concentrate on anything but his own thoughts. It also gave me time to prepare myself for whatever the doctor had to say. I didn't want Joe to see me panic or upset, so I turned on the radio. One of my favorite songs by Brooks and Dunn came on, and I thought Joe would get a kick out of hearing me sing along. I never realized how bad my singing was until he turned down the radio and said,

"Darlin', stop the car! I think you ran over a cat or was that you screeching?"

We laughed so hard that I snorted. He laughed at me laughing. It felt good to see him having a good time. Still the prospect of an unfavorable prognosis weighed heavy on my mind. *Please let him be okay.*

Joe must have dosed off. He wasn't aware we had arrived at the hospital. I shook his shoulder and he slowly opened his eyes.

"I was havin' such a great dream Rose. I dreamt we were in a hot tub filled with whiskey. And you thought it would be fun to snorkel down and take hold of my . . . "

I stopped him in midsentence. "Oh, no you don't. No sex talk before your doctor's appointment. You're stalling, and you know it."

"So you don't want to know how it ends?"

"Nope"

"Not even curious?"

"Nope"

"Oh well, I guess I'll have to put this dream on hold until after we get home. Now if that office has a secluded area maybe we could . . ." He whispered the rest in my ear.

"OH MY GOD JOE, will you stop it . . . I don't believe you!"

He gave me his now famous shit-eating-grin and helped me out of the car.

"Baby, sometimes even I can't believe the bull crap that comes out of my mouth. It just makes me laugh to see you so incensed."

We checked in and took a seat in the waiting area. Of course Joe's books where in the reading rack. Oddly, no other patients were there. We had the entire room to ourselves. I was happy because I didn't need any of Joe's fans hovering asking for autographs and photos.

The nurse came out and asked us to come with her. She performed all the preliminary procedure then walked us down the hall to the doctor's office. A few minutes later the doctor arrived. I was surprised he wasn't wearing a white jacket with a stethoscope hanging around his neck. He came in with a fancy cowboy shirt, jeans and boots. He could have been Joe's older brother or cousin. Or maybe it was the western attire.

"Hello Lash, aren't you going to introduce me to your daughter." Joe huffed, "Wow, an attempt at comedy. Thank God you're a doctor because you're a lousy stand-up comedian, but if I must . . . Amelia, this is my pain-in-my-ass friend and irritating doctor, Theodore Jacobs – Theo for short."

"How do you do Dr. Jacobs, my husband has told me a lot about you, most of which is too foul for me to repeat."

He and Joe laughed. "Lash, I love her already, anyone who can put up with your infuriating sense of bullcrap is a saint in by book."

Joe turned to me and said, "Darlin', this man is evil and should have been burned at the stake years ago for torturing his patients, like having me come back here just to check out this cough."

Theo smiled, "That's just Lash's way of telling me how happy he is to see me – but enough of the pleasantries."

Theo pulled up a chair and motioned for us to have a seat on the couch.

"Lash, I'm going to fill your beautiful bride in on our chart if that's okay." Joe nodded.

"Amelia, back in 1997, Lash has had three polyps removed all of which were benign. It was a simple procedure and he was back to being his ornery self in two weeks. If they have returned, we'll perform the same procedure but keep him overnight for observation. Of course, Amelia can stay with you if she'd like."

"Joe smirked, "Like I'd let her out of my sight for a minute.""

Like I'd let you out of my sight after an operation. I told Theo thanks and yes, I would be staying with him.

"Okay, then I'll see what's going on."

We all walked into the examination room, and Theo asked Joe to sit down on the stool. He adjusted the overhead light and examined Joe's throat with some kind of snake-like-tube thing. He palpated his neck.

"Hmm, well your throat is swollen and I feel two small polyps forming. Nothing to worry about I'm sure, but I would like to do a biopsy anyway. That should keep him quiet for a while so you can tell me how you two met and why in the hell you would marry this crippled up old rodeo man in the first place."

Joe cleared his throat, "You do realize I can hear you Theo."

He laughed, "Yes Lash, I know there is nothing wrong with your hearing. So, how about we get started. My nurse will be here in a minute to get you prepped and ready. Then we'll head down the hall to the procedure room. Amelia, there is a waiting room right outside if you'd like to wait there or you can wait here in my office."

I got up and walked over next to Joe. "I want to be near my husband if that's okay."

Joe took hold of my hand and kissed my palm. "I'll be okay darlin'. You hold on to that kiss until they're finished probing my tonsils and whatever they're fixin' to probe. I love you baby."

The nurse politely waited by the door, "Okay Mr. Montana let's get you ready." I hugged Joe and whispered, "I love you too Joe." He took off his cowboy hat and reformed the brim. "Hold on to this darlin' and don't let Theo steal it. It's my best Stetson and he's had his eye on it for years."

Doctor Jacobs laughed and handed Joe's medical file to the nurse. Joe joked, "Can I keep my boots on?"

She took hold of his arm, "Yes, you can keep your boots on. Quit your stalling – let's go cowboy."

As they walked away, I overheard Joe ask her if she was related to Big Nose Kate because she looked as though she could hold her own in a saloon fight. I could hear the nurse fussing at him as they walked down the hall and disappeared into the procedures room. I sat down by the window and pretended to read one of the magazines when Doctor Jacobs came in and sat down beside me.

"Why don't you relax and tell me how you two met. The procedure will take about 45-minutes and I'd like to get to know you better."

I told him about the library in Currysville and how much he infuriated me with his sarcastic wit and annoying obsession with coffee. But in time, I fell in love with the warm-hearted, sweet talking, romantic Montana cowboy who promised to love me forever; who kisses the palm of my hand so when we're apart I'll always have a kiss to hold on to.

Doctor Jacobs took off his glasses and rubbed his eyes. "I've never heard such an amazing love story before. It's epic when you think about it. How two people from opposite ends of the culture spectrum find each other and fall in love. It's the kind of love romance novels are based on. Maybe you should write a novel about your romance Amelia. Lash tells me you are or were an art critic."

"Yes, I was a columnist. I reviewed New York art exhibitions for a regional magazine called, *Beaux Art New York*."

He picked up a magazine from the table, "You write for this magazine?" I was shocked to find a copy in Montana! He thumbed through it and found one of my articles.

"Wow, you ARE good. I like the line, "Sculpture is something you bump into while you're backing up to admire a painting – very funny Amelia. You could be a humor writer. "

"I'm not much of a humor writer but I do know art. To be honest I miss writing. I would never tell Lash. He would feel responsible for me leaving my job. And if there were a choice between my job and Lash, the job would always come in second."

He laid the magazine back on the table and asked if I'd like a cup of coffee. He pointed to the Starbucks directly outside medical center. "We'll take good care of him Amelia. You hang in there, okay." I nodded and thanked him for his offer of coffee. A few minutes later, he came back with two large black coffees. He handed me one.

"Getting coffee from these fancy coffee cafés is such an anxious task. If you don't speak their lingo they look at you like you have three heads. And Lord help you if all you want black coffee, it's like a caffeine abomination. I thanked him for his sacrifice and apologized for his caffeinated humiliation.

I'd just started drinking my coffee when the nurse came in and told me they were finished. He was still a little groggy, but I could go in with him. She also informed me he would need to stay quiet for a day or so and the doctor would talk to us before we leave.

Joe was out like a light. He looked so peaceful. I'd never seen him so still. It was a little disturbing. I leaned over and kissed him. He mouthed, "Hello beautiful." I told him he wouldn't be able to talk for a day or two."

I shouted, "So, I guess you'll be emailing me if you need anything." He cringed then mouthed paper and pen. He quickly jotted "Damn it darlin' I can't talk – I ain't deaf."

It's an amusing phenomenon. When people are unable to talk you instinctively think they can't hear. He shook his head and wrote, "What am I going to do with you."

I whispered, "You'll find out what I'm going to do with you when we get home."

He wrote, "Nothin' wrong in that department." He grabbed my hand and put it on his crotch."

We heard the door open. Doctor Jacobs came in with Lash's chart in his hand. "Well Lash, this is a memorable moment for me. The legendary Montana Joe is finally speechless. He gave him the single-finger-salute and wrote, "When can we leave?"

"You can leave after I write the prescription for your meds and give you a list of things we don't want you doing – like trying to talk for one."

"Are there any physical limitations I should be aware of?"

"If you're talking about sex, he's fine in that department. He's in better shape than me and I'm ten years younger than him."

Joe gave him a high-five. I could feel my face turning red. It was like watching two bronc riders celebrating a rodeo victory. I was waiting for them to spit tobacco juice onto the hospital floor.

Theo went on to say other than talking or singing he's fine to do whatever he wants.

"Just try to keep him quiet for at least 48 hours. Drop by the nurse's station on your way out; your prescription will be ready and then it's homeward bound for the Montana couple. It was so nice to meet you Amelia, or should I call you Rose?" I told him Rose was fine. I'd become quite fond of the name.

"Take good care of my favorite cowboy writer and keep me updated to any changes in his condition."

Of course, we couldn't get out of the medical center without him stopping to sign autographs to the entire nursing staff. One gal had him autograph her nurse's smock; another asked him to sign her white shoes. They were like Montana's Angels of Mercy cowgirl groupies. We made our way to the door and got in the truck for the quiet ride home. The dancing would have to wait.

Joe insisted on driving home. I knew better than to argue with him because I had the advantage of talking. I didn't want him to strain his throat trying to convince me he was more than capable to drive his own truck. Before he got into the truck, his cell phone started to vibrate, and it was a missed message from Raymond. Joe put the phone on speaker and let me listen.

"Hello Montana, this is Raymond. It's Tuesday and I have your research cabin reserved for this week and was expecting you to arrive yesterday. I hope I didn't get the dates wrong. Of course, it's still available if you want it. And bring that beautiful wife with you – she's great inspiration for both of us."

With all our anxiety surrounding Joe's appointment we'd completely blanked out about his annually scheduled research trip. I asked Joe if he wanted me to cancel it. He shook his head NO, and quickly scribbling something on his pad.

"Tell 'em we're still comin'. It'll be good for me to write, since I can't talk. Tell 'em we'll be there Wednesday evening and have the coffee ready and waiting."

I expected the coffee comment. I thought, *He's feeling a little bit better if he wants coffee.*

I called Raymond and left him a message to hold our reservation. I also explained the mix up and apologized. He called back leaving a message saying he was more than happy if Joe wanted it for an extra week to recoup. We took him up on his offer. Joe was going to need some downtime from writing and what better place to relax than at Raymond's place.

Joe smiled, kissed my palm then wrote, *"Thank you darlin."*

He motioned for me to look into the glove compartment. There was a CD marked Travelin' Music. I popped it into the CD player. It was mixed music of his favorite songs, most of which were Creedence Clearwater Revival, George Strait, Brooks and Dunn. Joe cranked up the volume when CCR's, *Get Down Woman* came on. I had no idea he liked CCR. They were one of my favorite bands in college and *Get Down Woman* happened to be one of my favorites. I knew all the words and sang along. I noticed Joe continued to turn up the volume. I thought he enjoyed it loud until I realized it was his not-so-subtle attempt to drown out my singing.

We arrived home to hayed and watered horses and the aroma of something coming from the kitchen. Cecilia had stopped by and cooked dinner. She made a soup for Joe and left it on the stove. There was a note on the table.

"Dear Amelia and Lash, I knew you wouldn't have time to fix anything so I cooked up some soup for him and left you a platter of cold chicken and freshly made cob salad. I'll be back tomorrow to finish cleaning. Enjoy your research trip. Love, Cecilia."

Joe wrote, *"I don't know what we'd do without her, she's an angel."* I agreed.

After dinner, we took a much needed break. I put on some music to help Joe relax. It was comforting to rest in his arms and watch the sky turn from blue to violet and red, then full of stars. Still, in the back of my mind I was worried. Joe played down his condition, but I could feel his anxiety. I decided to put it aside and enjoy the moment.

Underneath the coffee table, I noticed a leather bound photo album. Funny I hadn't noticed it before. I reached down and picked it up.
He wrote, "That's my old rodeo album, can't believe I was that young and skinny!"

I couldn't believe how much he looked like Morgan - same solid jaw, hair and eyes. There was no denying that they were father and son. There was one photo of him being bucked off. The photo caught him in mid air about five feet above the bull.

He whispered, "Now that was a painful moment, thanks for reminding me."

We spent the next hours reminiscing about the early days of his career, why he decided to write and how much he loved western culture. I could have listened to him all night. Even though he was whispering, I could tell he needed to rest his voice. And, I needed sleep because we were driving to Raymond's first thing in the morning.

Chapter 13

It was early afternoon when we arrived at Raymond's place. He heard our truck coming up the gravel driveway. We were greeted with hot cowboy coffee and an herbal tea.

"Hello, my dear friends, I'm so glad you decided to come. Rose you get more beautiful every time I see you. It's a shame Joe just gets older and uglier."

Joe laughed and whispered, *"I love you too Raymond."*

Raymond handed me the coffee and Joe the tea. Joe frowned. He hates tea. Raymond explained it was an old recipe his grandmother made for them when they had a sore throat.

"It's fenugreek, ginger, honey and echinacea. Drink it while it's hot Joe."

Joe whispered, *"Can I put my damn bags down first and get a welcome hug from my old friend first."*

They gave each other the usual manly bear hug. Raymond walked over to me and kissed me on my cheek.

"And how is my beautiful Amelia. I see you're still married to this broke-down rodeo man. It's a shame I didn't meet you first or he would be old, ugly and lonely."

"Someone had to marry this broke-down-old-bronc-rider. I guess I drew the short straw and like you said he ain't gettin' any younger." I gave Raymond a hug and apologized for our forgetfulness.

Raymond totally understood and said no worries. "I'm just glad you both are okay."

Joe smirked then whispered, *"Hey, watch that broke down comment. I can still ride bulls and broncos, I just don't bounce as well as I used to."*

Joe and Raymond took the bags into the cabin. I sat outside taking in the lush greenery. A sweet blend of summer fragrances was on every breeze. I thought, *This must be what heaven smells like – so clean and fresh.*

Out of the corner of my eye I saw a hummingbird. I'd only seen them on nature shows – never in the wild. It flew around me so quickly I could barely keep it in my field of vision.

It hovered from side-to-side as if to say, "Hey city girl what are you doing out here?"

I was thinking the same thing. What was a girl who never envisioned herself leaving the big city life be doing in the wilds of Montana? It was such a different world – one that was slowly becoming familiar to me. I turned to look at it again and in the blink of an eye it was gone.

When Joe and Raymond returned, I told them what had happened. Raymond asked how long did it hover in front of you? I said almost a minute. I was surprised that it stayed so long and came so close to me. I was also amazed that it came back more than once.

"Amelia, I believe you've found an animal spirit guide. Some call them 'Aumakua' the animal that is there to help you communicate with those human spirits who have passed over."

I didn't know of anyone who had recently passed over. Raymond said it could be your great-great grandmother or father who wants you to know they are there for you. Or sometimes they appear to help guide someone over to the other side who had recently died or is dying."

I turned white as a sheet. I didn't want to think about anyone dying. Joe put his arm around me. I believe he knew what was going through my mind.

"For goodness sake Raymond, quit droppin' hints that I might be kickin' the damn bucket. I know you've always wanted my favorite gray Stetson, but I'm tellin' you right now, you ain't getting' it!"

Joe's comment lightened the mood. Raymond apologized if his statement made me uncomfortable. I told him it didn't but in all honesty, it terrified me thinking that Joe could die so soon after our marriage. This man was the love of my life and soul mate. I wanted to grow old with him. Death was not a subject I wanted to broach.

Raymond mentioned it was lunch time. He said he would bring it to our cabin so that we could get unpacked. I realized Joe hadn't taken his meds which he needed to take with food. I thanked Raymond for his generosity and being such a wonderful friend to me and Joe.

Before I shut the cabin door, the same hummingbird flew in front of me. I closed the door thinking, *Sorry pal, no one is dead or dying today.*

After lunch, I suggested Joe rest for an hour or two. He shook his head no and whispered that he had to start writing. I was amazed by his ability to block out his surroundings and write; how he was able to immerse himself in his novels. He said he would be leaving me for a while because he had to go to a little town called Beaver Rock, Arizona outside of Tombstone back in 1880 to finish off a gunfight with Sheriff Malten Dansville and outlaw Jake Buckslinger. He said old Jake had been terrorizing the town for months and was about to get his just desserts. I told him to be safe and to keep his powder dry.

He quickly typed a message on the blank page his laptop, *"I'm impressed at your choice of cowboy lingo – keep your powder dry, hah, next you'll be shooting single action Colt 45."*

I pointed my finger at him like I was shooting a pistol and blew the imaginary smoke from the barrel.

I noticed Raymond sitting on the porch and asked if I could join him.

"Joe must be writing. He gets grumpy if anyone disturbs him. I told him to put a sign on his door if he needs anything. It usually reads, *I'm not here right now. I'm somewhere in the 1880's. I should be back in an hour or two, thanks, Joe.*

"It makes me laugh just thinking about the places he travels to in his mind. Very strange people these writers."

Raymond was right. Novelists are a weird and unusual bunch. They get to come and go any place they want without leaving the comfort of their office or in Joe's case his research room.

We were still chatting when Joe finally emerged from the cabin with a hand written sign reading, "What's a cowboy got to do to get a cup of REAL coffee around here, I'm about to take a nose dive on my keyboard!"

"Oh, so you want coffee. Why don't you get the saloon gal in Beaver Hills or wherever you are to brew you a pot? I'm sure she would be pleased to serve coffee to the great Montana Joe."

He walked over and slapped me on the ass whispering, *"It ain't lady-like to sass a desperately under-caffeinated man by teasing him when it comes to his coffee. Darlin' I need it bad – coffee that is. Don't make me beg."* He pinched my butt and smiled. "What am I going to do with you Joe? You're horny even when you're sick! Okay I'll get you coffee and don't forget to take your meds." He crossed his heart then motioned his hand pretending to sip out of cup.

"Okay, okay I get the message!"

Raymond had already headed to the kitchen and started grinding the beans. I asked him if he would go back outside and keep an eye on Joe. He nodded and headed back to the porch.

I used a third of the coffee we usually use. I didn't want him too caffeinated. He doesn't need to talk any more than he needs to.

It didn't take long for the coffee to brew. I filled two cups and headed back outside. I could see them whispering. Joe noticed me in the doorway. He jumped up and held the door for me.

He wrote, *"Thank you darlin' I love you more than you'll ever know."*

Raymond laughed, "I guess you are wondering what we were whispering about."

I said the thought had crossed my mind but knowing you two I'm sure it was nothing good."

"Joe was saying that until his voice comes back he would write you emails, just like when you two were courting. He said it would be romantic.

"What a sweet way to communicate. And here I thought you were conspiring on how to sneak more coffee into the room while I was sleeping. To be honest, Raymond, I've missed his emails. They made me smile every time his name popped up in my email queue."

They finished their coffee. I picked up the cups and started back to the kitchen when Joe reached for my hand. Like always he kissed my palm and mouthed, "I love you Rose."

"I love you too."

Joe excused himself and said he was going back to 1880 and asked Raymond to keep me out of trouble for a few of hours.

We sat down on the porch steps. Raymond said, "So – Rose, what would you like to do? Not much goes on around these parts, but tonight I'm heading out to a drum circle if you'd like to come. I think you'd enjoy it."

I'd never been to a Native American drum circle. I got drunk once in San Francisco and stumbled onto a hippie drum circle; however, I'm sure this event wouldn't involve beer and marijuana. I told him I'd love to go.

I cracked the cabin door and told Joe we'd be going out for a while. He gave me a quick smile, blew me a kiss and went back to his writing. I was still dumbfounded by his intense writing concentration. I don't think I'd ever be capable of writing a novel. I can barely stay focused watching movies with sub-titles.

We left some soup and tea on the counter in case Joe needed an energy snack. We took Raymond's truck. It was older than me but very comfortable.

"The air conditioning is broke but the night is cool if you'd like to roll your window down."

The evening air felt good on my face. I thought about how hot it must be in New York with all that concrete. It was a different lifestyle in Montana. Nothing I'd ever known compared to the vastness of this amazing state.

We'd been on the road for about thirty minutes when Raymond motioned for me to look to the left. I could see a bright orange glow though the trees.

"That is the drum circle fire. It won't be long just a few more miles."

I was feeling excited but anxious. Would I fit in? Would they look at me as an outsider? Raymond must have sensed my anxiety.

"You will be well received Amelia. Remember we are all one nation; one brotherhood and you are a part of that nation. Now, if Joe was here we'd have a problem."

I questioned Raymond's remark, "Was it because he was a white man?"

Raymond chuckled, "No Amelia, his race has nothing to do with it. It's because he can be such a pain in the ass always asking questions about the old west, our tribal customs and so on. Sometimes we just want to have fun, dance and drum. Everything to him is research material– he needs to lighten up!"

His reply made me laugh and less nervous. It would be a fun evening. We turned down a dirt road, though a thicket of trees that opened into a large clearing. There must have been one hundred people in attendance. We parked at the end of the road and walked toward the crowd. There were children as young as 2-years old with their parents, grandparents and a few great-grandparents. Not all were Native American. People from all races were drumming and enjoying themselves.

I was taken aback by the friendliness and community of the crowd. I thought to myself, *I wish Joe was here to experience this with me, even though Raymond would prefer him to remain at the cabin. I'm sure I could keep his mind off of work for one evening.*

The drumming was intoxicating. I could feel my body becoming lighter with every beat. For a moment I felt as though I was floating. I mentioned it to Raymond. He said it was the ancient spirits of the ancestors embracing me – don't fight it, let them guide you on your personal journey. I was a bit apprehensive at first then decided to let go. I closed my eyes and let the rhythm of the drums consume me. In my mind's eye, I could see images and faces of what looked like tribal elders. At one point I swore I heard someone say, "Amelia, I'm not afraid to die, I'll forever be in your heart."

My eyes shot open like I'd seen a ghost, maybe I did. Raymond reached for my arm, "Are you okay, what did you see and hear?"

I told him about my experience. He could tell I was still shaken by it. He suggested we leave. I agreed. It was getting late and I wanted to make sure Joe was okay.

On the drive back, I replayed the experience in my head. I thought about Joe's pending test results and panicked. I didn't want to think about it. I just wanted to see Joe. I needed him in my life more than I'd admit.

I could see the light of the cabin. It seemed a hundred miles away. I needed to see for myself that Joe was okay. As we drove onto the driveway, I asked Raymond to stop the car. I jumped out and ran the rest of the way to our cabin. I could see Joe slumped over his laptop. It petrified me to the point I couldn't move. I shouted his name and he didn't move. I ran over and shook him hard and he finally woke up.

He grumbled, "Lord, woman can't a guy take a five-minute power nap without being shaken like a two-second bull ride!"

He slowly stood up from his chair, rubbing his eyes and hugged me.

"Did you have a good time at the drum circle?"

I was still frightened. If he hadn't been holding me, my legs would have buckled.

"What's got you so upset baby? I'm startin' to worry about you. You're actin' wackier than normal."

It took me a few minutes before I realized he was able to talk.

He smiled, "Must be that God awful tea Raymond has me drinking. It tastes like shit, but it's helpin'."

I told him on about the visions I saw and the voices I heard during the drumming. I was surprised by his casual attitude towards my drumming episode. He didn't seem at all surprised about what I had experienced. He tried to make light of it.

"Okay that's it, no more spiritual outings with Raymond. Next time, it's shopping at the local mall."

"Like it's not a spiritual experience finding Prada or Jim Choo at 50-percent off?"

He kissed me and said, "Baby, I think you need to get some sleep. In fact, I think I need to rest my voice and hit the hay too. And then I want to hear every detail about what you experienced. It might be something I can use in my book."

Raymond walked in just as Joe made the book statement.

"You see, I told you Rose, everything is a research opportunity for him – crazy ass white man!"

Joe laughed and told him good night and not to scalp anyone on his way back to his office. Raymond didn't turn around but flipped him the bird.

As soon as his head hit the pillow Joe was out like a light. I tried to sleep but kept thinking about what the voice said. I couldn't shake the feeling it was Joe. Maybe it was Joe; maybe he was trying to psychically tell me he would be okay even if the test results came back with grim news. I shut my eyes, snuggled behind Joe and drifted off to sleep.

We were so tired we'd forgotten to close the cabin curtains. The morning sun was so bright it woke me up. It must be past 8:00 AM. I stretched and rolled over to say good morning to my husband – he was gone. Thoughts of him wondering off into the woods, sitting under a tree waiting to die like old tribal elders would do scared the crap out of me. I sprang out of bed to look for him.

The door swung open almost knocking Joe over. He had two cups of coffee in his hands. "Whoa, girl where the heck do you think you're goin' and if'n you're goin' outside you might want to put some clothes on – it's a bit breezy out there. I realized I was standing in the doorway stark naked.

"Not that I don't like your choice of morning attire but you might give poor Raymond a heart attack. He being as old as he is and not seein' a naked gal in quite a while could cause problems if you know what I mean."

I ducked back inside hoping no one else saw me.

Joe said not to worry. Raymond had gone into town for supper supplies. He wanted to make us an authentic Blackfoot dinner.
"He'll probably scrape up some road kill and tell us it a tribal delicacy."

We finished our coffee on the porch. I asked Joe if he'd heard anything from the medical center. He shook his head no.

"Well, you know what they say . . . no news, is no news, so quit your worrying. Anyway I've got to write at least another five thousand words before I can take a day off. Sorry darlin', it's what I do. Now, tell me again why you fell in love with this crazy fiction writer?"

I stood on my tiptoes, put my arms around his neck and whispered, *"Why don't I show you? That is if you're up for a romp between the sheets."*

He brushed my hair away from my face, "Are you tryin' to seduce me into jumpin' your bones Mrs. Montana, because as you may know, I can resist those big brown eyes, your hot body and luscious lips. But then again why in the hell would any man on earth and in his right mind ever want to. What can I say darlin' I'm pathetically weak when it comes to you – disgraceful ain't it."

I whispered, *"Down-right-disgusting.* Now get them jeans off cowboy and let's see if you can hold on for more than eight seconds."

About an hour later, we heard Raymond's truck coming up the gravel road. I peeked out the door. He had two boxes filled with groceries and the mail. Joe and I put on our clothes and went out to help him unload his truck. We took the bags of groceries into his cabin.

"Rose the bag of caramels is for you." I thought, *How does he know I love caramels?*

"And Joe, there is a letter from the medical center." He thanked Raymond and shoved it into his back pocket.

He didn't seem anxious to open it. I suggested it could be good news about his test results. He said it could also be bad news and didn't want to spoil the last three days of our trip. I didn't want to argue with him. And to be honest I didn't want to know. I didn't need to hear any bad news. Joe said we'd open it when we returned home.

Joe had retreated back to our cabin to re-immerse himself in 1880, and I helped Raymond with dinner. I really enjoyed hearing about his ancestors and his childhood growing up in Montana. Unlike Raymond, my family was scattered all over the world. I was 7-years-old when my mother died. For years it was just me and my dad. He remarried when I left for college. I have two stepsisters who never keep in touch and a stepmother who was too involved with her own career to give me the time of day. My dad Arthur died shortly after marrying Crystal – whom I lovingly called, Bitchzilla. He was the only person in my life who never disappointed me. A talented poet, he taught me how to create beautifully written works of art in the form of Haikus, as well as my appreciation of the fine arts.

Raymond asked me if Joe and I had talked about starting a family. To be honest I'd never thought about it. It was something Joe and I hadn't discussed.

I said, "Children are a huge responsibility. Joe never had the opportunity to raise Morgan and it might be a wonderful gift if he was able to have a family of his own with me. Morgan might think it was cool to have a little brother or sister. Or he might think we were completely crazy to think about having kids when we were perfect examples of arrested development."

Joe was a month away from turning 48-years-old and I would be 38-years-old December. We continued to talk about Joe's health. Raymond suggested he cancel his speaking engagements until he had a chance to heal. I laughed saying it would be like telling him not to breathe. Joe was extremely loyal to his fans – that's why they loved him so much.

Joe walked over from our cabin with an empty cup in his hand.
"What's a fella' gotta' do around here to get a refill on a cup of coffee."

Without looking up Raymond said, "The last time I looked there was nothing wrong with your hands and legs – go get it yourself."
I had to laugh at the bluntness of Raymond's reply then said, "I'd like one too, if you wouldn't mind."

Joe huffed, "Excuse me but what did your last butler die of . . . boredom – get up off that pretty little ass and get it yourself."

I asked Raymond if he'd like some caramels – he said no and that he'd better go start dinner. He headed off to his cabin.

I got up from my chair and sat down on the porch steps. I couldn't help worrying about Joe. He was putting on a brave face but I know the test results were weighing heavily on his mind. I didn't want him to see me upset. I took a deep breath to clear my mind and stay positive.

I heard the screen door open. Joe came outside and sat down beside me.

"Here's your coffee darlin' let me know if there's anything else you need perhaps extra cream, lumps of sugar, or maybe a bevy of muscle-bound hunks to fan you."

"That's what I love about you Joe. You are so kind and caring – not a thread of sarcasm running though you."

"Yes indeed, that's me – sweet, kind and sarcastic cowboy . . . sugar?"

Joe reached behind him and pulled a couple of packs of sugar and the letter from his back pocket.

He leaned over and laid his head on my shoulder. "Rose, I wanted to open this privately but that wouldn't be fair to you. You're my wife and I don't want to keep anything from you, especially something like this. Good or bad we'll get through this together. Now don't go tearin' up on me – deal?"

I shook his hand to seal our deal.

He ripped the side open and slipped out the letter. We both held out breath while we read it. The first part was mostly test information informing us of the types of tests that were performed. The second part was the results.

Joe read the test results one-by-one. All of them showed negative for any signs of cancer or unusual cell formation. However, the doctor wanted to keep his eye on one of the polyps. It was a bit larger than the other. He said it may be nothing to worry about but he'd like to see Joe in two weeks – just to be on the safe side. Other than that everything looks good.

I don't remember standing up or how I wrapped my entire body around Joe's. Joe let loose a cowboy style yeehaw and swung me around in circles until we both fell down on the porch floor.

Raymond ran out from the kitchen not knowing what all the commotion was about. He had a large butcher's knife in his hand. "What in the name of heaven is going on – you both almost gave me a heart attack with your screaming."

Joe let out a sigh of relief. "Heaven's gonna have to wait Raymond – my tests came back negative!"

Raymond sat down in one of the porch chairs and wiped his brow. "We'll that is something to shout about – that's very good news my friend. I had no idea what was going on. You almost got scalped!"

Joe laughed saying that his knife wasn't sharp enough to cut hot butter and that whatever he was cooking smelled like it was burning. Joe was right, something was burning. Raymond leaped out of the chair and dashed back into the kitchen.

He yelled, "The pot boiled over a little bit. It's okay nothing to worry about compared to your good news my friend."

It was great news. Joe was okay. He asked me what Raymond and I were talking about.

"I peeked out the window and you two looked as though you were having some serious conversation."

"Raymond asked me if we thought about having kids. I told him we hadn't discussed it.

Joe rubbed his chin, "Hmm, I never gave it much thought. A baby is a major responsibility. Through no fault of my own I wasn't there for Morgan, hell, I didn't even know I had a child until he was grown. I don't want to do that to our child. I want to be there for them every step of the way."

Having children and trying to balance a full time career were not on my agenda. But things have changed. I have no career. However, I do have a wonderful man who I would love to share the bond of a child with.

Joe asked, "So does that mean you'd like to have a kid?" I nodded, "Yes, I'm as ready as I'll ever be. I'd like to have a baby with you Joe, if you're up for those 3:00 AM feedings and endless diaper changes."

I leaned over and whispered, *"In fact, maybe we could start practicing tonight after dinner?"*

Joe flashed his infamous shit-eating-grin. "YES MA'AM!"

Raymond poked his head out of the door and announced that dinner was just about ready. We walked back to our cabin to clean up. Joe and I decided to get dressed up in honor of Raymond's Native American feast. Joe put on pale blue embroidered western shirt with his black jeans and I wore my favorite white summer dress and squash blossom necklace.

Raymond came from the kitchen and saw how nice we looked.
"I didn't know this was going to be a formal affair or I would have worn my full head dress."

The table was set with beautiful tribal colors and flowers from Raymond's garden. Everything looked delicious. Raymond said it was an old recipe from his mother. Roasted chicken with wild rice and yams. There was a pitcher of sweet tea and homemade rolls. Joe said Cecilia better watch out because Raymond could give her a run for her money in the cooking department.

Raymond smiled, "I don't make this very often - only on special occasions. And this is a joyous occasion; celebrating Joe's good health and the beginnings of a new family."

I was surprised by his *new family* statement and asked him how he knew we'd decided to start a family.

Raymond shrugged his shoulders, "I would like to say it was a message from the great spirit of my ancestors or my Native American sensitivity but it was plain old fashion eavesdropping. What can I say – I'm nosey."

I don't think I'd ever laughed so hard in my life. Raymond was quickly becoming my best friend. I loved his outlook on life and his droll sense of humor.

After dinner Joe and I offered to clean up but Raymond wouldn't let us lift a thing. He insisted we go back to our cabin and start working on our new family member. Joe asked him if he would be eavesdropping on the baby-making activity.

"I'm nosy, not a pervert! Good grief Joe, sometimes I worry about your sanity."

Raymond winked at me, "You see, what did I tell you Rose, crazy white man with nothing but tumbleweeds between his ears. Goodnight all – I'll see you in the morning."

I kissed Raymond on his cheek and whispered, *"Thank you so much for taking care of Joe and me, sweet dreams my dear friend."*

We walked arm-in-arm back to our cabin. The moon was so large it looked like it was sitting on the horizon. Joe walked up behind me resting his chin on my shoulder.

"Now ain't that the best baby-making moon you've ever seen. It's so bright. Bella Luna, that means beautiful moon in Italian. What say we start working on that buckaroo?"

It was a night of love making I'd never forget. I'd never felt so fulfilled and satisfied in my life. If a baby wasn't conceived it wouldn't be for the lack of trying. Joe called it practice – I called it amazing. Afterwards, I slept better than I have in years. Who knew procreative-sex could be so relaxing. It was better than a shot of whiskey.

I sat up in bed and watched Joe sleep. I thought about what a good father he'd be and how much he would love our child. The words *spoiled rotten* crept into my head. I grinned and stroked his face brushing back the tuft of hair hanging over his eye. I got up to get a drink of water when I heard Joe stir.

He mumbled, "So-o-o, do you think you're pregnant?" I said no and told him to go back to sleep.

"Okay, wake me up when you're ready for round two. A baby will be made tonight I promise you that."

I said, "How about we take our time and enjoy the trying-to-make-a-baby part." He said he really liked the trying part, and we'd continue tomorrow.

We spent our last four days relaxing. Joe hadn't taken a writing break in weeks. Raymond took him fishing. He taught me how to make his famous Blackfoot chicken and rice dish. Tomorrow we'd be leaving. Joe's research trip was over. Soon it would be back home and back to his nonstop writing sessions. He had compiled lots of data, stories and had written twenty thousand words into his next novel. As much as I loved Raymond's place and being on a working vacation, I did miss the ranch. I missed haying Daisy and Bailey, riding fence checking the barbed wire for weak spots with Joe. I missed our bed. I wanted to conceive our baby in our bed.

Joe woke up before me and brought fresh coffee back to the cabin. "I hope you slept well Mrs. Montana. And have I told you how much I love you today?"

"The day just started."

"Then I'd better start now. I love you, I love you so much Rose, always have; always will."

I questioned his "always have" statement. He said he always knew he'd find me; he just didn't know where or when, but he knew I was out there.

For a moment, I reminisced about how our paths crossed back at Currysville library and how fate brought me to that town and how Joe's persistence kept me interested. One missed green light, one road accident, one rest stop for another cup of coffee and we wouldn't have met. Was it completely coincidental or was it something bigger than both of us that allowed us to find each other; as though the universe brought us together for a reason? Maybe it was to help Joe with his writing or to stand by him through his health scare.

Staying at Raymond's place brought about an untapped level of spirituality within me – energy and feelings I'd never experienced. Maybe Joe and I knew each other in another life. Maybe we were meant to be together all along. Either way I'm thankful to have this amazing man in my life.

Joe had already started packing the truck. Raymond said there was a basket of leftovers in the refrigerator to take along with us.

He told Joe that there is nothing worse than roadside fast food.

"That stuff is poison and will kill you quicker than a rattlesnake. And if she's pregnant she'll need to eat healthy."

We had a quick breakfast with Raymond and afterwards said our goodbyes as Raymond walked us to the truck.

"Have a safe trip. I miss you both already." He hugged Joe, then me. He whispered something to Joe and patted him on his back. Joe laughed out loud and said he would. He hopped into the driver's seat, and we waved goodbye until the cabin was out of sight. A few minutes into our drive I asked Joe what he and Raymond were laughing about. Joe said it had to do with us getting pregnant.

"He said don't forget to eat lots of oyster because they'll keep my pecker rock hard for hours of baby making, if she isn't already pregnant."

I blushed at the thought of Raymond suggesting such a thing.

I said, "I can't believe some of the things that come out of that old man's mouth. He never ceases to amaze me."

Joe laughed and said, "You're right darlin' but you got to love him and his infernal honesty."

I put a CD into the player to keep Joe awake and alert. It was his favorite mix of songs. I must have looked extremely tired because he hinted that I should take a nap. To be honest, I was exhausted. Waiting for those test results to arrive was nerve wracking. I never want to go through that again. I leaned back, propped my feet on the dashboard and dozed off.

Chapter 14

The package was addressed to Keough Teal Montana. The postal delivery person left it on the porch. It looked as though no one had picked up the mail for a couple of days. A rusting old red pickup truck with a large black dog passed the mail truck and parked beside the cabin. An old fellow wearing a frayed straw cowboy hat stepped out of the vehicle.

"What the hell is this? I didn't order anything."

He tossed the box through the door and picked up the pile of mail from the porch chair. He whistled for the dog – a huge black lab. It jumped out of the truck bed and followed him inside. The cabin was cluttered with books, old newspapers and rodeo gear. He flung the mail on the kitchen table and headed to the refrigerator.

"Hmm, I'm almost out of beer. Better put that on my repetitive-shit-to-buy-list." He'd been out of town for a week visiting an old rodeo buddy. He thought, " *It's good to be home.* "

He lowered himself into an over-stuffed recliner and popped the bottle cap off a long neck, taking a swig.

"Okay, now where was I?"

He pushed the back of the chair, raising the foot rest and at the same time reached for the book beside his chair. It was a dog-eared copy of *Montana Joe's, Lost Trails of Sweet Grass Canyon.*

"Let's see how my big-shot-son-the-western-writer writes his way out of this situation."

Lash's father had been following his career, cutting out press clippings, buying his books and keeping bits and pieces of his rodeo days. He, in his own way, was proud of his son's success even though he hadn't communicated with him in decades. K.T. had been banned from the rodeo circuit due to his reckless drinking. He became a liability to himself and the other riders. They gave him his walking papers, and he never looked back. After he sobered up, he headed to Mexico and tried his hand at ranching again. That didn't seem to work out either. It only took one fight and he was back to drinking again.

He headed back to Montana, found a small cabin in the high country and spent his time doing odd-jobs. He'd pawned most of his rodeo buckles and was living off his meager social security checks. His black lab, Lucky-Lou was his only companion. K.T. re-read the article announcing Lash's marriage to Amelia.

He looked down at Lou and said, "I should have called my boy and congratulated him, but why would he want to hear from an old drunk who left him and his mamma. I ain't never done nothin' for the boy in his life except give him life. It's the only thing I've ever been proud of, and I destroyed that with my drinkin'. He don't need some old coot comin' into his life now."

K.T. had just turned seventy-seven years old. He was in pretty good shape for someone his age and with his history. He got up, looked in the mirror and ran his fingers through his thick white hair.

"Hah, I ain't no Sam Elliott, but I can still turn them fillies' heads. I just can't catch 'em like I used to."

He sat back down and continued reading Joe's book. Lou started sniffing the box that K.T. had thrown on the floor.

"Oh shit, I plum forgot about that Lou. I'd better open it and see what's in it. Huh, it could be something from Publisher's House. Probably some free samples of something I don't need like that last box. What dumb-ass in their right mind sends an old man a trial sample of maxi-pads?"

He ripped open the box and found an autographed copy of Montana Joe's latest novel, *Chase Down the Wind*. He'd forgotten he'd ordered it.

"I must be getting' old Lou. I ordered this last month when they had the author's special edition event."

He rubbed his finger over the signature as if to trace his son's handwriting.

"I'm proud of you son – you're doin' well for yourself. Maybe it's best if you continue thinkin' I'm dead." He rubbed his sleeve over his tearing eyes.

"Hell, maybe I'm better off bein' dead to him. It ain't his fault that I'm a drunk or that I left the only woman I ever loved for whiskey and rodeo."

He took a blue bandana from his back pocket and wiped his eyes, then put the book down beside his chair with the rest of Joe's books. He picked up the bottle of beer and walked into the kitchen. Staring at the sink, he turned the bottle upside-down.

He muttered to himself, "I miss ya', I miss ya' real bad son. I want you to know I'm proud of ya' but I'm afraid you won't want nothin' to do with me. I don't blame ya' if you told me to rot in hell for not bein' there for you and your sisters."

A ringing phone snapped him back into reality. It was his brother Kurt. Kurt Jonah Montana was K.T.'s twin brother. Joe never knew his father had a twin – neither did his sisters. K.T. answered the phone.

"Before we get started, I got no money, you ain't gettin' no more of what I ain't got, and you owe me money! Now what the hell do you want?"

The voice on the other line replied, "Yeah, and I love you to lil' brother. I'm five minutes older than you so shut the hell up and listen. I ain't callin' about money or the lack there of, I'm callin' to let you know that my nephew, your son, will be at a book signing in Billings, if you're interested. It says Saturday, September 14th at the Billings Marriott Hotel. That's three months from now."

K.T. paused, ". . . now tell me, why in the world I would be interested in what my son's doin'. He ain't never been interested in what I'm doin'."

Kurt's voice raised two octaves.

"That's because he thinks you're dead ya' dumb-son-of-a-bitch! You buy every damn book he writes, you know them by heart and you're so proud of him you can't see straight. Why don't you just grab what's left of your wrinkled balls and let him know you're alive and living in the same damn state."

K.T got quiet. He knew his brother was telling the truth.

"I'll think about it Kurt, but I ain't gonna promise nothin'! Now unless there's something else you wanna tell me I'm gonna hang up!"

Kurt grumbled, "You're the same old pig-headed fool you've always been. How's it workin' for ya'?"

When Kurt heard the dial tone, he knew his brother had hung up. "Stubborn son-of-a-bitch! The bastard hung up on me – again!"

K.T. sat out on the porch for a few hours to mull over Kurt's suggestion. Maybe I should tell my son I'm alive, maybe he'd like to know that I still think about him and follow his career. Or maybe he'll tell me to burn in hell.

He thought, *"I'm already in a livin' hell being estranged from my family."*

"Oh well, I never know unless I own up to my son. Maybe I will hang out in Billings for a couple of months. Might be interesting, might not, but it's a hell of a lot better than sitting here talking to a dog – no offense Lou. "

He packed his things including his new Montana Joe book and left a note for the postal service. He motioned for Lou. "Hey boy how'd you like to live in Billings for a while?" Lou wagged his tail as if to say of course!

"Then come on – I guess we're headin' to Billings."

Chapter 15

"Wake up Rose, we're home darlin'." I couldn't believe I'd slept the entire time, so much for me keeping an eye on Joe.

"Why didn't you wake me up Joe? I could have helped with the driving."

He kissed my palm, "Now why would I do something stupid like that when it was so sweet watching you sleep and drool all over my jacket. And, yes I did take my meds while I was filling up the truck at the gas station."

I raised my eyebrows, "You mean we stopped and you didn't think to tell me? Maybe I was hungry or needed to pee."

Joe wrote something on his writing pad, the one he'd used during the trip to Raymond's. In big letters he wrote I'M SORRY!

"Very funny Mister Montana, you'd better hold on to that sign because I predict you'll be using it for the rest of the evening!"

He winked and wrote, "So there'll be no talking during sex?"

I grabbed the pad out of his hand and laughed. *He seems to be feeling a lot better.*

However, I was tired and as much as he tried to hide it, so was he – I could tell. He didn't look his chipper self. I told him I'd bring in the luggage if he would brew a pot of his infamous cowboy coffee. I knew he had some barn chores to do as well as some edits to his work.

Cecilia had stocked the refrigerator and did some necessary food shopping. The drive left me parched. I was filling my glass with ice when I noticed two gallons of my favorite ice cream. *Thank you Cecilia!* She'd also left two jars of her famous canned sweet pickles. I made a mental note, *She must teach me how to can.* I reached to open one of the jars then froze – *ice cream and pickles?*

Does she know something Joe and I don't know? I chuckled to myself contemplating the connection and the possibility of me being pregnant. Maybe I should call Raymond. He seems to know more about this spiritual psychic stuff than I do. Maybe Cecilia is psychic?

I popped a pickle into my mouth and went to check on Joe. He had gone out to the barn to check on the horses. I sat down on the couch and thumbed through our stack of mail. There was a letter from the medical center addressed to Joe. I held it aside. Most of the mail was junk but one piece stood out. It was advertising baby clothes and nursery items. I stuffed the circular under the coffee table.

Way too many pregnancy references for one day.

Joe walked in the living room and plopped down beside me on the couch. He whispered, "So how's my *baby.* Are you glad to be back in our own *crib?*"

I jumped up and shook my fist at the ceiling as if I was talking directly to God. "Okay, okay enough of the pregnancy hints, for Christ sake."

Joe looked at me like I had lost my mind. He didn't know what was going on. "So you won't talk to me but you'll scream at God? What in heaven's name did God do to you? Hah, that's funny . . . heaven's name, God. I take it you're not amused?"

Joe had no clue what had just happened. In less than five minutes I'd received more than a half dozen pregnancy references.

"Joe, what if I'm pregnant? Are you sure that's what you want? Do you really want a baby?"

He paused for a moment and said, "That's the dumbest trilogy of questions I've ever heard. Darlin', I know I'm great in bed, in fact I'm a real stud stallion, if I do say so myself. Do you think I endured five hours of hard lovemaking if I wasn't tryin' to get you pregnant? Okay, the last two hours were just for fun, but quit tryin' to change the subject!

YES, I hope you're pregnant, yes, I'm ready for a baby and yes, I want to have one with you. Now can we eat somethin', I'm starved. Where did Cecilia put my jerky? I'm kidding. I know I can't eat it but, like I said I'm starved."

We had a light dinner and afterwards Joe opened his mail. I noticed he left the one from the medical center to read last. I felt his mood change when he read it. He took a deep breath and put it back in the envelope.

I sat beside him and put my arm around his shoulder, "What did it say? Tell me Joe, what is it?"

"Well it seems they want to do another biopsy on the larger polyp. They've scheduled it two weeks from today. Just routine, better-safe-than-sorry sort of thing I guess. But hey, that's in two weeks let have some fun now. How about we go for a midnight ride or swim or just sit outside until morning and watch the sun come up. Maybe tomorrow we'll go into town and by one of them home pregnancy test to see if my boys fulfilled their mission"

I knew exactly what he was doing and played along.

"I like the sitting and watching the sun come up idea. I'll even bring you some coffee."

He took the old Indian blanket onto the deck and I headed out to the kitchen for our coffee. Between the living room and kitchen I couldn't hold back my tears.

I can't, no . . . I won't think about the worst. He's going to be okay.

I handed him a cup and sat beside him. It felt good to be cuddled in his arms. He had such strong arms. *Who else would hold me if something happened to him.* I didn't want to think about it. I didn't want to think about anyone else holding me but Joe. We fell asleep on the deck.

He must have carried me into the bedroom. By the time I woke up Joe had already headed into town to pick up a few things for his printer and the EPT for me. My cell phone rang it was him asking if we needed anything else. I said no just hurry home I'm eager to find out whether or not we're pregnant. He said he liked the sound of that and would be home soon.

A few seconds later my cell rang again, it was Jannine.

"Hey girl, how are you? How was the research trip?"

"It was wonderful and in fact you might be an aunt." Her screaming hurt my ear. I could hear her telling Morgan the possible good news. He was just as excited.

We were still talking when Joe's truck pulled up. He was waving the ETP out of the window like a flag. I told Jannine and Morgan I'd call them later and let them know the outcome.

I took the test out of the package and headed into the bathroom. Joe put his hands together as if to say a prayer. I was in there for 10-minutes. He knocked on the door and asked if everything was okay. I opened the door and said no everything is not okay. He's face went pale.

"Nothing will be okay for at least 18-years. After he or she is in college then we might be okay but I highly doubt this household will ever be okay again."

The test showed a positive response. I whispered, *"Mister Montana, congratulations you're going to be a daddy!"*

I'd never seen Joe's knees wobble. I thought we was about to pass out. I helped him over to the couch. "Good Lord, I'm gonna' be a dad – A DAD!" He grabbed his crotch giving it a squeeze and said, "Good job boys, well done!"

We called Jannine and Morgan back with the good news. I don't know who was more excited Jannine or Joe. Morgan was so sweet. He said, "Any child would be blessed to have you as a mother."

After the commotion I walked outside to reflect on my good news. For a moment, it overshadowed the news of Joe's upcoming biopsy.

The next two weeks were a blur. There were lots of conversations about baby clothes, baby furniture, birthing classes. We'd almost forgotten about his appointment. It was tomorrow morning at 9:00 AM.

We arrived early at the medical center and headed to Dr. Jacobs office. He was talking to the nurse when we walked in. He and Joe gave each other the usual guy hug. He asked him how the research trip went. I thought it best not to tell him about the pregnancy until after the examination. He walked over to me and hugged me.

"Hello Rose you look even more beautiful than before. You are glowing – you must be pregnant."

I was shocked! I looked over at Joe who was already laughing. "Hey I didn't tell him anything. It must be that glow that you pregnant gals give off."

Doctor Jacobs was surprised. "Really, you're pregnant? I was only joking, but my Lord you look simply radiant! Congratulations to you both."

He asked us to sit down. He said after reviewing Joe's test results he wasn't pleased with the size of the polyp. It was bordering on the size of a tumor and wanted to be on the safe side so he set up an MRI. He asked Joe if he had any trouble swallowing, hoarseness, any changes since his last visit. Joe said none that he noticed. I did say from time-to-time he'd complain about ear pain. He said it was because I'd been bitchin' at him about something or another. He said if you check, you'll also find I have a pain-in-the-neck referring to me. They laughed but I didn't think it was a laughing matter. I wanted this to be over in a positive way.

The series of tests took two hours, most of which was waiting for them to be reviewed. I headed across the street to the Starbucks for coffee. I got Joe his usual and an herbal tea for me. I was leaving the shop when I heard someone call my name.

"Hello Amelia, or should I call you Rose, fancy meeting you here."
It was Paul the British truck driver. I was surprised to see him and even more surprised he remembered me. He asked if my emergency worked out. I smiled saying yes it did, in fact I married it.

He winked and said, "Good on you girl, I'm happy for you. He's one lucky bloke, chuffin' lucky I'd say!"

I asked him if he was still driving. He nodded and said he was headed to California to drop off his load.

"I was in need of a caffeine and petro break. Then I remembered there was a Starbucks here."

We discussed Joe's condition. Paul was genuinely concerned. He reached in his pocket and handed me his card.

"If you ever need anything, anything at all you call me – and I mean it, poppet. I was hoping to meet up with you again, just not under these circumstances. But I must say you do look simply radiant. You wouldn't be up the duff would you?"

My puzzled look asked him for a translation.

"Up the duff means pregnant, love."

Can everyone tell I'm pregnant? I nodded yes and I thanked him for his card.

"That's brilliant; best to you, the hubs and the new addition. It was good seeing you again. Take good care of yourself Amelia."

He watched me until I reached the center's door then waved goodbye.

Whenever I had some sort of a personal crisis, Paul was there to help me out like my own British guardian angel. Maybe it was Karma. For a brief moment I felt relaxed. Then reality set in – Joe's diagnosis. I hurried back to Dr. Jacobs' office and waited.

His nurse poked her head in the office and asked me to follow her into the examination room. Doctor Jacobs was looking over Joe's results. He sat down beside me and took a deep breath.

"Amelia, I'm just going to cut to the chase, I'm not happy with the look of this polyp. It's not shrinking. In fact, it's grown by a half a centimeter. I'd like to start aggressive treatment. Now, I know Joe will baulk at it but I really need your help in insisting he go along with my treatment plan. Can I count on you?"

I had such a lump in my throat that I couldn't answer him. All I heard was my husband had some sort of growth that didn't look good, and it could be bad news. I told him I would do anything and everything to help Joe.

"Okay, I'm going to schedule surgery this afternoon to remove the polyp then we'll send it to pathology. I'll know more after that. Now comes the tough part – I need to convince Joe to agree to the surgery. That's where you come in, he'll listen to you."

We walked down the hall into the examination room. Joe was autographing the nurse's stethoscope. She looked a bit embarrassed, smiled and left the room.

Joe smiled and said, "Gotta' keep the fans happy. And why do you two look like you're ready for a shoot out and realized you've forgot to load your guns?"

Doctor Jacobs didn't waste any time trying to sugar-coat his plan. He told to Joe his concerns and about that he wanted to remove the polyp today. The doctor was ready for a fight but to his surprise, Joe agreed.

"This thing needs to be taken care of now. I'm not going to drag Amelia back and forth to this place any more than I need to. Let's get it out and over with so we can move on with our life." Joe glanced over at me. "Do you agree darlin'?" I nodded yes.

"Alright, let's get this cowboy prepped for surgery. I'll get the paperwork ready while you meet with the anesthesiologist."

Joe sat back on the examination table and handed me his cowboy hat.

"Here, take this. If anything happens to me don't give it to the goodwill – it's my favorite hat. And, please don't give it to Raymond. He'll stick feathers all over it and wear it to one of them drum circle hootenannies."

I couldn't hold back my tears any longer. I broke down in his arms. He let me cry for a few minutes then held my chin and said, "Listen to me, I'll be okay. Did you hear me Amelia, everything will be okay."

"How do you know…how can you honestly tell me everything will be okay? I can't lose you Lash, I can't!"

He kissed my palm and put my hand over his heart. "That's as close to a promise as I can give you baby. You know my heart doesn't lie. I love you Mrs. Montana. Now come over here and talk dirty to me before they prep me for surgery." I mustered a pathetic smile.

"Wait a minute; did I just see a smile? Hah, I did! That's my cowgirl."

He hugged me as tight as he could. We held onto each other until the nurse motioned for me to leave. It was time.

I must have fallen asleep in the waiting room. I didn't hear the nurse come in to tell me the surgery was over and that I could sit with Joe in the recovery room. She said he would be out for another hour; however, she was sure he'd want me there when he woke up.

I walked into the room, and he was out like a light. It was good to see him sleeping. He never slept well when he was immersed in his writing. He looked so peaceful. I kissed his cheek and brushed the tuft of hair from his forehead. I remember how sweet his hair smelled the first night we slept together. The lavender scent brought back sensual memories of our lovemaking. I closed my eyes for a moment wanting to remember every detail.

I opened my eyes when I heard a hoarse whisper, "Tell me ma'am how long before the next stagecoach leaves for Santa Fe? I got a pretty little gal waitin' for me at the Red Horn cantina."

I leaned over and said, "Joe, Are you awake?"

"Nope, I'm dreamin' so please don't let my wife know I'm winkin' at some sexy señorita or she'll cut my throat worse than the doc did."

I took a huge breath and sat down. The anesthesia was wearing off. It took him another hour to realize that the surgery was over and that he was in the recovery room. Doctor Jacobs came in to check his stats.

"He seems to be doing well. I'd like to observe him for another hour. The pathology report will be available in the morning and we'll know more about his course of treatment then. You'll be able to leave once he's fully awake. I'll phone the pharmacy and you can pick up his meds on your way out. Go home and get some rest, and I'll call you tomorrow. Are you okay to drive?" I assured him I was and that I would be extra careful.

Joe was fully awake and getting dressed. I was about to put his hat on the bed to help him with his shirt - he caught it before it hit the sheets.

He whispered, *"Whoa darlin', don't you know putting a cowboy's hat on a bed is bad luck? Whew, that was close. I'm gonna need all the good luck I can get."*

I thought, *"Good luck and a lot of prayers."*

We arrived home late in the afternoon. I nudged Joe. The procedure took more out of him than he was willing to admit. I told him not to bother getting undressed and just go to bed. I helped him off with his boots. He didn't argue with me and went straight to bed. I brought him a glass of water and something to help with the pain. It wasn't long after he was sound asleep.

It had been a long and stressful day. I wanted a shot of his 100-proof Bourbon. Joe didn't drink much because of his father being a heavy drinker. He said he'd never wanted to go that route nor did he want his children to see him drunk like he saw his dad. He'd jokingly say that bourbon was for medicinal purposes only.

I thought, *Well Joe, this is one big ass medicinal purpose.* However, in my condition, orange juice would have to do. After getting Joe settled, I took what I thought would be a quick nap on the couch.

The sound of hungry horses and coffee woke me up. Joe was still sleeping. It was 6:00 AM and the coffee was starting to perk. I mouthed, "God bless you Cecilia."

I needed to get up and start the ranch chores Joe would normally do. I walked over to the barn and pulled a bale of hay from the lower hay loft. It was heavier than I expected. *Mental note to self – must started upper body weight training after the baby is born.* After they finished, I let them out into the pasture. I loved watching them run and buck after they've been fed. I could only imagine Joe riding one of those bucking broncs.

He must be freaking nuts to ride something that could stomp you to death. I rode a mechanical bull on a dare at some local New York bar. Falling off onto an air mat was easy. Falling off onto a hard dirt area – now that's another story. Like Raymond says, "Youth has no fears and no brains."

I bent over to pick up the feed bucket when I felt a hand on my ass. "That had better be my husband or Sam Elliott."

Joe laughed then whispered, "Well, I ain't Sam Elliott but will an old cowboy-bearing-decaffeinated-coffee do?"

His voice was still hoarse, but I was surprised how much better he sounded. To be honest, I loved the hoarseness – it was deep and sexy. We sat down on a bale of hay and watched the horses graze.

"It just doesn't get any better than this does it darlin' – how are you feelin'?"

"My back is a little achy from all of our traveling but other than that I felt pretty good." He reached over and rubbed my stomach.
I said, "It's hard for me to wrap my brain around the fact we were going to have a baby.

Joe agreed. It was an unbelievable whirlwind of events.

He explained, "It feels like only yesterday we were at each other's throats. You didn't like me at all. But I knew from the first moment we met, you were my angel. And now we're havin' a baby. How amazing it that Rose."

Our lives had changed in the blink of an eye. I almost felt guilty having so much happiness happen so quickly. I had a new life, a new home, new husband and a new baby on the way.

"You know Rose, sometimes I wonder how I would have turned out if my father has stayed with my mother. Would my life have turned out differently? I guess I'll never know. I reckon he's in prison or someone had the good sense to put him out of his misery. Nonetheless, I'll be there for our baby. I promise you that I'll never leave you high and dry like my father did."

I'd never heard Joe open up about his father like this. I think it was the fact that he was going to be a dad and didn't want to make the same mistakes with his kid.

He said, "Morgan is an amazingly talented and handsome kid, no thanks to me. His mother and aunt are to be commended for his turning out so well."

I took a sip of my coffee and replied, "And you don't think any of your genes had something to do with it?"

Joe smiled, "Well of course, where do you think he got his incredible good looks."

We finished our coffee and headed back to the house. Joe said his throat was starting to hurt a bit and that he should quit talking for a while. I reminded Joe to take his pain medication. He took one with the reminder of his coffee and headed back to the bedroom.
I was washing up the coffee cups when the phone rang.

"Hello, Montana residence. Hello, is anyone there?" I could hear someone was on the other end but whoever it was didn't say a word. I was about to ask again when I heard a dog bark in the background then nothing - whoever it was hung up.

Chapter 16

I finished packing our things for Joe's book signing in Billings. I couldn't believe three months had passed but when I looked at my baby belly I realized I was into my second trimester. Joe seemed excited about the Billings trip mostly because his voice was coming back and he was feeling good. I enjoyed watching him prepare for his fans. He would go through the same routine saying it was good luck and wasn't about to change it. He would get a professional shave, his hair trimmed buy the same gal and have his signature gray Stetson steam cleaned. His lucky shirts were hanging in a separate closet along with his western belts and buckles.

I was having breakfast when he walked down the hall and into the kitchen.

"Well, I do declare who is this handsome man? Don't tell my husband you're here or he'll shoot you dead between the eyes."

He looked at his reflection in the toaster and pretended to straighten his eyebrows. "I am a handsome devil ain't I? Good morning baby. And, good morning to you too, Rose."

He kissed his palm and gently rested it on my stomach. He stooped down, "Now you be good to your momma and no somersaults while we're driving to Billings. Hah, like you'd listen to me. Heck, your momma doesn't even listen to me. Hmm, must run in her family."

I laughed and told him it was time to leave and reminded him to take his meds. "Yes mother, I've already taken them and the rest are packed in my overnight bag." He leaned back down towards my stomach, "See what you have to look forward to – nag, nag, nag."

I said, "I'll keep on nagging if it will keep you healthy."

The drive seemed longer due to my constant restroom breaks. *Was it going to be like this for the next 4-months? I feel like I'm releasing an ocean of pee every ten miles.*

We arrived at the hotel and not a moment too soon. My bladder felt like it was going to explode. Joe turned the keys over to the parking attendant while I hurried to the lobby restroom. I remember passing an older fellow with a dog. Oddly, he reminded me a lot of Joe.

I wonder if Joe will look like that when he gets older. He looked like Tommy Lee Jones only older and with longish white hair. I'd just walked out of the stall to wash my hands when a woman came in. She politely smiled and looked at my belly.

"Oh, how I remember those days, honey. Having to pee every minute of the day, knowing where every rest stop in the United States was located. But when you see that little piece of you smile for the first time it's all worth it. And by the way, you look absolutely radiant."

I thanked her and said how much I appreciated her compliment because I felt like an elephant trying to squeeze through a keyhole. I'd never weighed more than one hundred and twenty pounds and I'd already gained fourteen. Joe said it was just more of me to love but I felt like a blimp and it would only get worse. At least I looked good or so she said.

I met up with Joe in the lobby. He'd already checked in and the hotel attendants took our luggage to our room. I noticed the man I'd passed was still sitting by the elevators. I glanced over causing Joe to look. He did a double take but never said a word to me. It was as though he'd seen a ghost. I asked him if he knew the fellow. He said no, but he looked very familiar. I hadn't noticed the large black dog lying beside him. The elevator doors opened and we walked in. By the time we turned around, the man and his dog were gone.

Joe's book signing was scheduled from 7:00 PM - 9:00 PM in the Grand Montana Conference Hall. I couldn't believe how many people showed up. Reality finally hit me that I was married to a very well known writer with a legion of loyal fans. I felt embarrassed that I'd never heard of him until that day at the Currysville library. The line of people waiting to have their copy of Montana Joe's, *Chase Down the Wind* autographed was impressive.

I was about to check on Joe when he came up behind me. "Ma'am it ain't polite to jump the line. There's enough Montana Joe to go around, you'll have to wait your turn like everybody else."

I nonchalantly turned and said, "That's not what happened at the Currysville Library. You practically leaped over the table to give me an autographed copy of your book."

He grinned, "Okay, you can jump the line this time, you being pregnant and all, but after this little fella or gal is born you'll have to wait your turn. However, if you sleep with the author he'll give you more than an autograph. He flashed his shit-eating-smile and kissed me.

"Okay darlin' it's time to turn on the Montana charm and greet my fans. Now give me a big wet one and let me get to work. And don't stay too long because you need your rest is that understood Mrs. Montana."

"Yes, it is Mr. Montana, now get going and thank your fans. They've been waiting a long time and I am getting a little tired."

He got half way through the door then turned around and whispered *I love you*, then disappeared into a crowd of cheering fans.

I walked toward the elevators then decided to go outside for some air. The night air helped me sleep. Joe's kid had a habit of twisting and turning whenever I thought about sleeping. I rubbed my back and sat down on one of the benches. There were rocking chairs in the hotel's garden all of which were taken. It was then I noticed the old man with his dog leaving. He walked by me then turned around.

"Pardon me, ma'am but you shouldn't be sittin' on that hard bench, bein' in the condition you're in. Why don't you sit in that rocking chair I was sittin' in?" By the time he'd finished his sentence, someone else was sitting in it.

He walked over and asked the guy if he would move and let me sit down. He frowned, told him no and continued his cell phone conversation.

The old man gave a sharp whistle and the dog lifted his leg and peed on the man's pants.

The man shot up out of the chair cursing a blue streak and left. He walked back over to the bench and helped me up while the big black dog guarded the rocker.

"Here you go ma'am, some folks ain't got any respect for a gal in your condition. Sometimes they need a little reminder on manners."

I was laughing so hard the baby started kicking. I said, "That was so cool. How did you train your dog to do that?"

He grinned and said, "Because I have an exceptional ability to piss people off, so I taught my dog to do the same. You have a good evening ma'am and congratulations to you and your soon-to-be youngin'."

He started to walk away when I said, "Thank you mister . . . "

"Teal, the name is Keough Teal, ma'am. And your rocker sentry is Lucky Lou. I'll thank him later with a hunk of jerky."

What a charming man. You don't find many gentlemen like him anymore.

Still, he seemed very familiar. Maybe it was his style or his mannerism. Then it dawned on me that he had the same shit-eating-grin as Joe. I smiled and thought, *"Must be a Montana-thing."*

I headed inside. The fresh air gave me a second wind. On my way to the elevators I decided to take a peek in the conference room. Fans were still lined up waiting for autographs. I asked Joe's publicist, Hanna to tell him I was going back to our room. It was the first time I'd met her. Hanna C. Vagando from what I've heard is one of the best national and international publicists for novel writers. She's handled all of Montana Joe's publicity from his early days until now and works out of Kansas City, Missouri. Joe said she had a good head for promotion and knew how to kick ass when necessary. She assured me she'd let him know as soon as he was done and would have him call the room to let me know he was on his way.

"Don't worry Amelia, I won't let any starry-eyed-buckle-bunnies lay a hand on him. You go and get some rest. We have the room for another twenty minutes. I'll wrap things up afterwards."

I told her thanks so much for looking after my husband and me. "Oh and please call me Rose, everyone he works with does. To be honest, I've grown very fond of the nickname."

She laughed and said, "Okay – then Rose dear, leave and that's an order young lady, now scoot!"

I already loved Hanna. Like me she was a take charge gal. No nonsense. I knew Joe would be in good hands and I could get some much needed rest.

I took the elevator to the 16th floor. I was so tired I didn't remember passing the other floors. I got out and noticed my rocking chair hero was standing by the other elevator waiting to go down.

I whispered, "Well, hello again! And where is my four-legged-hero?"

He chuckled, "He's in the hotel kennel. They wouldn't let him stay in the room, something about a No Dog Policy. Heck, I told them he ain't ever been caged in his life, so I've got to walk him on a leash every two hours or so. I need the exercise so it's no big deal."

The doors opened, and he said goodnight then grabbed the door. "Excuse me ma'am, seein' that we're slowly becoming hotel acquaintances, I apologize for not asking your name. I could continue callin' you ma'am, but seein' we've shared a rocking chair . . . "

"Amelia, my name is Amelia Montana, however, my husband has nicknamed me Rose. He's the writer at the book signing. He writes under the name of Montana Joe. And since you and I are so well acquainted, I'd love for him to meet you or at least give you a couple of autographed copies of his books for being my rocking chair hero. Maybe you'd like to join us for coffee tomorrow? I'll be drinking juice of course, but I'd love you to meet him. In some way you remind me of him.

Keough let the doors close. *That's odd, no goodnight, not a thanks but no thanks, hmm very odd.*
I was too tired to think about it. I took a long hot shower and crawled into bed. About an hour passed, when I heard the door open. I turned on the light.

"Hi baby, how did everything go? I can't wait to hear about it."
Joe whispered, "Sh-h-h, go back to sleep darlin'. I'm going to take a quick shower and hit the hay. I'm plum tuckered out."

I could hear Joe coughing above the running water in the shower. It was hoarse and deep. He must have coughed for two minutes straight and then I heard a thud. I jumped out of bed to find Joe on the floor still in his clothes. I called the hotel manager and asked him to call 911. We needed an ambulance right away! A minute later Hanna was banging on the door.

"Amelia, it's Hanna – open up!"

I rushed to the door. The emergency medical team was right behind her. Joe had regained consciousness, feeling very embarrassed.

"Whoa, now that was some ride, did I stay on for eight seconds?"
I cried, "Baby, you passed out. You were coughing so bad you passed out in the bathroom."

I noticed blood on the front of his shirt and around his mouth. He was coughing up blood. They rushed us to the hospital emergency room. I asked one of the nursing staff to contact Dr. Jacobs. They assured me they'd already called him. Hanna made all the other necessary calls. I sat in the waiting area feeling numb. Another nurse came over to me and said once they checked him out and everything was stabilized, I could go in. But in the mean time, they wanted to check my blood pressure. My pressure was sky high so they took me into an empty room and checked the baby's heart rate.

The nurse said, "Her heart beat is strong and steady." What made her think I was having a girl? We chose not to find out until they were born. But she seems very certain about it being a girl.

She said, "I've been a pediatric nurse for 25-years, and I haven't been wrong yet. Hope you want a girl. Maybe your next child will be a boy but I'm betting my nursing credentials on a girl." *Next child - what did she mean, next child?*

For a brief moment, her humor eased my fears. She said she'd check on Joe's status and find out if it was okay for me to join him.
I sat up on the edge of the bed and cried. *This can't be happening, not now, not with our child coming.*

The nurse said it was okay for me to go in and let me know that they've given him a mild sedative to help his coughing. I walked into his room and tried to smile.

His smile was forced and very fatigued.

"Well darlin' that was not what I had planned for tonight. They won't let me pounce on you until Theo gives them the okay and I'm released."

"Joe, I'm not worried about that… I'm afraid. I'm really scared. I'm trying to be brave, but I'm so hormonally upset I can't think about anything else but you getting better." I dropped into his arms and cried.

He kissed my palm twice saying one was for me and the other was for the baby. I mentioned that the pediatric nurse seems to think we're having a girl.

"Well I hope she's right. I've always wanted a little girl." Like they say a son's a son till he takes a wife but a daughter is a daughter the rest of her life. How sweet will it be to have a little Rose running around the ranch?"

I said he'd have plenty of time to spoil him or her when he got better. I climbed into bed next to him and dozed off.

The sound of curtains being drawn back startled me awake. It was Theo. He helped me out of bed. Joe was resting comfortably. We left the room and sat in the doctor-patient conference room. Theo sat down close beside me.

"Rose, I'm going to shoot straight from the hip. I'm not happy with his test results. The growth is getting larger, and it's beginning to affect his vocal cords. We're running some tests here; however, if we don't start aggressive treatment now I'm worried it could destroy the cords and he'd lose his ability to speak. I know this is a lot of medical crap to take in, but I respect you and Lash too much to beat around the bush. That's not his style and it's definitely not yours."

Theo put his arm around my shoulder. "To be honest Theo, I heard about a third of what you've said. All I wanted to hear was my husband and my baby's father would be okay."

A few minutes later, the other doctors came in. They confirmed everything Theo had said and wanted to consult with him about procedures.

I needed to be with Joe. I walked back to his room and sat in the chair next to the bed. He looked tired. Not the usual been-on-the-road-too-long tired, but, I'm-done-fighting-this-shit tired. I knew I had to be strong for all of us. Hanna peeked in and motioned for me to come into the hallway.

She hugged me and said, "Rose, I need you to know that I'm here for you both. If you need anything and I mean ANYTHING you call me. Now, I've got to leave for an hour to get his things and wrap up the signing contracts, and I'll be back ASAP! Lash tells me you are one hell of a strong gal. Well, I need you to prove him right. Hang in there honey, okay?"

I nodded and went back into his room. I asked the nurse if I could have a glass of water. While I was waiting, Joe started to stir and woke up. He was still drowsy from the sedative. I sat on the side of his bed and asked if he needed anything.

"I just need you to love me baby. It's going to be a rough ride but I know we'll be riding it together."

I thought about what Hanna said and told Joe to fight, fight hard and like everything else we'll get through this together.

He smiled and said, "That's my gal. I know you're scared to death and to be honest so am I. But let's keep that between you and me, okay. I wouldn't want Theo calling me a yellow-belly."

I cracked a brave smile and said, "Never! You are one of the bravest men I know Mister Montana."

I asked Joe if he wanted me to call Morgan and Jannine. He said not to bother them until we had more information.

"Don't worry the kids if there's nothing to worry about. Anyway it's late. We can call them in the morning. For now, I just want my immediate family to be here. If you haven't figured out who they are, it's you and that little person inside of you."

I got back in bed with him and snuggled behind him. Suddenly, I felt the baby kick! Joe jumped and asked me to quit poking him. I told him it wasn't me; it was his kid. He said, "Wow, they've got one hell of a soccer foot."

I rolled over and put his hand on my stomach. They did it again. "That's one of the best feelings in the world feeling your baby kick for the first time! I'm falling in love with our kid already Rose. Boy or girl it doesn't matter. They've got my entire heart forever."

Joe dosed off again so I left and let him sleep. Plus nature was calling for the umpteenth time. I walked down the hall to the restroom and saw the old fellow from the hotel. What was he doing at the hospital? I made a quick dash to the restroom. When I came out he was still there talking to the nurses.

"Hello Keough, what are you doing here? Are you okay? I don't think I can take anyone else getting ill tonight."

For a moment he looked somewhat nervous as though he didn't know what to say. He finally said he was okay just checking on a friend. He turned the conversation around asking why I was here and if the baby was okay. I told him I was fine but it was my husband who was admitted. The blood left his face as if I'd walked over his grave.

He stammered, "My bo . . . I mean your husband Lash is sick! How is he? What happened to him Amelia?"

I told him the details then thought, *"I never told him my husband's name was Lash."* Not many people know his real name because he goes by L.J. Montana.

I said, "I'm curious Keough, I never told you my husband's first name. How do you know it, and I'm also curious to know how you know so much about him, because if you are a whacko stalker, I'll kick your ass myself! I don't have time to play fiddle-fuck games with you. Tell me how you know Lash!"

He walked over and sat down on the waiting room couch. I followed him and stood over him.

"So what the hell is going, and again who the hell are you?"

He slowly rose to his feet, took my hand and kissed my palm and said, "Hello Amelia . . . I'm Keough Teal Montana. I'm Lash's father."

It all started coming together. The kiss on the palm, Keough Teal, K.T., the mysterious phone call with a dog barking in the background – everything was beginning to make sense.

"Now, before you have security kick me out, I just want to know how my boy is doing."

I said, "Why should I tell you how your son is doing? You haven't cared for decades! You left him and his sisters, not to mention your wife Charlotte, who by the way died years ago."

His eyes welled, "I know I ain't been a good father or husband. I know he won't want to see me, but I care about him more than you'll ever know. I left because I didn't know how to be a father. I was afraid he'd turn out a drunken saddlebum like me. So I left them. And from the looks of things, he was better off without me. Now, I ain't asking for forgiveness, I just want to know if he's okay."

I screamed, "NO, he's not okay! He may never be okay again and that scares me to death. I don't want him to die; he can't die . . . HE CAN'T!" Keough caught me as I collapsed into tears. He went to the nurses' station and came back with a cup of water. After I regained my composure, we sat on the couch, and I told him about Joe's illness and how he passed out at the hotel.

Keough stood up and stared out the hospital window shaking his head.

"A man ain't supposed to outlive his children. I'm old, worthless and ready to die. Lord, why don't you take me instead. I just wanted to come see my son, even if it was from the back of a conference hall. I wanted to tell him how proud I was of his success. I couldn't give him much back then, but I always wanted him to have everything. And from the looks of things, he's accomplished just that. Beautiful wife, baby on the way, successful career – everything I wanted to give him but couldn't."

He walked over to the elevators and pushed the down button.

I said, "And where the hell do you think you're going?" I put a death grip on his wrist and dragged him down the hall.

"You are going to see your son. Even if he tells you to take the express train to hell, at least he'll know you had the balls to face him."

Keough slowly looked down at my hand wrapped around his wrist. "Gal, you've got one hell of a grip. No wonder my boy loves you so. Where did you learn to fight like this?"

I said I was born in New York City. He flashed the same shit-eating-grin as Joe and said, "Well, that explains everything."

I opened the door and Joe was sitting up. I told him he had a visitor. He said if it's that nurse with the man-hands wantin' more of my blood she'll have to wrestle me for it." I said it's not a nurse. Keough walked from behind the curtain. He stood silent for a minute.

"You're that fella from the hotel. You look really familiar but I can't rightly place where I know you from. What's your name?"
He mumbled, "Keough Teal . . . " Joe said, "Speak up I can barely hear you."

He took a deep breath and said, "Keough Teal, my name is K.T. Montana – your father."

I waited for Joe to blow a gasket, but oddly he remained calm. Maybe it was the sedative.

"So, you finally got the guts to come face me man-to-man. How's life been at the bottom of the bottle? Did you know mom died from a broken heart?"

He nodded yes. "I go to visit her grave every week. Who do you think planted the prairie roses? They were her favorite flower."

Joe continued. "We all waited for your sorry ass to come home. But you never did. And now you come waltzing in here like nothing happened. You've got some nerve old man."

I looked at Keough and whispered, "Tell him. Tell him why you left." He pulled up a chair next to Joe's bed and proceeded to tell him his story. I left the room so they could have their privacy.

I came back an hour later and they were still talking. I thought, *If they decide to kill each other at least they're in a hospital.*

I saw Theo and two other doctors at the nurses' station. They were involved looking at charts and I didn't want to disturb them, but I needed to know Joe's prognosis. I started walking toward him. Theo came over to me. I didn't like the look on his face.

Theo asked me to step into the doctor-patient conference room. The other doctors were already there. He took a deep breath and held my hands, "Amelia I'm going to give it to you straight. Joe's condition has worsened. The growth is malignant and has metastasized to one of his lungs. That's why he's coughing up the small amounts of blood. We can start treatment but to be honest I don't know if it will do any good. I'm willing to try . . ."

I stopped him midsentence, "How long Theo, I need to know how long does my husband has to live?" Theo removed his glasses and rubbed his eyes. "Eight months, possibly a year with treatment, I'm so sorry Amelia but that's the best we can do."

I don't remember leaving the room. I couldn't feel my body. If it wasn't for Lash's kid kicking my ribs I wouldn't have felt anything. I walked over to the couch and sobbed until I had no more tears to shed. I felt a hand on my shoulder. I looked up and Raymond was standing over me. I didn't know how he knew – but he knew.

"Rose, I had a feeling you needed me, so I'm here. I believe the spirits guided me. How is Joe?"

I told him what the doctors had told me. Raymond assured me that western medicine can be wrong and that Joe had a strong spirit, even though he was a pain in the ass.

"There – I got you to smile. Keep smiling Rose. Joe will need that smile if he's to stay strong and so will that little girl you're carrying."

Why does everyone except me believe I'm carrying a girl! Either way I wanted Joe to be there for the birth. I looked up at the sky and shouted, "No dying until this baby is born--do you hear me?"

Raymond smiled, "Shouting at the spirits won't get you a return invite to our drum circles. Now, let's go check on Joe."

I suddenly realized I hadn't told Raymond about Joe's father and that he was in the room with Joe. I explained their history and how tumultuous their relationship was. Raymond said it was good that they made peace with each other. He didn't want Joe taking on any bad energy. He needed all his strength to fight this thing if that's what he chose to do. I questioned why Joe would not want to fight. All of his life he'd had to fight for his place in the world no thanks to his father. Raymond explained that some people choose not to fight because they have a higher purpose to attend to. It's possible Joe is needed elsewhere in the universe. I told Raymond I needed him right where he is and the happy hunting grounds would have to wait their turn.

"That's what I love about you Rose, you're such a warrior. You have enough fight for both of you. Stay strong and keep that mind-set."

I couldn't wait any longer, I had to see Joe. Raymond and I hurried down the hall to Joe's room. His father stood up, leaned over and gave Joe a hug.

Raymond whispered, *"Looks like they've worked things out. That's very good medicine for Joe."*

Joe was happy to see Raymond. He introduced him to his father. I kissed Joe and I asked if I could talk to my husband in private. Raymond said he would fill his father in on his son's life and for us to take our time. He knew we had much to discuss.

"You look tired Rose. I don't like to see you this worn out and upset. I'm sorry darlin' to have to put you through this."

"Put me through this, what the hell is wrong with you Lash? I'm so worried about you that I can't see straight and all you're worried about is me!" I broke down again.

"Come here baby, let me tell you something. I would die a thousand times if it meant not having to put you through this stress and pain. And the fact that you're carrying our child, you don't need this kind of upset."

I stopped crying and got angry. "Don't you dare tell me what I can and cannot do! If I want to be upset then I'll be upset, and if I want to fight for you then I'll fight for you. Is that clear?"

Joe sighed, "Yes Mrs. Montana, whatever you say Mrs. Montana, now come over here and give me a big, wet, sexy kiss."

I wiped my eyes and thought, *"Now that's the man I married."*

The door cracked open. It was Raymond and Keough. Joe was still drifting in and out of consciousness from the strong sedative they'd given him. Theo knocked on the door with some paperwork for me to sign. It was permission for Joe to start chemo treatments. Joe must have subconsciously overheard our conversation. He tried to sit up. I adjusted the hospital bed to a seated position.

"Rose, if you love me, you'll listen to me. I don't want to prolong the inevitable. I want to spend what time I have left with you and my family. I want my boots beside my own bed. I want to go home."

Theo looked at me and I looked at Raymond. "Then we'll go home Joe."

Keough started to leave the room.

"Not so fast old man, where do you think you're going? You're comin' with us. I may not like you, but you're the only father I've got. I need you . . . we'll need you. Maybe you'll be a better grandfather than you were a father and redeem yourself. What do you say, deal?"

"It's a deal, son. Thank you for giving me a second chance even if it's under the most horrible of circumstances. I promise I'll be there for you and *your* family. Keough walked over to Joe and extended his hand. They shook on his promise.

I helped Joe on with his shirt and jeans. He put on his hat and adjusted the brim. "Okay baby, it's time to go home."

Chapter 17

Jannine and Morgan were already at the house when we arrived. They caught the red-eye from New York immediately after they received my phone call. Jannine came running to the door and gave me a huge hug. Morgan quickly followed her helping his dad into the house.

Joe was weak from the ordeal but insisted he could walk on his own. Raymond and Keough brought his books and writing gear into his office. I was surprised by how well they were getting on, like old college buddies at a class reunion. They were close in age and had a lot in common.

Morgan helped him onto the couch and asked if he needed anything.

"What I need is for all of you to stop doting over me and brew me some coffee. That stuff they have at the hospital tastes like frog's piss, not that I've ever consumed frog's piss or would ever want to. I've had some bad whiskey and got tore-down-drunk on Tequila, eh . . . what was I sayin?"

Joe continued to rattle on. It must have been the residual effects of the sedative. Raymond headed into the kitchen to make a pot. Joe asked him to make it strong because he had lots of work to do. Raymond said okay then looked over at me. I nodded. At this point I didn't see any need to fight with him about slowing down. His work was his comfort and gave him a purpose. Not to mention it was the last in a series of novels he'd been writing. All it needed was a cover design and editing. He'd been tossing around titles with no luck. I asked him if I could try my hand at the title and book cover.

"Now, why didn't I think of that – you're hired Rose. Now let's talk salary. Actually, we can discuss salary tonight in bed, wink, wink, ya' know what I mean, darlin'!"

Morgan and I looked at each other and smiled. "He'll be okay Mom; he's strong and ornery just like us."

Mom, Morgan called me mom. I didn't know what to say. I was shocked and happily surprised. I gave him a lingering hug and expressed how happy I was our baby would have such an amazing big brother.

"I'll need all the help I can get Morgan. This parenting thing is new to me and Joe." He promised to be there for all of us. Jannine chimed in that she would be the best aunt ever.

"I can practice changing diapers on the cat!"

Raymond came in with the coffee. Joe had dozed off again. We thought it best to let him sleep. I brought a blanket from the bedroom and laid it over him.

We gathered on the deck to talk. His care and treatment needed to be discussed. Morgan and Jannine volunteered to be his daycare providers. Raymond said he too would be happy to stay.

"I need to go back and close for the season. Then I can come back. It won't take more than a day or two. I would like to stay here with you Rose if that's okay. You'll need extra hands to take care of the horses." I told him of course, and he could stay in our guest house.

Keough picked up his stuff. "It looks as though you've got everything worked out Rose. If you don't need me I guess I'll be headin' home. Lou and I will be out of your way first thing in the morning."

Without realizing it, I'd took a swing at Keough landing a punch on his arm. I think I shocked the shit out of him.

He let out a holler. "Ouch, why'd you do that?"

"Because I'm angry at you for thinking you're not needed. Joe is going to need all of us. Is that clear? And that means YOU and my rocker guardian – right Lou?" Lou ran over and sat beside me.

"Now, Lou had made his choice. How about you, are you stayin' or are you gonna' leave your family like you did in the past?"

That got his attention. He looked like he was going to slug me then decided it would not be in his best interest. Although I was pregnant, I was still agile enough to cold-cock anybody who pissed me off. I called it a knee-jerk reaction from my old Bronx neighborhood days.

"My son married a damn saloon fighter. Not a bad punch for a gal in your condition. I bet you can hold your whiskey too."

"If I wasn't pregnant, I'd drink you under the table old man! Mister Jack Daniels and I are well acquainted, thank you very much. Now then, if we're finished with this pissin' match, get your shit and take it to the guest house. You'll be sharing it with Raymond. And by the way, I could use your help with dinner tonight. This gang gets really ugly when they're hungry."

He mumbled to Lou, "I think I like this gal, but don't tell her Lou or she'll think she's won this round" He winked and smiled the same shit-eating-grin as his son.

Lord have mercy, I've got to deal with two of you? As if on cue the baby gave me one hell of a rib kick.

"Okay, the three of you! I swear you are as ornery as your daddy and grandpa'."

I thought back to my own childhood. I never knew my grandfather. He'd died long before I was born. The only thing my father told me was that he had mixed heritage – part Native American and black. My birth mother was part Italian and black – hence my, love of Tuscany, Mediterranean food and hair-trigger temper. It was comforting having such a diverse family, in blood and community. I hope this is the kind of world my child will experience. There's way too much hatred and bigotry. To be honest, we're all just a gene or two away from being related. The baby kicked me again.

"Okay, let's get you fed because I know the rest of the family is starved."

The rest of the family, that's something I never thought I'd hear myself say.

It was almost time for dinner when I realized I'd forgotten to take my vitamins. I grabbed a glass from the cabinet, and poured some orange juice. The vitamin bottle top was child proof. I thought, *"Why do they put child proof caps on prenatal vitamins when they know this is our first child?"*

Joe walked into the kitchen still woozy from his nap.

"I thought you all would have dinner ready by now. So much for being waited on hand and foot."

"Joe, don't push this waited on hand and foot crap too far or it'll be bread and water for you the rest of the week."

"That's no way to treat a dyin' man darlin'. I deserve a decent meal before I bite the big one."

I spun around and threw my juice in his face.

"Don't ever say that to me again! It's not funny Lash. I don't want to hear any talk about you dying or preparing to die. I won't accept the fact that you may or may not live to see our child grow up."

He brought me another glass of juice and apologized for his lapse in judgment.

"I'm awful sorry, Amelia. I'm just trying to take some of the tension away from this horrible situation. It's not death that's frightens me – it's leaving you. I'm afraid of never waking up feeling your body next to mine. I'm petrified of leaving you and our baby. For the first time in my life, I'm scared shitless!"
His entire body began to shake and he broke down in my arms. We fell to our knees in the middle of the kitchen floor and I rocked him in my arms. He needed to cry and I knew that I needed to stay strong.

Once we regained our composure, we sat at the kitchen table and talked about worst case scenarios. He told me his lawyers had his estate affairs handled. I said I had my own money and would put a large percentage of that into a trust fund for the baby. He said he contacted his finance people the moment my pregnancy test showed a plus sign. His lighthearted comment eased our tension, then back to reality.

The more we planned, the more I realized we weren't talking about divvying up rodeo memorabilia and low-premium life insurance policies. Montana Joe was a brand – a western novel empire with global connections. *I needed help and more importantly, I needed someone I could trust to be a liaison.* It was a lot to absorb. I told Joe to put the rest of this conversation on hold until I could collect my thoughts. He agreed.

Dinner was unbearably quiet. Everyone was trying to act as though nothing was wrong. I finally put my fork down and said, "Someone needs to say something. This quiet is driving me crazy!"

Joe cleared his throat and slowly stood up. I thought he was going to leave the table. He tapped his glass with his knife.

"May I have your attention? Now my beautiful wife knows how much I hate to sing and to be honest I can understand why. The last time I attempted to sing, we had to replace all of the glasses and windows in the house. But she says it's too quiet so I'm going to sing a little number for ya'. I'm willing to give it a whirl if y'all are willing to listen."

He proceeded to belt out the most horrendous rendition of *Friends in Low Places* I'd ever heard. Jannine and Morgan didn't help. They 'egged him on' and tried to harmonize making the entire performance worse than it was. Even Lou started howling. Keough howled with Lou. Within a few minutes, the whole table was laughing. Raymond went into the kitchen and threatened to cut off his own ears. I laughed so hard the baby kicked me in the ribs three times as if to say, *"This is what I have to look forward to? Please someone stop Daddy from singing . . . he's terrible!"*

It was a horrible but humorous break from the deafening tension. Joe took a bow and announced tips were appreciated.

I said, "Here's a tip . . . never sing again!"

"Rose, I take offense at that lame attempt at comedic advice. Unlike my lilting vocals, your singin' sounds like an injured coyote caterwauling at the moon. It would drive me insane if I weren't already goin' deaf from your snoring."

Jannine gave him a high-five. "Whoa! Nice one Joe. You feel my pain. Now imagine that screeching waffling into my reception area. It's enough to make me throw my Pradas at her."

For a moment we'd forgotten about the gravity of Joe's condition. Still the gnawing reality of losing him crept into my thoughts. I decided it was best to let it go for now and enjoy the time we had together.

After everyone had gone to bed, Joe and I talked about the baby's future. I told him if it was a girl I wanted to name her Charlotte Rose. Joe said if it was a boy he'd liked the name him Mathew Lash. He said he didn't care either way as long as they were healthy. Joe rubbed my belly and kissed me goodnight. We had a rough journey ahead of us.

Chapter 18

I lifted my large child-laden body off of the couch. I needed to pee. I always need to pee. It seems I can't go five minutes without running to the bathroom. I think the baby is using my bladder as a recliner. It was the first of December and I was entering my eighth month. Because of Joe's deteriorating health we decided to find out the sex of the baby. We were having a girl. Charlotte was due the end of December possibly the beginning of January. I'd been experiencing soft labor pains but nothing serious.

Joe was getting worse. He'd lost over forty pounds. It was becoming more and more difficult for him to write. But that didn't stop him. He continued writing short stories and western articles. His publishers were amazingly supportive of his condition and said they had enough Montana Joe books in stock to keep his fans happy for years. This made me feel a little bit better because Joe was in a constant state of lethargy. He wasn't able to eat much but he'd never turned down my cooking saying as long as I can get a couple of teaspoons down it was worth the pain.

His publicist Hanna called almost every day. She didn't want Joe to worry about his publicity saying, "If you and Joe need anything please don't hesitate to call me. I love you both. You're like family to me you know that, right? I need to be in California next week so I'll drop by on my way back to Missouri if that's okay."

I said, "Of course, we'd love to see you. It will be good to see you too." She said to give Joe her love and she'll call again when she gets to the west coast.

Jannine took a leave of absence to help me with the baby. I said it would be good training for her if she ever decided to have a kid.

"Amelia, if I could find a man like Joe I would have a kid in a New York heart beat." I indirectly pointed at Morgan. She blushed. I'd never seen Jannine blush. I thought, *"These two are closer than they're letting on."*

Morgan, Raymond and Keough took care of the ranch. Cecilia said she would stay on as housekeeper. That took a huge weight off my shoulders. I took care of Joe. He was my husband, and I didn't want anyone else to do it. He would do the same for me.

Lou lumbered over and sat beside me. He was my constant companion and wouldn't leave my side. When Joe found out we were pregnant, he brought me a lovely antique rocker. He planned on being up for the late night feedings and said a rocker would help both father and baby drift back to sleep. I stroked Lou's head and said, "You were my rocking chair sentinel then and you'll be my rocking chair sentinel now.

Lou laid his head in my lap and pressed his nose against my belly as if to say, "And I'll be Charlotte's protector when she's born."

It was time for Joe's meds. We invested in a medication organizer. I gathered his half dozen evening pills and took them into his office. He was reading some of his older works. I sat beside him and read over his shoulder. He took my hand and kissed my palm.

"It's been one hell-of-an-adventure hasn't it, Rose?"

I told him the adventure wasn't over yet until this baby was born and in our arms. He took his glasses off and wiped his eyes. He looked frail and tired.

"Rose, when the baby is born I want you to do me a favor. Let her know how much I loved you. Tell her about how we met and what a nuisance I was trying to impress you. That way if she ever meets a persistent cowboy she'll have the good sense to run the other way."

We spent the rest of the evening reminiscing about how our lives changed in the blink of an eye at Currysville library.

"Ours is an epic romance, Rose--one I'll never be able to write in the time I have left. I've written most of it down so that our Charlotte will know the kind of man I was and how much I loved her and her momma. Not that my fans every will let her forget. The daughter of Montana Joe has a legacy to live up to. She's gonna need to be tough like her momma and able to handle that kind of pressure. Teach her to be tough, Rose. I've also written some private messages for you to read. Don't get them mixed up or our daughter will know more about our sex life than she'll care to know." I chuckled thinking how good it was to see that twinkle back in his eyes.

I still couldn't handle Joe talking about himself in the past tense. We made a deal that I could cry once a day without being teased, twice if the baby was acting out."

Jannine helped me get the nursery ready. We picked out a horse theme with a night lamp that had different color horses galloping across the top of the ceiling, a full sized stuffed pink pony and lots of room for her growing wardrobe. Keough put together the baby furniture and Raymond blessed the room with sage.

Joe came into the room and sat in the large white rocking chair. Hanna had brought us a small chair just like it for Charlotte.

Joe smiled, "It's beautiful. Our daughter will love it. Tell Hanna thank you. I do have one more surprise for Charlotte."

He asked me if I'd open the closet. I opened the door and found a brand new saddle with her initials engraved on a small silver plate mounted on the backside of the saddle.

"Teach her to ride, Rose. Show her how to sit tall in the saddle and never be afraid. I've also left my prize buckle and rope. They're hers if she wants them. Teach her to love Montana the way we've grown to love it."

I had to stop for a moment and catch my breath. Between Joe's final instructions and the baby's activity I needed to sit down and compose myself. I was also experiencing a dull throbbing pain in my lower back. I told Joe I probably needed to pee again. He came over to help me but started to cough. I tried to help him but my pains were getting stronger.

"OH MY GOD, I think I'm going into labor but it's too soon!"

I screamed for help. By the time everyone ran down the hall, Joe had passed out on the floor. He wasn't breathing well. Keough, Morgan and Raymond helped Joe up while Jannine called 911. My labor pains were getting stronger by the minute. I was so worried about Joe's condition; it was Raymond who noticed my water had broken.

Raymond said, "I don't think this little one will be born at the hospital. I think she wants to be born here." I yelled at Raymond to help Joe.

"Don't worry about me, please help Joe, please help him!"

Jannine helped me into our bed and Keough and Morgan carried Joe in and laid him beside me. He was barely conscious but realized what was going on. *Where are the EMTs?*

Theo was the first to arrive. "Where's Lash?" A distressed Keough pointed and rushed to the bedroom.

"Help my boy doc, don't let him suffer, I'd trade places with him if it meant he'd live!"

Morgan tried to console Keough, but nothing seemed to help. Lou ran over to Keough and sat by his side whimpering trying to comfort him. He hugged Lou around his neck then wiped his eyes with his bandana. He whispered, *"I love you son, hold on!."*

Theo noticed I was in labor and asked how close the pains were coming. I said, "Don't worry about me; help JOE!"

"Lash can you hear me, this is Theo." His breathing was labored but he was able to respond.

"Hey there Theo . . . had garlic bread for lunch again, eh. Where's Rose?"

"She's right beside you Lash, and she's in labor."

Joe reached over, felt for my hand and held it tight. "Hold on baby' I'm here. Let's bring our daughter into this world together."

I didn't care how much pain I was in I just wanted Joe to be okay. Theo examined me. I was fully dilated to ten centimeters.

"Okay, Rose it's time to push and PUSH HARD!"

I pushed and squeezed Joe's hand. Jannine held on to my other hand and was breathing with me.

Theo looked up at me, "Rose, I can see the head, another hard push, you can do it, one more!"

I pushed as hard as I could. A few minutes later I felt as though my entire body had fallen out – then a cry.

Theo placed the baby on my chest, "Charlotte Rose welcome to Casa Montana." Theo wrote down the time and date of birth and noted it was an emergency home-birth. The EMTs had finally arrived. They started setting up to work on Joe, but Theo instructed them not to. At this point, there was nothing they could do for him and Lash had already signed the DNR (Do Not Resuscitate) forms. He had them check out Charlotte, then me. One of the EMTs said baby and mother are fine. Theo filled in the rest of the birth records.

Jannine was still breathing beside me, with her eyes closed and was about to hyperventilate. Raymond told her to open her eyes. She looked at Charlotte and cried louder than the baby. "Oh my God Amelia! She is so beautiful and tiny. She looks just like you...only small and slimy.

I turned toward Joe and smiled, "Here she is Joe; here's our daughter. Charlotte Rose, say hello to your daddy."

Theo placed her on Joe's chest. Keough helped Joe up so he could see her. He smiled and kissed her forehead. "She's beautiful Amelia, just like you. She's a true Montana. I love you Rose." He raised my hand to his lips and kissed my palm. As his grip weakened, so did his breathing...then nothing.

"Joe, Joe, JOE talk to me. Joe, oh God no . . . NO!"

Theo held me tight, "He's gone Amelia – Joe's gone."

Chapter 19

We began preparations for Joe's memorial service. It would be a small private ceremony for family members only. Hanna took care of all the media and press. There would be a larger public event later in the week. I don't know what I would have done without her. I wouldn't have been able to handle it. I was still in shock. I found myself calling Joe for dinner, reminding him to take his meds and reaching for him in bed. His treasured gray Stetson was still sitting on the cedar chest in our bedroom. I picked it up and held it to my nose. It still smelled like his lavender shampoo. Jannine and Morgan came in and sat on the bed with me.

Morgan held my hand, "You know he loved you more than life Amelia. I've never seen my father so happy and youthful, until he met you."

I leaned over, kissed him on the cheek and brushed the tuff of hair off of his forehead. He looked so much like his father. Charlotte started to stir. Jannine said she would check on her and for me to concentrate on Joe's obituary. As a writer I knew I needed to do this myself. I wanted every word to be perfect.

I could hear Joe telling me to keep it short and sweet. "Darlin', they don't need any long-drawn-out speech."

Raymond said he would be honored to minister the service.

"I joined you two together so it seems appropriate for me to oversee his untimely physical departure. You know his spirit lives on in you and Charlotte." I thanked Raymond for his thoughtfulness.

Keough helped Hanna with the flood of cards, letters and flowers from his fans. I watched as we all performed our heartbreaking but necessary tasks. A little over a year ago, I didn't know any of these people and now we were one united family. A diverse tribe of cultures gathered together by one special man.

Hanna gently knocked on the door informing me that I had a phone call. It was Patrick and Daniel. They were terribly upset about Joe's death. I could hear an announcement in the background that flight 817 to Billings would be loading at gate 9B. They must be on their way to Montana to attend Joe's funeral.

Patrick said, "Did you think we would let you go through this without us. Plus, someone's got to be there to touch up your makeup. Funerals are dreadful on mascara." I chuckled.

"I heard a chuckle . . . Daniel I got a chuckle out of our girl." I heard Daniel say, "Tell her I love her very, very much, lots of kisses and we'll see her soon."

"Did you get all that Amelia – gotta' go girl our plane is about to leave, ciao sweetie, love you!"

The evening before the memorial I went for a drive to clear my head. I'd finished the obituary and wanted to collect my thoughts on Joe's death. So many emotions swirled within me. I found myself getting angry at him for dying and then collapsing into tears because I missed him so much. All I wanted to do was to fall apart – but I couldn't. My daughter needed me, and I needed her. She looked so much like Joe.

I strapped Charlotte into her car seat and drove to the end of our property where Joe proposed. Charlotte was still sleeping when I took her out of the car. I held her close to my chest and looked up at the sky.

"Your daddy always called this Big Sky Country. This is where he asked me to marry him and this is where he wants his ashes to be spread."

Charlotte cooed and blinked as if to say, "Yes, I know!"

"But I'm sure you already know that baby girl. God, you are so much like him. Not quite two weeks old and you're already a Montana – strong and opinionated."

I raised her tiny little hand to my lips and kissed her palm. "That's from your daddy. Hold it tight and remember he loves you."

I put her back into the car seat and headed home.

It was after 9:00 PM when I arrived at the house. Lou met us at the door, tail wagging and yawning. The house seemed so quiet and so large without Joe. Morgan and Jannine were curled up on the sofa fast asleep. Everyone was exhausted. I tried not to wake them, but Morgan heard Charlotte whimpering. She was hungry.

"Give her to me Mom, I'll feed her. It's time me and my little sister to get better acquainted."

Mom . . . he called me mom. I started to cry then heard Joe's voice mocking me.

I looked over at his hat and said, "You're still making fun of me and you're not even here."

Raymond came in from the barn and overheard me.

"What do you mean he's not here? He's always going to be here Amelia – in your heart and in this home. He has good spirit and will always be with you, always."

Keough walked in from the deck and hugged my shoulder. It felt the same as Joe's hugs.

"How are ya' holdin' up darlin'? Let me know if there's anything I can do for you."

I nodded and thanked him.

He started to leave the room then turned around, "Oh, by the way, someone named Paul called askin' for you. I left his phone number on the kitchen table."

I called and got Paul's voice mail. It didn't seem appropriate to leave a message. Ten minutes later my phone rang – it was Paul.

"Hello Rose, this is Paul. Sorry I missed your call love: however, it seems I need a favor and thought I'd cash it in."

I couldn't get the words out but knew I had to tell him what had happened.

"Paul, Joe died last week."

There was complete silence then, "I'm on my way!"

Patrick and Daniel arrived early afternoon. It was good to see them. They had been my rock for so many years. I introduced them to everyone and it was as if they were long-lost-family members. They fit right in.

Daniel walked over to Charlotte's bassinet and smiled. "Oh Amelia she is so beautiful. What a gorgeous baby!"

He picked her up and introduced himself, "Hi precious, I'm your Uncle Daniel and that's your Aunt Patrick. He's a bit of a diva but you'll learn to tolerate him."

Patrick rolled his eyes and said, "Honey, don't listen to that Madonna-wanna-be. He'll have you wearing last year's Gucci with this year's Prada."

Jannine laughed and hugged them both. "I've missed you two so much. Maybe we can get matching pairs of cowboy chaps and go riding."

Patrick said, "No way honey, I don't ride anything that doesn't buy me dinner first."

It was time to feed Charlotte when I heard a large motor rumbling towards the house. I recognized the cab, it was Paul's truck.

How did he get here so fast? He jumped out of the truck and headed toward the house. I met him at the door.

"Rose, I'm so sorry to hear of Joe's death. I'm here to help in any way I can. Consider it my favor paid in full."

I thanked him for his thoughtfulness and introduced him to everyone. It was like the United Nations and Gay Pride had thrown a party for Joe.

I know he's watching and thinking, *"Well damn it, looks like I'm missin' one hell-of-a-bash."*

Then I remembered Paul's phone call and him needing a favor. He said he had a mandatory three-day down time and needed a place to park his cab. He knew we lived near Billings and had enough space to house an 18-wheeler with or without the trailer. I told him of course, and he could stay as long as he liked.

"I would be honored if you could stay for Joe's memorial. After all if it weren't for you, I would have missed the email that literally brought us together."

Paul smiled and said, "Of course, I'll make arrangements with my company to attend."

The morning of the memorial service was somber. I knew it would be a difficult day. We decided to have the service at an outdoor chapel. Raymond had changed into his tribal attire. Hanna had set up lovely photographs of Lash on a table with two daffodils in a crystal vase. Beside his portrait were his saddle and his prized gray Stetson. There were a few people I didn't recognize. As I sat down with Charlotte, they came over and introduced themselves. It was Lash's sisters Kathleen and Trish. I'd never met them and apologized for meeting them under these circumstances. They walked over to their estranged father, exchanged a few words and then hugged. I was happy they'd put aside their differences. I thought, *"Joe would be so proud of his family."*

I noticed Keough sitting in the back. *I thought he was sitting with Morgan and Jannine?* I looked, and he was still sitting with them. *This is freaking weird.* I headed over to the gentleman and was shocked. He looked just like Keough. As I got closer he stood up.

"Hello, Miss Amelia, My name is Kurt, Kurt Montana. I'm Keough's older twin. I'm sure my half-wit brother hasn't told you about me. I'm sorry for your loss ma'am, but I just wanted to come pay my respects and to say goodbye to my nephew."

Keough walked over and hurled a string of abuse at his brother for not letting him know he was coming. I told them to save it for later and that they were both welcome to stay and pay their respects.

The memorial started with Raymond walking to the front and asking everyone to stand for a moment of silence.

"There are so many diverse people in attendance today, and I thought it best that everyone pay their respects to Lash in their own way. Let Lash know that he was important to you and how much he made a difference in your life. Tell him how memorable his kindness, wit, humor and selflessness was and how it will always be with you. The spirits gone before him will guide your messages to him."

Raymond then asked if anyone would like to say something about Lash. Everyone had a story to tell, a joke, fond memory of Lash. After an hour, Raymond asked if I'd like to say something.

At first I shook my head no, but I could hear Joe saying, *"I don't believe you Rose. You always have something to say about everything. Get your pretty little ass up there and say somethin' about me. Just to tell them I WAS hung like a horse. That'll get their attention!"*

I stood up and took a deep breath.

"Lash Jackson Montana or Montana Joe as he was known to his millions of fans was one of the most annoying, self absorbed, tenacious men I'd ever met. He was obsessed with coffee, he never got enough sleep, and his lust for life was larger than the state that shared his name. Now I know most of you know him as a tough, hardheaded, no nonsense, rodeo cowboy. That was the professional persona he wanted you to see. He once told me he didn't want people to know the real Lash. His fans wanted the wild and raunchy cowboy who wrote stories about his rodeo days. But privately he was a sweet, sentimental, exceptionally witty and tender man. This was the Montana Joe I knew. No one knew the hard working writer who slept on the floor of his office when he had to finish a manuscript, the man who kissed my palm, the gentle man who brought me fresh daffodils with my morning coffee, who knew my heart, shared my bed, who believed our love could survive all obstacles. The man who no one knew is the man I fell in love with-- the handsome, romantic, cowboy who lovingly called me Rose and who I called Joe – simply Joe.

I paused for a moment.

"I know he's upset that I've gone on-and-on about how much I love him. Well that's too bad Joe, because I want everybody to know the true Montana Joe. I miss you like crazy Joe'."

I kissed my palm and placed it over my heart then sat down. Everyone was weeping including me. It wasn't my intention to preach about Joe, but I wanted them to know the man I knew. I had to do something to break the silence.

I stood up again and hollered, "And as my Joe would say . . . for God sakes, would you sons-of-bitches please quit your sniveling and let the drinkin' and dancin' commence!"

The chapel erupted into laughter. It was good to see everyone smiling. I know Joe would have smiled too.

Raymond came over to me and said, "Even in death, he has to have the final word…arrogant white man!"

After the reception, the crowd started to disperse. I thanked everyone for their attendance and for their kind thoughts and words they said about Joe. Raymond said he would take care of closing the area and Hanna dismantled the memorial. Jannine and Morgan said they'd take Charlotte home if I wanted to stay a little longer. It was the first time that I'd been alone since Joe's death. The sunset was beautiful. I grabbed Joe's Stetson and placed it on my head then picked up the urn containing his ashes. The sun was sinking low in the sky. I stared at my palm. I swear I could feel his lips gently kissing it.

Hanna slowly walked over to me and said, "Amelia – honey, it's time to go home." I thought, *"Home? There's no home without Joe."*

Chapter 20

Three months had passed since Joe's memorial. Charlotte was getting bigger and looking more and more like Joe. I was extremely happy Cecilia stayed on as housekeeper and nanny. Joe always said she was worth her weight in gold and that's why she loved to eat. Sometimes I think she knew Lash better than I did. She said he was always a happy man but wasn't truly happy until he met me.

Keough stayed on to help run the ranch. Every now and then his twin brother Kurt came by to help. Joe's death had brought them closer together. At least they weren't at each other's throats as much. My dear sweet canine friend and sentinel Lou never left my side.

Keough would say, "I do believe that dog loves you more than he's ever loved me. And I've noticed he's very protective of Charlotte. You'll never need to worry about her when Lucky Lou's around."

Paul kept close tabs on me and Charlotte. He would make it a point to drop by every two weeks to check on us. Jannine and Morgan went back to New York. They called daily always sending their love and support.

Montana Joe correspondence continued to pour in from all over the world conveying messages of support from his loyal fans. It was difficult to sleep without Joe by my side. I would stay up until midnight sending thank you emails. I don't think Cecilia was able to sleep either. She would stay up late cleaning the house. I watched her pick up Joe's urn to dust the mantle. I thought, *"It's time Joe."*

I called Raymond and told him to meet me tomorrow morning at the place Joe wanted his ashes to be spread. I told him it was time to fulfill my promise to my husband. He said he would be there.

I'd just finished our call when Cecilia came into Joe's office. "I've put Charlotte down for the night and if you don't need anything I think I'll go to bed." I thanked her and said goodnight.

I sat down to log off my laptop when I saw two email notifications. *Who could be writing me at this time of the night?* I clicked on the first email. My heart nearly stopped. It was from Joe's email account. *If this was some horrific hacker joke it wasn't amusing!* I was about to delete them when I thought back to the first time Joe sent me an email. Had I deleted it my life would have turned out completely different. I wouldn't have married Joe and more importantly I wouldn't have Charlotte. I decided to open them.

To: Rose
Fr: Montana Joe
Subject: **Convergence by Jackson Pollock & other jokes of art, Part 1 of 5**

Hah, thought you'd be rid of me just because I'm dead. I am dead, right? I must be because my lawyer sent you these emails. How was my funeral? You didn't sing did you? That would be a really lousy end to my life (just jokin' darlin'). I hope everyone enjoyed Raymond's eulogy. He did minister my passing? I told him not to say anything embarrassing about me like the fact that I was hung like a horse. I hope my dad attended. It was good to finally make peace with him. Tell him I understand why he left and that all is forgiven. And please tell him to be a good grandfather to Charlotte. That little girl is going to need him as much as he'll need her.

Be that as it may, there are a few things I wanted you to know after my death and it made sense [to me] to email them to you. Since it's the way we got together in the first place.

1. Don't give Daisy sweet feed. It gives her a terrible case of gas and makes for a very unpleasant ride for both you and the horse.

2. The switch for the thermostat in our bedroom is busted. Never saw fit to fix it seein' that you're the hottest woman in Montana, except for them cold feet.

3. Don't give my treasured gray Stetson to anyone. I want Charlotte to have it. She can wear it, hang it in her room, or save it for her kids. I placed a photograph for her inside the crown label. It's the one I took of us on our honeymoon ride.

4. When I'd drive, I'd find myself talkin' to you. Yes, I know you weren't there but I'd talk to you anyway. Wonderful conversations they were, mainly because it was the only time you'd ever listen to me, hah. I'm a loony darlin'. But you already knew that about cowboy fiction writers.

5. . . . and, like head lice, they are extremely difficult to get rid of, so you're stuck with me – even after death, scary huh.

So my darlin' sweet and beautiful wife, Amelia Kristen Montana aka Rose, I hope the service went smoothly and you're seriously thinkin' about spreadin' my ashes. It'll give you closure and its one less thing Cecilia needs to dust. I love you more than life Rose, and I'm a man who has enjoyed livin' life to its fullest. Adios, baby!

Love, Joe

I was determined not to cry. Knowing Joe he's probably placing bets in heaven on whether or not I would or wouldn't. I took a deep breath I clicked on the second email. I smiled when I saw Charlotte's name.

To: Charlotte Rose Montana
Fr: Daddy
Subject: **Convergence by Jackson Pollock & other jokes of art, Part 2 of 5**

Rose, you'll need to read this to her because I'll be gone long before she's able to. Explain our silly title joke and how it brought us together. Let her know how much I looked forward to holding her, kissing her sweet little face, teaching her to rope and ride like I taught her momma. Tell her that life can be unfair and loved ones do die. It's a lesson I want her to know early because it'll help her understand my death. Tell her I didn't leave her by choice – it was just the lousy hand I was dealt.

Now Charlotte, the first thing you must know is your momma can't sing. Yes, I know she'll tell you it ain't as bad as I'm sayin' but trust me baby girl it is. And, your daddy wouldn't lie to you darlin'. Also, your momma is one of the most talented and intellectual women I'd had the pleasure of calling friend. She's witty, tough and charismatic with a heart so warm it would melt the sun. Every now and then call her, "Cuppy" and watch the sparks fly, hah.

Speaking of the sun, she once teased me about naming a star after her. When I heard my prognosis I decided to do it. In my desk drawer on the left hand side you'll find two manila envelopes one addressed to you and the other to your momma. You both have your own stars. Yours is named Prairie Rose-1 and hers is Rose Darlin'-99 the year we met. Now when you look at the sky take the enclosed star guide with you and you'll find them and think of me. If you wave I promise I'll wink back at you.

My dear sweet baby Charlotte, there is so much I want to tell you about me, but I'll leave that up to the discretion of your momma. She'll tell you more when you're old enough to understand mostly about how we met and how we fell in love. You've inherited a huge western writing empire from the legendary Montana Joe. Keep it going and know how much I regret not being there for you. Behave for your momma and give her a kiss on her palm every night from me. And remember your daddy loves you more than all the stars in the sky.

Love, Montana . . .

[End of email conversation]